From

The Women's Pr

34 Great Sutton Str

Nina Sibal holds BA and MA degrees in English literature; from 1969 to 1972 she taught English at Delhi University. She joined the Indian Foreign Service in 1972, and was First Secretary in India's Permanent Mission to the United Nations in New York between 1976 and 1980. She chaired the UN group which drafted the Convention on the Elimination of Discrimination against Women. From 1983 to 1986 she studied law, received her LL.B in 1986, and now works as a diplomat at the Indian embassy in Cairo. She published *Yatra*, a novel, in 1987 (The Women's Press), and is currently at work on another.

NINA SIBAL

The Secret Life of Gujjar Mal

and other stories

The Women's Press

This book is for Kapil.

First published by The Women's Press, 1991.
A member of the Namara Group
34 Great Sutton Street,
London EC1V 0DX

British Library Cataloguing in Publication Data
  Sibal, Nina
  The secret life of Gujjar Mal and other stories.
  I. Title
  823 [F]
  ISBN 0-7043-4271-5

Typeset by Input Typesetting Ltd, London
Printed and bound by BPCC Hazell Books
Aylesbury, Bucks, England.
Member of BPCC Ltd

Contents

The Secret Life
of Gujjar Mal

I first met Gujjar Mal when I was a very young man, just out of college in Delhi. My father had set up a new publishing business for me in Meerut. My father was a rich man. His father had come up from Calcutta to be Diwan to the Nizam of Wasirpur in Uttar Pradesh – a long way to come, but he had the right ambitions; we all respected my grandfather. The Nizam had given him a large piece of land which my father inherited and used for a sugar-cane plantation. Then he set up his own factory just outside the small sugar-town of Daurala, which would handle everything from the actual extraction of juice from the sugar-cane, to the final processing of the sugar. He imported the latest machinery from the United States and took me around his factory with great pride, hoping to persuade me to join him. But I saw the weary line of carts loaded with sugar-cane waiting for entry, the heat and dust of Daurala, the noise and rubble, the absolute desert of a small town. My heart sank and a terrible depression settled over me. My father is a wise man, he agreed readily that I should not live in Daurala; he would manage the factory on his own. He did not want to take chances with those depressions. My mother suffered from them all her life, and they say depression is hereditary.

Meerut was a larger town, close enough to Delhi, the Usha publishing house would do well here. Gujjar Mal was one of my first authors and he has stayed with me since then. I do a lot of text books, which brings good money, but the real income comes from guides. They are the mainstay of university education in Uttar Pradesh: students would be lost, they would not pass exams without them. Although these guides or 'dukkis' are cheap, both in printing and in facts, they nevertheless sell for ten to fifteen rupees each, a clear eighty per cent profit, as I don't have to pay much to the authors. But other things are necessary to add interest to life in Meerut, so I publish fiction from time to time. And I publish Gujjar Mal.

The manuscripts are erratic since he went away into the mountains. I don't know where he posts them, he gives no address. I can't send him payments, or contact him. The manuscripts arrive in a battered condition, envelopes torn, showing the writing inside, sometimes with sections defaced by water- and finger-marks. We do the best we can with them, I edit them myself: strange, beautiful stories. One day he will win the Sahitya Akademi Award, and I will be famous as his publisher, but how will we locate him?

I have to write a story about Gujjar Mal, the writer, whose own beautiful creations are polished and hard, perfect little compositions flowing from a centre which I can only watch from outside. Maybe it is a story about this centre. Maybe all the details are not true and yet all of it is true, because who am I to choose, the choice is made elsewhere.

Gujjar Mal, Rewati Bai, the woman he sleeps with, and the Himalayas, are characters. And Manimala his wife. Is it Anup Basu, BA from Delhi University, proprietor of the Usha publishing house, Meerut, who writes these stories? It is not likely. I have the name of Gujjar Mal, witness and participant. We change and interchange. Whose voice is below the words, reposing in the cells of a honeycomb, rich and silent, the surface completely still, yet light with movement?

Before his move to the mountains Gujjar Mal sat all day in a shop full of lights, they stayed switched on to display his wares. He sold electric fittings, lampshades, little pieces of crystal to hang on the ceiling, wall brackets, or candelabra with small bulbs jutting out from candlestands. It is an important shop for these items, on the busiest road in Meerut, the road to Delhi, which is full of traffic and people who peer out of the windows of cars, rickshaws and scooters, just idly looking.

They see Gujjar Mal sitting there, up front, behind the cash counter. Monolithic, a large, rough-hewn man, very still until he moves to count money, give directions, make out a bill, or show a customer something which might interest him, and then he is all movement, slightly awkward, eccentric movement, but full of an incipient force, riveting attention. Sometimes customers look at him curiously, slightly alarmed by his compressed energy, but they learn soon enough that he is an infinitely gentle man.

Every day at lunchtime he climbs stairs to the living-quarters above the shop. Manimala is there, her long plait of hair moving busily behind her as she goes about her work. She does all the housework herself, except for the help of a little girl who comes in to sweep and wash the floors. There isn't much work, as they have no children who would need much caring and looking after. And her husband manages well by himself. She sits beside him as he eats, watching the food move slowly. In fifteen years of marriage, he has never once commented on its quality.

The whole town, except Manimala, knows that every evening, after the shop closes, Gujjar Mal goes to Rewati Bai, a Nepali prostitute who lives on the other side of town, beside Katra Neel Kamal. But he is back every night, scribbling his stories into the early hours of the morning.

What happens when a character in a story speaks? Where does the voice come from? I always wonder about this. Maybe it is the voice of God, coming from his soul. Gujjar Mal tries to follow each voice to its source. He finds it difficult to speak. Keeping a shop, dealing in figures which have definite relation to abstract truth is easier, cool and restful. Like wrapping your head in a wet towel when a fire's going on inside. Gujjar Mal appreciates silence. Someone told him it was not necessary to talk to prostitutes.

'When are you going to Delhi?' Manimala says.

'Tomorrow.'

'Can I go with you?'

'Yes, of course.'

Each time he goes to Delhi to buy stock for his shop, she goes with him. These are the high points, being alone in Delhi with Gujjar Mal, everything comes alive. He always takes her, yet each time she feels it necessary to ask.

Manimala's family lives in Delhi. Her father was an official in the Income Tax Department who took enough bribes to build himself a house in Patpar Ganj, across the Jamuna river. They could easily stay with her parents during these visits to Delhi, everybody lives with relatives, but not Gujjar Mal. He and Manimala stay in Hotel Ram Lal in Chandni Chowk.

'This is where my business is, where I buy and pack my things. There is no point in staying in Patpar Ganj.'

Neat brown boxes tied with twine, packing material peeping out of gaps, pile up in the room in the boarding-house. The door pushes into them each time it opens, and she squeezes through a narrow passage between the piles to reach the bathroom. In the morning, after he leaves, she takes a bus to meet her parents. Each time Delhi is a new city, it welcomes her with open arms, waiting to swallow her, there is no way in which Gujjar Mal's shadow will shelter her, he is a man without shadow. Yet she rushes back to be there when he returns in the evening, that's the whole point of coming to Delhi, to be with him.

'Shall we go out a bit?' Their boarding-house is right at the top of a huge, beetling building facing the Sisganj Gurudwara. She could look from the window at its gleaming white marble façade, its sharply curving dome and curling edges. In the morning the sound of chanting and prayers, the sweet, heavy voices of devotees, came floating up through the air. Now there are street sounds, and traffic, heavy and thick on this main street. Lines of shining cars are parked on the roadside, to be skirted carefully by pedestrians and rickshaws, buses and trucks.

'I have to hire a tempo to get all this stuff back to Meerut.'

'When are we leaving?'

'Tomorrow.'

'Already?! It always seems too short.'

'You like living in Delhi?'

'Yes.'

'Would you like me to set up a place for you here? Somewhere near your parents? Then you could live in Delhi.'

'And you?' He just stands there smiling at her, the boxes rising around him.

'No,' she says, 'no!'

He turns towards the door; she can no longer see his face; the cheek forms a sharp angle like rock against the light. His gesturing hand appears enormous in shadow. 'Come, then, shall we go?'

She follows him down a long, narrow staircase. It zig-zags between the floors and smells of urine. Red betel-nut stains are blazoned on the walls, like revolutionary posters. She picks her way between piles of rubbish, carefully following the steps taken by his large feet in black slippers, through banana peel, crumpled paper bags, inexplicable rags.

The sound of traffic hits them in full fury as they emerge. Shops are closing up, the road is full of headlights and honking cars preparing to depart. He stops to buy two bags of peanuts. Then they are at the crossroads, and going across to the grounds in front of the Red Fort.

'Oh look! A puppet show.'

A group of Rajasthani puppeteers has set up their stand in the middle of the grounds, close to an electric pole. Their lanterns and electric lights are a bright patch in the fading half-light of dusk. The show is just beginning.

'We are grateful to the government for making it possible for us to perform in Delhi.' Some chairs have been put right up in front for officials and their wives. Manimala pulls Gujjar Mal right beside the honoured guests.

They are performing the story of Amar Singh Rathore. The puppets move in and out of a colourful, low tent which is the chief prop, erected on a platform draped in black. The puppeteers are shadowy, bulging figures behind the tent, or pushing out against the swirling black drapes below.

It is a story of true love and courage, of faithful honour and betrayal. Simple things, like calculations in Gujjar Mal's red ledgers, related to a careful system of known relationships, profit and loss, love and marriage, devotion to king and country. Amar Singh Rathore, resplendent on his brave horse, wins the hand of his beloved princess, fights to save his lord's kingdom, and is betrayed by a jealous relative, stabbed in the back as he climbs through a difficult window. A trio of singers squats on the grass nearby. They are singing the narrative, their voices and music rising into the darkness. The king stands over the fallen body of his faithful subject. 'I had heard of Amar Singh Rathore, and I longed to meet him. Now he is lying here, and I see that he is exactly as I expected.'

Manimala turns to him in the middle of the clapping and cannot find Gujjar Mal. He might have been gone a long time. The crowd is pressing up firmly around her, but she pushes her way out.

It is quite easy to spot him in open space, his large, square body outlined in a loose kurta, faint light reflecting from his spectacles. He is walking along the wall of the Red Fort, looking up at the dark battlements silhouetted against the evening sky. Watchtowers are dense pools of darkness, and the sandstone walls seem soft as velvet in discreet electric lighting.

He is almost at the edge of the ground when she catches up with him, he would have gone straight on for ever if she had not stopped him here, panting as she runs, her bangles jangling ridiculously in her ears. A great fear fills her.

'Why are you going away like this?'

He turns and walks back with her to the boarding-house.

In Meerut, Rewati Bai waits for him in the evening. Since

she has at least one regular customer, she has been given a separate room in the warren of rooms which run like a barrack–dormitory behind Katra Neel Kamal. Her pimp takes a month's payment in advance from Gujjar Mal.

He comes early, an hour before his usual time. A 'bandh' or strike was declared in the whole Meerut Bazaar, to protest about the beating up of a shopkeeper by the police, so all shops closed at 5 pm. She is fast asleep in the narrow bed under a window, her limbs spread in innocent abandon, her enormous breasts, the part of her anatomy which draws the principal number of her customers, spill over the edge of the bedding, hooks and buttons pushed loose, skin exposed to a faint breeze which comes in from the window.

Gujjar Mal strips off his clothing at great speed, and moves her body into the centre of the bed in one small movement. Her body is thin and narrow, it fits easily between his hands. Her eyelids flicker. A small dribble of spittle stands at the corner of her open, sleeping mouth. He wipes it carefully, then makes love to her.

'Oh yes, oh yes, I am happy here,' Gujjar Mal says.

Rewati Bai turns over and goes to sleep again.

Gujjar Mal lies on his back, his naked body feels perfectly at ease in the room. Where do these images come from? Rewati Bai wakes to find Gujjar Mal looking down into her face. His eyes are large and expressionless.

'You are a girl from Nepal, land of beautiful, sacred mountains. Why did you leave the Himalayas?' he says.

'I left with all the others. They said they would give us jobs in India. They collected us in Dehra Dun, then they sent us off to different parts of the country. I came to Meerut, I thought I was going to work on the roads. This is better.' She smiles happily at him, her body stretching and contented after sleep. 'Listen, Gujjar Mal. I'm going to have a baby.'

'Oh.'

'It could be your baby.'

'That is not necessarily so. It could be anybody's baby. Lots of men come here to you.'

'That's true. But I feel it is your baby.'

'Yes, it could be my baby.' He puts his hand on her stomach. The tender, fair skin ripples involuntarily under his palm. He bends down to kiss it. Then his tongue runs over it. She reaches down to press his head down into her, giggling.

'What are you doing?'

'You don't like it?'

'Yes, it's OK, it's nice.'

'I'm going away, into the Himalayas. You want to come with me?' he asks.

'You would never go. How can you go? You have a wife, a family business. What will you live on if you give up the business?'

'I said, will you come with me?'

'Oh, they would never let me leave.'

'Nobody can stop you, if you want to go.'

'You're always dreaming. Now it's the mountains.' She clucks casually, and turns over, her high little bottom pushing into him.

'Besides, you can't go now. Gujjar Mal, I told you, I'm going to have your baby.'

He runs his hands over her body, and bends to suck briefly at her beautiful breasts. Then he leaves to go to the Usha publishing house, beside the Bata shop, in the Meerut Bazaar, to see me, Anup Basu, his publisher.

The shutters are down, following the call for a bandh, no use taking chances with this kind of thing. I am out in the open yard, at the back, alone, with a couple of cane chairs beside him. The stars hang heavy above his head, and a pale watery moon.

'Anup, where do the stories come from, and the images?'

'I don't know. You're the writer, I'm only your publisher.' Gujjar Mal watches my face, with its large, rounded nose and thinning hair. My hesitant apologetic eyes which can sink so quickly into oblivion, reach towards him through the gathering gloom. 'What do you think?'

'One or the other thing, a picture, a person, comes to me perched on the rim of a turning wheel. With Rewati Bai I had freedom, she opened me to an area of chaos where I was free to roam and select. All the riches of the world lay around me. But now the question comes, who selects? Who gives the stories and the images? Now I'll have to leave, to find out.'

'What do you mean, leave? Are you going somewhere? Where will you go?' I am sitting bolt upright, tilting my chair forward, eager to hear. A gong is beginning to beat in my brain, the sign that one of my deep headaches is coming on. If Gujjar Mal goes, one of the chief supports of my life will disappear, and I am almost certain that Gujjar Mal will leave.

'I don't know. It doesn't matter too much. Perhaps to the mountains where Rewati Bai comes from.'

'But . . . '

Just then a procession connected with the bandh descends upon the Meerut Bazaar, with a panoply of loudspeakers, drums, slogans, and hundreds of people ringing the bells of their bicycles, clapping their hands. They set up the squat effigy of the chief municipal councillor just outside my office, and begin preparing to burn it.

Pain and lethargy are spreading through my body but I must make some effort to get the crowd to move on, find another venue. Anything could happen from flying embers, they could set my whole place on fire. Even as I argue with stalwarts in the crowd, I continue to look around for Gujjar Mal. I need him; I must ask him at least one more question, but he has disappeared in the commotion.

Manimala, Gujjar Mal's wife, comes to me in my living-quarters behind the Usha publishing house. For days, depression has claimed me completely. I am beset by anxiety and irritability, a deep inertia possesses me, I have lost all desire, nothing interests me, to move seems an enormous effort. I lie on my bed all day reading Gujjar Mal's volumes of short stories, one after the other, small, blue, hard-bound books with the logo of the Usha publishing house on the cover. There is something unfinished about them, they do not reach out to me, answer my questions. Surely this lady cannot answer them?

I have no difficulty recognising her, though I can barely see her through the haze in my eyes.

'Where is Gujjar Mal?' she says. 'My husband.'

'I don't know.' I lean out towards the pile of small blue books beside me, and push them over. 'I only have these. Why don't you sit down?' She sits lightly on one of the cane chairs, and waits for me to speak. 'He's gone to the mountains,' I say at last.

'What will I do then?' But I close my eyes. I fall deep into the throes of my depression when I find her bending over me, her hands cool on the back of my neck, pressing my shoulders, gently, tenderly, letting out the pain. Then she pushes me over a bit, and lies beside me. Her flesh is clean and smooth, it smells of roses, her hair is unbound and lies over us like a curtain, everything is safe and dark behind Manimala's hair, I can climb back, back into her utter safety. 'Don't go to your empty rooms,' I say. 'Don't leave me now.'

The first battered manuscript from Gujjar Mal arrives. The stories are different, quite different. I wait avidly for each one, as the answer accumulates, like a flood each time, the river depositing a layer of fertile silt.

Then I begin to visit Rewati Bai in Katra Neel Kamal. No one visits her now, it is off-season for her, she is heavily pregnant. The veins in her stomach stand out in blue networks as the skin stretches to accommodate the growing baby. Her breasts are larger and even more beautiful, swollen and heavy with pregnancy, and they pull at her narrow body. When I hold them in my hands, they spill over in all directions. Her pimp is no longer interested in her, he does not wait at the bottom of the stairs for an advance; he is elsewhere, looking for alternative sources of income during this lean period.

'Has Gujjar Mal come back?' Rewati Bai asks.

'No.'

In a desultory way she is already gathered into the warm swelling stream of her body. 'Did he tell you where he was going?'

She shakes her head. 'To the mountains,' she murmurs.

'He writes about you, in his new stories. I received one lot yesterday.'

'He knows about the baby,' she says.

Anup Basu goes to see the baby as soon as he hears news of its birth. A boy who looks exactly like Gujjar Mal, square face and beautiful, curved lips, outsized hands and feet, a long body.

In the early morning light, Manimala watches from behind a curtain in my house as Rewati Bai slips into the back yard of the Usha publishing house. She props the bundle of her baby gently against the wall. He begins to cry, and she squats to feed him. Her breast is enormous, bulging with milk, it overflows from the baby's mouth. Manimala holds her own breasts, she feels a tugging against the nipples. Rewati Bai feeds her baby until he sleeps, dropping from her breast in a satisfied ball. Then she puts him down again and bends to kiss him. She looks swiftly towards Anup's house before she leaves, but Manimala is hidden.

Rewati Bai's pimp comes looking for her in the Usha publishing house. Her child has been born, her holiday is over. Now it is business as usual. He scratches his hairy cheek and passes through the retail outlet, piled with blue, hard-bound books. He reaches the living-quarters at the back.

'I know nothing about Rewati Bai. How can I tell you where she is?' I say.

'She came to see you. I know she came here, just before she disappeared.'

'What can I do about that? Maybe she has gone to the Himalayas to look for Gujjar Mal.'

'But I love her, she is my woman, I must get her back. She must have told you where she's going?'

'Has she left Meerut?'

'You should know, you have her baby. I know that is her baby, which your woman is holding to her breast. You can't fool me, I'll get the police, you've stolen her baby.'

'No,' Manimala says, 'this is my baby, don't you see, it looks just like my husband Gujjar Mal.'

I smile. I push the deflated intruder out of the back door.

By His Death

Bhisham Chand: They've all settled in, the plane is ready to leave. Mr Vir Bahadur Singh will look after himself now, doesn't need me. OK, he is right there, across the aisle. Come what may, I have to make sure he is comfortable, otherwise he might make the next trip abroad without me. How difficult it is to get these trips abroad. So worthwhile. Everybody in the ministry in Delhi knows that I am travelling to Rhidus. Not many people manage to get a trip there. Everybody goes to Paris or Rome, London or Frankfurt, but Rhidus is different, tucked away in a corner of the Sea of Brisbane. My father-in-law was a great traveller, his job with the United Nations took him all over the world. You wouldn't believe it, looking at him now: short and stocky with the fat in rough layers all over his body. Only his nose is sharp and thin, like a beak, always stuck into my business. Shubha, my wife, dotes on him, they have the same thick, fleshy lips and slightly bulging eyes, always whispering counsel to each other. But still, it is useful to be married to the daughter of someone who had been so high up in government. Very secure, entering the network in a space already cleared by your father-in-law, like entering a tomb made to size. Also like entering Shubha. Warm and succulent, held in from all sides. Sometimes women are rough and thorny as rose plants, I'm told.

Wonder what Ms Anna Dorai feels like, inside? She's quite magnificent, isn't she, seated across there with Mr Vir Bahadur Singh? I haven't looked at her in detail, why should I bother, I am a married man? Though one is free to look, of course. The whole issue is confusing, it's often better to avoid it, take the simpler way out, just do what people tell you and carry on your life in these safe areas. Like taking care of Mr Vir Bahadur Singh's baggage, seeing that his tickets are in order. Ms AD laughs at him. How can you laugh at an officer of such high status, a senior officer? My father-in-law never made it to an ambassador's post, he tried very hard, didn't he? Shubha is still very indignant. A family grievance against the whole world, that Mr Prahlad Joshi was never appointed ambassador. His last post was counsellor in Kathmandu, that's quite high too. Never mind, you don't have to mention the post, enough to say, 'When my father-in-law was posted in Yugoslavia . . . ' or 'I've heard a lot about your country, madam, from my father-in-law who came to Rhidus for a UN conference some years ago.' No need to say what he did in the conference, ran around with papers like an office-boy, I'm sure.

Ms Anna Dorai: The Lebanese from Orly Airport should be on this plane. He was boarding at the end of the line, his portly figure distinctly interested in striking up an acquaintance.

'I'm taking a Rhidus Airways plane to Mesos, we will organise a garments fair for the government. What about in India? Can't I do something there? You're in the government, you can help with this, get me a contract. You can be my agent, I'll give you a commission.'

'I'm not in that kind of government job. I'm the Director of the National Museum. Nothing to do with trade fairs. But I can tell you who to contact in Delhi. We all know each other after all. The official network. And I'm not interested in a commission.' How to explain to him the way government worked in India.

'Oh, come on, you're too gentle. Too quiet and idealistic. How do I know? I can sense it, I read people like a book. That's why I do so well in business, or whatever I undertake, a fair, a film, anything. I'm always successful. Remember that. Any contact you give me, it will be a success. And you must profit from it too. If you do work, you should get money. At least that's what I believe. I was doing very well until these wars came along. But I guess we should be used to wars. Before I was born, Lebanon was such a battlefield. Palestinians and Israelis, and hundreds of factions. Fortunately it was almost all over by the time I was born, the Western countries had given Lebanon over to the Syrians to pay for their help in the Gulf War against Iraq. My mother told me the stories. My father was killed by a stray bullet right before the truce. He wasn't at all involved in the fighting, he was just a shrewd businessman dealing in shoe-uppers. A case of destiny, I guess. And you, you're a nice, soft woman, what are you doing waiting in Paris for a flight to Rhidus? It's no place for a woman.'

'Why not? Are there no women in Rhidus?'

'They haven't told you about the Marmots? They're spread all over the island, an army of occupation, cutting even the capital city of Mesos in half. You'll see them there, striding the wall which separates the occupied portion from that still under the Magdalene government's control. In fact, the government is lucky that the United Nations came in so fast and saved the airport. Otherwise the little island would have been cut off from the rest of the world.'

'I've heard. It's been an active UN question for a long time. The Marmots hate the Magdalenes in Rhidus. They came in from Kasmira on the mainland, and invaded the island. When was it, some ten years ago?'

'That was the second invasion.'

'But I don't understand how they've been able to stay so many years. Has nobody put pressure on the government of Kasmira to withdraw?'

'Why should they? Who's bothered about the little island of Rhidus? And if the sect of the Magdalenes is wiped out, it wouldn't hurt anybody outside the island. They would just say, 'Oh the women-worshippers! Too bad!' But the Magdalenes keep talking about India, I think they look to you for help.'

'We're so far away. And anyhow, it's an internal affair, how can we come in?'

'Why are you going?'

'To plan an exhibition on the development of Magdalene culture and civilisation. We want to show it in New Delhi, Bombay and Calcutta next year.'

'Then you will stay in Mesos for some time?'

'A few days, not too long. I'm going with these other people. Just a week, I think.'

Ms Anna Dorai: Here is Mr Vir Bahadur Singh, what a joker. But what can one do with him? With his sheer, hearty presence. How can he be so energetic for God's sake? Doesn't stop talking. He even greets children on the road as if he is Father Christmas. Learns all the words of greetings and 'Thank you' in a foreign language as soon as he arrives. Last time in Jakarta he was picking up little bits of Bahasa Indonesian, and mispronouncing it of course. But that's really his business, I'm not responsible for him. Wagging his large head at the children. Imagine, to be stuck with him twice. Just my luck. They congratulated us back in Delhi, How nice being able to travel together to Rhidus, since you already know him. We made a great effort to get you there at the same time, just before the prime minister's visit. In fact he arrives the day after you, which means tomorrow the prime minister will arrive in Rhidus. The active Vir Bahadur Singh will be there to greet him, bumbling and submissive, running around to make arrangements. Or Bhisham Chand will do that, they always travel together. Vir Bahadur Singh is bow-legged and so shabby in his pyjamas, I felt sad; he was so diminished by taking off his suit. The phone between our rooms was not working, he came to tell me we had to leave early. Even then he was nibbling a biscuit. He is always eating and drinking. His lantern jaw is like a pouch, specially constructed to take in all that stuff. He's descending on the first meal of the flight. He's to be in charge of the preliminary talks until the prime minister takes over. My visit's just been tagged on. Finalising this exhibition will add weight to the prime minister's speech, he can refer to it. A major exchange in the field of culture is being planned between our two countries. Your country with its great cultural heritage, and ours which goes back well beyond Mohenjodaro. How long have the Magdalenes been in Rhidus? Anyway, well after Jesus Christ, AD, my own initials. Mary Magdalene, an off-shoot of Jesus Christ. With her long beautiful hair and perfume and myrrh, for his poor worn-out feet. Bathing them with her tears. How soft and tender. What did she feel as she cried? It must have been the first time she cried at a man's feet. Maybe it loosened up what the years of pain and silence had deposited inside her, and it floated out, all of it, like huge icebergs lumbering out into a warm sea, freeing her from the weight of her past. Floating out into a warm sea, the Sea of Brisbane, for example. Deep blue, a very special colour they say, it is all around the island of Rhidus, and right below us now, here, from the plane windows. He leans across, pressing his striped jacket of shiny terry-cot into my side. What a wonderful view, how beautiful! I'm the great detective, following his every move, I track VBS down to the centre of his being.

Myself, I'm quite easy to track as well. Just follow me to the museum. A huge building in red sandstone which has bleached to a gentle pink over the two hundred years since the British built it. Their cupolas and umbrellas of stone, to which we added modern galleries in glass and marble. My shelter and my hiding-place, my garden where I bloom. Our last exhibition of Mughal Miniatures was most successful. They glowed on the new walls as the prime minister lit a lamp to mark the opening of the exhibition. He stopped to look in all directions, and everyone clapped, waiting for his eyes to arrive at them. VBS had stationed himself in the direct line of the lamp, but the prime minister's gaze stopped short at a carved wooden door which our designer had propped against the wall for effect, then swept back across the path it had come. What magic in that prime ministerial eye. But VBS can make up the shortfall now, the prime minister is bound to see him, and VBS has an important bureaucratic post. How did he get it, considering the level of his intelligence?

Economic co-operation, joint ventures, how can we join up with little Rhidus? He will prepare the ground now for the prime minister and the Minister for Economic Affairs, arriving in their chartered plane from Frankfurt. Gondwana-land was their last stop for a state visit. Vir Bahadur Singh and Bhisham Chand arriving in advance, towncriers before the circus, preparing the way. Here you will tread, these are the thorny paths of inter-state co-operation. Rhidus waits for them. And for me.

Vir Bahadur Singh says, 'What about the Magdalenes and who are they? You know everything, Ms Anna Dorai, so, please, tell a little bit about them. I will have to give a speech when they welcome us at the airport, standing on the tarmac with flowers.'

Ms Anna Dorai says, 'I can give you a book, it's right here. *History of the Magdalenes, 1100–2100 AD: a study in cultural development*. It has a special section on the human figure in early Magdalene art, which you don't need to read. Actually, it is the only book on the subject, written by Dr Kiranos, my counterpart in Rhidus, head of the Department of Antiquities.'

Vir Bahadur Singh says, 'Oh yes, a book is all right, though I would prefer to hear a lecture from you, in your sweet way. I am a great reader, my house in Delhi is full of books. I will read it tomorrow morning. I wake at 5 am always. No matter where, or at what time I go to bed, 5 am. Just like that. But, you know, the speech, I should like to hear it now. Tell me a little bit. Then I will also read. Will Dr Kiranos give me a copy of his book?'

Ms Anna Dorai: They talk about Kiranos in Delhi and in Srinagar too.

'I haven't met him,' she says, 'I was in the States when he visited India, and, in any case, it was before I became Director of the National Museum. But you can ask him yourself. I have only the copy he sent to the museum, it's a recent book. But he did original research in Kashmir. Jesus Christ is supposed to be buried at Rozabal, Khanyar, in the interior of Srinagar city. A book published more than a century ago by an Indian historian, F. Khurshid Taing, entitled *The Next Day*, talks about it. But the local people did not let Dr Kiranos enter the tomb, since it has become a local pilgrimage spot over the last two hundred years. He went instead along a route Christ is supposed to have followed when he escaped from Jerusalem after being taken down from the cross. He headed for the Himalayas with Mary Magdalene. They went to Bukhara, and then to Samarkhand and Kashgar in Central Asia. I went there myself once, after a visit to the Soviet Union. We were doing a bilateral exhibition at the Hermitage. They took me to Tashkent, and from there I went on to Bukhara and Samarkhand. It's the usual tourist trip, like foreign visitors going to Jaipur and Agra, the Golden Triangle, when they come to Delhi.'

'You travel a lot, Anna! Very lucky. I love visiting foreign countries.'

'I like travelling. If I stay too long in one place, I get restless.'

He has finished his drink, and is poking around at the bottom of the glass for a green olive with a red centre. It rolls tormentingly over the smooth, heavy crystal. He gestures to a steward who peeps into the executive-class section at that moment, who then sends an air hostess. They haven't seen her before. Vir Bahadur Singh is completely bowled over. She has softly permed, shoulder-length hair and heavy blue eyes, a strong American accent, slightly faulty English, and exquisite pearl-like teeth which bite gently at pouting lips painted crimson.

Ms Anna Dorai: Is this girl actually getting his order right? Does she really work? Am I jealous of her lightness, of her pretty, balloon beauty which makes her float casually up and down the aisles?

Vir Bahadur Singh launches into her presence with

immediate gusto. 'Your airline is great. I am liking very much this journey. We have come a long way, from India to Kuwait, then changing again at Paris for Rhidus Airways. The flight from Kuwait to Paris was terrible. The worst airline that I have ever used. I was very much upset. Mariana Airlines. But yours . . . and now especially as I have met you. What is your name?'

'Sonia.' She is smiling down at him. Anna Dorai looks out of the window.

Ms Anna Dorai: We know what happened in the Mariana Airlines. He quarrelled with an air hostess when she asked him to pay for a tin of caviar. He insisted that it was part of the free menu. The head steward told him if he didn't pay, the air hostess would be liable, from her salary, and she could not afford it.

'You remember what happened in the Mariana Airlines?' He is dragging Anna Dorai's attention away from the window, she is nodding at him, clearly hoping that the conversation will carry on without her, but her input is needed.

'I agree with you,' she says. 'If you were expected to pay for the caviar, they should have told you before.'

'Oh I stuck to my rights. I don't let people push me around.'

The young goddess has disappeared with his order. He lumbers up in search of her. The plane is steady as a house, the executive cabin full of soft light as the staff prepares for dinner. He returns with a triumphant plastic bag held to his side. 'I got what I wanted. I knew these people are very good.'

Both sides of the bag are printed with the logo of Rhidus Airways, long strands of a woman's luxuriant brown hair, crowned with a circlet of tears. 'Sonia – that's the pretty girl who took my order. I knew I would be able to charm her, she just loved me, gave me a whole stack of complimentary chocolates and three half-bottles of champagne. Now I don't feel so bad about the hassle on Mariana Airlines. Sonia lives in Mesos, where we are going.'

He pops the plastic bag into a huge black briefcase with green stripes across it.

Ms Anna Dorai: One doesn't usually think of an air hostess living anywhere; she belongs to the world inside the aircraft. VBS has taken her out, and put her in the world down there, in Mesos. Now she appears as a follower of Mary Magdalene.

'Anna,' he is sipping a fresh drink now, Sonia has just left in a whirl of perfume, 'you have still to tell me about the Magdalenes. Who are the Marmots? I should not make stupid mistakes at the airport. Maybe I will not have to speak, and we can go straight through to the hotel, but, who knows? Everybody says I am a bull in a china shop. Once I bought my wife a bottle of perfume which turned out to be air freshener for bathrooms. She flung it across the room at me and it smashed against the wall. You can still see a huge yellow stain on the whitewash.'

The dinner trolley has arrived in the aisle beside them. Vir Bahadur Singh quickly clears the serving tray in front of him ready for the goodies which are to follow, tucking away his whisky glass. It is to be a formal meal, elegantly served, with a neat menu card, indicating choices, placed at each corner of the tray. Vir Bahadur Singh is whispering his refrain with delight. 'What a wonderful airway.' A square hairy hand cleaves possessively to a long-stemmed glass of chilled white wine. It forms tiny drops of moisture which run into his thick fingers. 'And wine too,' he murmurs, 'all for us.'

Ms Anna Dorai: The Lebanese from Orly Airport is here, seating himself in the last line, looking around for me. What is he doing here? I don't think he's looking for me because of a sudden attraction, he must want something. Everything in his outer layers is very pleasant, very warm and congenial, but once you begin to go into it, you hit something, something dense and hard as rock. I imagine it would be difficult to move him from anything he attaches himself to, despite all this very accommodating charm. He's looking around for me. Here, this is me, my head thrown back behind VBS's large turban. But I am busy, as yet unapproachable; we are eating dinner. Maybe later. What more does he want to talk about? He has told me already of a family which moves rapidly across the violent faces of the Middle East. His father was in ordinary business, but the son is being pursued by terrorists, for an unmentioned reason. Do I believe a good story which gains my sympathy, that of an innocent victim being ruthlessly pursued, anything said in his soft, tender tones? Sonia is bending over him, the fairy lady of VBS's dream. She must be saying, move back to your own seat in economy class. They get a different dinner back there, I'm sure. Nothing fancy like this. But the Lebanese is rich enough not to care, not in the desolate way of VBS and the caviar. But he is attached enough to good food. He is peering into BC's dinner, gauging the delights to come. He catches sight of me watching and waves a fat hand, his eyes, a pale brown, merge with the gold of his skin. VBS looks up, ham rolled around a swirl of prawn pâté.

'Fish will be very good in Rhidus, it is an island,' he says. 'Oh wonderful, there she is. Sonia, Sonia! You aren't serving us dinner. Of course, I have no complaints, everything's fine, but it would be nice if you were here.'

The Lebanese is poised over a good dinner, about to dig a casual fork into a circlet of ham. There is no question of moving him back to economy class if he wants to stay here. His warm, fat confidence is like newly-baked bread, rising all around you, ready to smother you. Sonia extracts herself and arrives at VBS's side, smiling down at him.

Ms Anna Dorai: Is this politeness? Maybe Sonia actually likes VBS! But she has other duties. Sonia of the American accent and bleached, ash-blond hair, nothing wrong with it, she really is beautiful. Her pouting lips have taken themselves off and away to do her work. Yes, of course, the Magdalenes, what are their rites of worship? No one who does not belong to the Church can participate.

'The great point of controversy is where Mary Magdalene is buried. Khurshid Taing of Kashmir is the only Indian historian who supports the claim of the Marmots that she is buried in Kashgar. All the others say she came to Rhidus, even that she is buried in Sirocco, in the northern region of Rhidus. It's a pity we will not have time to go there. I have seen photos of a grand tomb, full of marble and gold, like a palace. After her difficult life, perhaps her bones deserved this. The Marmots have built their own tomb for her in Kashgar, a small, quite elegant thing, decorated with lapis lazuli from Afghanistan, more in keeping with her truly feminine nature, they feel, and they have their own separate set of bones. Sheikh Marmot was one of Mary Magdalene's principal disciples in Central Asia, and started the whole line of the Marmots. They look upon the Magdalenes in Rhidus as heretics and liars, who have persisted in holding to a wrong view of the scriptures, and they would willingly wipe them away from the face of the earth, to destroy their heresy. The Marmots look upon themselves as the stern, ascetic guardians of the faith. All the men wear beards and square leather shoes with gold work along the sides, showing the fierce, five-pointed flower of Sheikh Marmot, and their women go veiled in public. They long ago left off worshipping Mary Magdalene, though she is part of their pantheon, and, according to them, buried firmly in Kashgar. They worship a male line descended from Sheikh Marmot. But all our historians, with the exception of Khurshid Taing, hold that she came on here from Kashgar, crossing the sea to Rhidus in a small boat belonging to Arab traders. The people of Rhidus feel very close to India for that reason . . . They feel we are holding up the basic foundation of their faith, even though we have never broken off diplomatic relations with the Marmots of Kasmira. Dr Kiranos became something of a hero in Rhidus when he disproved Khurshid Taing's theory through his research in Srinagar. In fact, when the Marmots invaded Mesos, they wanted to kill Dr Kiranos. But he had the protection of Mary Magdalene, in her tomb in Sirocco; and they could not find him.'

'Magdalenes and Marmots. This is very interesting. But what can I say about them in my speech?' Vir Bahadur Singh has decided his choice from the menu, and put it back on a corner of his tray. He is sipping wine with gusto, collecting his hunger for the coming meal. He glances down the aisles in search of Sonia, of more drink, more food, and picks a scrap of ham from his plate.

'You needn't speak too much about either. After all, we haven't severed diplomatic relations with Kasmira, so from a government functionary, they will not expect loud denunciations. But make sure to mention Mary Magdalene arriving on the shores of Rhidus, establishing the great monastery of Silenus up on the hill. About two hundred years ago, when their religion had got very conventional and orthodox, there was a great battle up on the hill near Silenus. The young ascetic monks in monasteries all over the island banded together and forbade entry to women, saying they were congenitally rotten, and should be banished from the faith because they were causing the downfall of the Church. The other lot opposed this vigorously, saying that as we worship Mary Magdalene, who was the essence of all womanhood, how can we forbid women to enter Silenus? The Marmots saw a good opportunity and excuse to invade the northern part of the island. As the Magdalenes were not equipped to defend themselves, the Marmots spread in small settlements all over the island. Ten years ago they invaded a second time, more thoroughly. Now they have consolidated their position so well that no Magdalene can even enter the area occupied by the Marmots. So, in effect, the island has been divided.'

Bhisham Chand: She has forgotten me completely. She looks sometimes at that fat chap who has sneaked in from the economy section. He must have come from her, a Punjabi brain always notices these things, she was sitting with him at Orly Airport, talking a great deal. Maybe she likes him, though it appears difficult to see why. She's beautiful, collected, rolled tightly on herself. He spreads himself in oily ease. I envy his confidence. He could easily pass over my small clerical prickles, like a steam-roller, flatten me out. Who knows? He might have decided to plot some deal through her, maybe he's assessing the possibilities. I do not miss his narrowed eyes, and the way they follow every movement without the least tension in his body. He seems to have attached himself to her for the time being, but he would have no qualms about moving on if it suited him. I think he'll add interest to my trip. Will whisky be cheap in the airport? One must take back all these goodies. I have VBS all taped up, he depends upon me completely. I am his soul. That's my revenge, and my reward for crawling on the floor for him. Not a bad fellow really. She laughs at him, it is quite obvious she laughs, and sometimes she is very irritated. Wants to fling away from him. Her head swings back, I see the long sweep of her throat, pale gold in artificial light. How must it be, to touch that skin, run the palm of this hand over its smooth surface? I don't know if he sees it: her neck, the beauty of her body. I have been telling her so often, he has a good heart, a heart of gold, though I'm not sure it is simple, like that. He's pretty sharp, he knows how to look after his own interests, even how to be kind to me. He knows that I am useful. Last time he went out on a trip, he bought me a shirt from Dubai, white terry-cot with red and black stripes, very bright, wonderful to wear on holidays, Shubha likes it very much, VBS is a good chap. But she is beautiful. I can see her long, lovely, straight, thin nose, beyond VBS's face when I bend a little forward. He eats so much, it tires me to see him, it seems to go on for ever. She has masses of hair, thick like a forest, and full of life. She could have married anybody, but she was involved for years with that Bengali person from Calcutta. Mr Rabindra Nath Khokkar. Then it broke up, and we never understood why, nobody gave any reason. Now it's a little late for her to get married, she's past the age . . . there's a proper age for everything. Very safe to be married. Everything is arranged between me and Shubha, I have my rights. Otherwise to approach a woman like AD would be, for me, absolutely impossible. To bear the heavy presence of a woman to whom one is not related. Mother, sister, wife, cousin, once the labels are established, everything else is possible. But to take on the weight of an unknown woman! That is something else. She is very clever, Ms AD, knows so much, I am a drop in a wave of admiration. She is telling this long strange history of the Magdalenes to VBS. Will everything be all right in Rhidus?

Ms Anna Dorai: A long history, everything should be clear to him now. It is still possible that he will make a mistake, but he is not my responsibility, he carries himself and his own sins. Also his own virtues. He has worked out his survival techniques quite well, he is constantly filling himself out, needs to make himself substantial. We hear so much, about his fishing, and his son who chases butterflies with a camera. And constantly about his collection of coins, and how it is developing over the years.

'I am only an amateur. Mr Bhola Nath, the great authority on the subject, said to me, 'Vir Bahadur, one day your coin collection will be good enough to find a place in a museum.' I am waiting for that day. But already I am invited to seminars and people write asking my opinion. One women's magazine interviewed me last year when it proposed coin-collecting as a good hobby for its readers.'

Ms Anna Dorai: I can just see Mary Magdalene arriving at the coast of Rhidus, her small, shell-like boat skirting huge rocks which lie along the shore, her long, loose garments swelling in the wind as in paintings of the event. Everyone considers the moment of arrival to be an important one, the first step she took on the soil of Rhidus is venerated. You can see it in the holy pictures. In some areas of New York, they do a thriving business in turning these out (for Rhidus refugees from the occupied territories who settled in the US), framed in white plastic with edges of gilt, or just in plastic cases, easy to carry against your heart, to protect it from breaking. Mary Magdalene with a flat brown face and beautiful shining eyes, lifting up her heavy hair, stepping on a strange and utterly unknown shore. It could have been inhabited by cannibals. Why didn't Jesus Christ go with her? Why did he abandon her at Kashgar? She would have fol-

By His Death 33

lowed him to the ends of the earth, anywhere he went, whatever he wanted from her. She was utterly devoted to him. He had captured her soul, drawn her into the centre of his being. Yet he abandoned her at Kashgar, sent her off in a boat across the high seas, to carry the word into unknown quarters. I wonder if someone went back to tell him where she had reached, to establish contact between Mary Magdalene and her Saviour. But I'm not sure of the dates. He could already have been dead by the time she reached Rhidus. Journeys took a long time, in those days.

Ms Anna Dorai says, 'After Kashgar, Jesus came back to Balkh, taking the route along the bank of the river Indus, and reached Sind. After crossing the five rivers of Punjab, he reached Rajputana and wandered from place to place till he reached the Valley of Kashmir, where he came to be known as Yuz-Asaph. That's his connection with India. But Mary Magdalene was no longer with him at that time. He had sent her off alone to Rhidus.'

Sonia is at her elbow, bending to whisper. Vir Bahadur Singh gazes at the air hostess in sheer delight, and at the bowl of fruit she carries. She had taken away the dessert which was on the menu, American cheesecake, 'I never eat this. It's been years. Whenever someone serves cheesecake, I think of some way to avoid it. Makes me too heavy and fat. Dear, dear Sonia, can you get me some fruit instead?'

She is placing the bowl before him, piled with red, glowing cherries, two bananas arranged decoratively, oranges from Rhidus, their bright skins flecked with red. She has poured a drink which releases a strong, acrid smell. 'You must try some of our Rhidus brandy.'

'You know, Sonia, I love these cherries, I could make a meal of them, a meal of fruit.' Though he has already eaten everything else.

'The gentleman, madam, at the back of the cabin. He would like to talk with you,' Sonia says to her.

Ms Anna Dorai: Maybe, by the time they reached Kashgar, he wasn't interested in her any more. It could be true. That happens, anything can happen, between two people. Rabin stopped calling me. Just disappeared. Nothing mysterious. Just dropped like a stone into the political life of his party. Even now I can't believe that he doesn't love me any longer. The phone rang and rang in his apartment. I could almost hear its echo in the empty rooms, and then I couldn't imagine the rooms any more, I was possessed only by the sound in my ear. For months I imagined coming across him suddenly, at an airport, or at a party, at a wedding, in a garden, in the shops. Walking down Khan Market and seeing him on the pavement. Turning to find him watching me, his dark eyes full of smiles. But none of these happened. He just went on, somewhere, and I was left behind. To travel restlessly, like this.

Anna Dorai is nodding at Sonia, 'Yes, OK, I'll go over.' The Lebanese is watching her without a smile, his eyes fringed with dark lashes. He knows she will come.

Bhisham Chand: She doesn't need to sit so close to him, almost leaning over the arm of the seat. He is a fat fellow, his flesh is yielding and soft, like cotton-wool, maybe he's even fatter than VBS but he is casual, relaxed. VBS carries his ugly rolls of fat jutting awkwardly from tight shirts and trousers which perch on a protruding shelf of a stomach. This chap is confident. Maybe that's what one needs with AD. To be confident and outgoing. Just to go out and get her. But that's not in my nature. I'm not made that way, and I'm not trained in that culture. It's Western culture. No loyalty, I tell you. Why doesn't she stick with us, instead of fraternising with a foreigner, and a Middle Eastern guy at that, not even European? She turns away, laughing, then goes back to an animated conversation. So different from the bored, flat look she had talking to VBS, telling him all that history stuff. I can't hear what they are saying. This fat fellow, surely he is a diamond merchant or something exciting like that? He looks rich, as if he is prospering, and determined to survive that way against all odds. He is whispering to her.

Ms Anna Dorai: Our very first meeting seduced me. Drew me for ever into this cocoon which holds me. The first time, with Rabin, and all the times after, whirling round him like a hula hoop, a bright red ring, wrapping him, and me, in constant movement, until it all comes to a stop.

The Indira Gandhi Centre is celebrating its centennial. Opens with a huge, glittering reception on its grounds near Rajpath. This used to be a very active boat club, and boats have once again been provided for the guests. They rock the evening breeze under clusters of fairy lights which reflect from the water below. Oars are neatly crossed, the boats are ready. If only it were not so hot, but you can't get away from the actual date of an anniversary, it must be celebrated. I tug at my high necklace, it is such a formal occasion. I am not accustomed any more to wearing jewellery. The knot at the back is stuck. If I could only loosen it, take it off, no one would notice, the reception line has been negotiated already and it is dark in the shadows beside the canal. My fingers are slippery with sweat which only tightens the knot. A large cool hand settles on my back, and, within moments, the necklace is loose, lifted off. I turn with fear, a thief, and he is looking into my eyes. He is handsome and intense, and the scene is just right for the beginning of a romance.

The plane is to land soon, the Lebanese beside her prepares to go back to his regular seat in the economy class. 'Who are these people you are travelling with?' He turns his round, dimpled chin towards Vir Bahadur Singh. 'It's always nice to meet Indians.'

'A senior official in the Ministry of Defence Production. I'll introduce you, if you like.'

He bends over Vir Bahadur Singh solicitously, then settles into a seat beside him, leaving Anna Dorai standing aimlessly in the aisle. Sonia appears, brisk in her landing procedures, and gently propels her beside Bhisham Chand. She collects an untouched brandy glass from Vir Bahadur Singh. 'Oh, you didn't like our Rhidus brandy!'

'Very much, very much. But there was no time to drink it, you gave me so many other things.'

A coldness in the elbow which brushes his arm upsets Vir Bahadur Singh. He snaps at Bhisham Chand. 'See, I told you to finish it for me. Not to upset her in any way. She has promised to give me two bottles of champagne as I disembark.' He looks anxiously at Sonia. The Lebanese gentleman beside him does not impose an alien presence, he is introducing himself without abrasion, layer by layer, into the fluid life of the group.

'Maybe she will give you two bottles of Rhidus brandy, instead!'

Vir Bahadur Singh looks at Anna Dorai as if she had dealt him a mortal blow. Recovering, he says, 'Whatever it is, I do not have a single enemy, everybody is my friend.'

Anna Dorai has been abandoned by the Lebanese. He's a shrewd businessman, Vir Bahadur Singh is a better contact, she has no power to influence things, to make deals. It makes sense that he should have settled in firmly beside his new acquaintance, and begun assiduously to cultivate him. One fat man beside another, they belong together.

'Oh, look, how many people to receive us!' Vir Bahadur Singh waits at the top of the gangway. Sonia has been faithful to her word. He is clutching a Rhidus Airways bag with the two bottles. Sonia handed it to him quietly as he passed her, followed firmly by the Lebanese. He stopped and murmured a long time. She nodded and smiled, the three of them jammed in the narrow space of the pantry.

A bunch of people moves to the foot of the gangway, their dark heads clustered in welcome as the honoured visitors descend. Flowers rustle in large bouquets 'And so many flowers, what exquisite flowers!' VBS whispers.

'Only for you, sir, they have come to receive senior official of government of India,' says Bhisham Chand, settling a large briefcase decorated with a green line carefully on the tarmac beside Vir Bahadur Singh.

Only two detach from the reception group to greet them.

The others smile abstractedly towards the gangway. 'We are waiting for your minister to welcome him.'

Sure enough, the minister's wide trousers emerge, he has been kept to the last, after all the other first-class passengers have left.

'Oh, was he on the plane with us? Are you sure? We didn't know anything about it.'

'Maybe because of security. He is a cabinet minister after all. Security is our paramount concern. And then, later, your prime minister comes. Both from India, such a friendly country. We cannot afford to take any chances with terrorists and all that,' says Mr Bashir Fennel. He hands her an enormous bunch of orange lilies. Spotted tongues heavy with pollen wave at the centre of each flower. 'I am the protocol officer attached to you during your visit. Anything you need, please ask me.'

Ms Anna Dorai: What will you give me, if I ask? Will you give me back Rabindra Nath Khokkar, who just disappeared from my life a few years ago? I've even forgotten how many years, time expands and contracts, it is a well-known law of physics. It wasn't like a death or a crucifixion, a sudden, terrible event, or like coming upon your man sleeping with another woman. Something which breaks you up, destroys you with pain. But it's there, staring you in the face, and there's nothing you can do about it, except get over it, like a mountain you must climb. But Rabin's slipping away like that, just fading, didn't even give me the chance for grief. A crumbling, gradual erosion which ate away my life, left me with nothing except this awful anxiety about being passed by, of being suffocated by sterility. This final flattening which goes on behind the walls, until one day there is only emptiness behind them. There's lots of loss and longing on this invaded island of Rhidus. Mary Magdalene brought it here, exiled from her lord, despatched here in a cockle-shell boat, arriving here to set up monasteries, propagate the faith, while her heart was breaking. This is hard tarmac, firm and black beneath my feet, not the soft sands of the beach where she stepped from her boat and the vast sea, with the unknown, fearsome island of Rhidus, empty of Jesus Christ, before her. A wind pulls at my hair as we stand here, perhaps it will rain soon. The sky is grey and dark.

Bhisham Chand: She leans forward to talk to me, the soft silk from her sari cascades over my shoulder. I want to wrap myself in it, to snuggle up very close to her. I can feel her breath against my ear. Of course, I did not know that the prime minister was in the plane, nobody tells me these things. Perhaps VBS did not know either. His usual expression for the boss, of watchful alertness, struggles with his disappointment that the flowers and reception were not for him.

'You won't have to make a speech now. Be grateful for that. You can forget about the Magdalenes and the Marmots. Let the minister do the work.' She is comforting him, dissipating his foolishness.

'Oh, here you are, Vir Bahadur Singh. I hope you are carrying all the relevant files. The prime minister might want to touch upon this topic, you know, the new computer deal. How are you, Ms Anna Dorai? So, the museum is all set for the exhibition?'

Bhisham Chand: He must not notice me, I am small fry. Must not impinge upon the consciousness of men in such god-like positions. I will disappear behind those two cabinets lined with artifacts: ancient mouldy vases supported on iron rings, terracotta pots: in my village they make them much better. She is standing right there examining them, I can see the blue folds of her sari below the edge of wood. The protocol people are taking care of the minister now, he is sipping some strong coffee from tiny cups. Who can wet even the base of one's throat with such tiny quantities? They are looking for me now, carrying a large mug of beer, I was the only one who ordered beer. Oh, the fat man from the plane is taking it. What is he doing here anyway? Who let him in? Maybe they thought he was part of our entourage, he was walking so close to the heels of VBS. In fact, I have the feeling that from now on he's going to be around a lot, pushing into the centre of our lives for his own reasons. What are those reasons? I will watch him, like I watch everyone. That's the task of all successful underlings. He is the huge pancake with secret pockets and empty combs for honey and molasses. I am the spoon that will dig him up. But this extraordinary fascination with Ms Anna Dorai deflects me.

The party is split for the long journey from the airport to the hotel. Bhisham Chand, very uneasy, travels with Anna Dorai. For the first time on this trip Vir Bahadur Singh is separated from him, travelling in the car just in front, with the Lebanese.

Ms Anna Dorai: I can see that the Lebanese is not interested in me any more. Well, I guess he wasn't attracted to me or anything like that. Just the contacts. How to get on in life. Make the right touches. And VBS is the correct one for that. It's good the Lebanese has tapped VBS the joker, he's the important one here, with government contacts. And he knows it. Under all this nonsense, our bumbling bull is sharp. He uses all his advantages, such as they are.

'His son's book on butterflies, with that huge, beautiful picture of *Seraphina Mineur* on top, who published it? I see it in every minister's office in Delhi. Your boss has been presenting it, I suppose,' she says to Bhisham Chand.

'Young master Nirod is a good photographer, the book is published by the government press, very good quality, you can see I am carrying, carefully, many copies for presentation by Mr Vir Bahadur Singh.'

Ms Anna Dorai: Anyway, doesn't seem to work, I'm not interested in the Lebanese myself. It was proforma trying, an obligation to being alive and sexually attractive. Don't want them saying, not yet, well, middle-aged lady. Why should anyone know how much I have lost? I can't build a monastery like Mary Magdalene, but I suppose one has to do something. Like make eyes at the Lebanese, flirt with him a bit. One must kick around, show signs of life. Not, of course, like VBS, spilling over in all directions. Rabin is always with me, like a feast for a hungry person. Always the sight, the sound, even his smell is here, close to me, inside my soul. My friends said, what does it mean? Why do you mourn? He was not worth so much longing and desire, so much love. It's not relevant to count how many days we spent together. Someone like Bhisham Chand would make the computation, and dismiss him as not important. But I'm different, I'm murdered by different instruments. You only knew him for a few months, Anna, forget him, let him go. He did nothing which you asked, made no commitments. He was like a bit of mist which touched the ridge of a big, black mountain, which Mary Magdalene climbed to build her monastery, and tried fruitlessly to rid herself of the memory of Jesus Christ, who lived always with her, even on Rhidus, this faraway chunk of earth rising from the sea.

Bhisham Chand: Seems like a very long way from the airport into the city of Mesos. We are to stay at the Hotel Alinda. It is my duty to find out all these things beforehand. Supposing he turns to me to ask beginning, 'Bhisham Chand' in his hearty voice, emerging through layers of sleep and food. As soon as he is in a moving car, VBS goes to sleep. He must be snoring up ahead, slumped beside the fat man from Lebanon, his head nodding crookedly against the back seat. He did not sleep in the plane, he was all excited about the wine and the air hostess. Didn't like her myself, our AD is much more beautiful. Older, but substantial. Her long neck is like the iron pillar in Kutab Minar. I could reach around it endlessly, and my hands would never meet at the back. I would love to be pressed up against AD. But she's not interested, of course. I couldn't imagine her interested in someone like me. She always appears to be mooning after that lost love, the fellow who left her. That's really stupid. If VBS asks, 'And in which hotel are we to stay in Rhidus? What is the price of scotch in the airport?' I should know all these answers, to be safe. My head is rattling with bits of random information. Sometimes, sometimes, I have problems pulling out the right piece. Did we know the minister

was on the same plane, reposing in first class while VBS
negotiated for bottles of champagne? He would have gone
up front to pay his respects if he had known. Maybe he is
blaming me for the lapse, punishing me by going away with
the Lebanese. Waiting on the pavement for the limousine to
draw up, he did not even look around for me, simply left,
climbing in, his bright black polished shoes flashing against
the velvet upholstery. His luggage was left in a pile, waiting
for someone to load it into our car. AD was cursing about
that. She doesn't understand these things, spends all her feelings in words, while I store them up cautiously, waiting for
the right time. One day it will arrive.

'I don't know how you can stand him for such long
stretches, Bhisham Chand. You practically live with him,
when he travels abroad. Minister to his every need! But
what does he mean, going off with that wretched foreigner,
leaving us to carry his luggage?' She was irritated.

Ms Anna Dorai: Really, is the airport so far? Oh I forgot,
this is an occupied country. The city of Mesos is divided,
troops from Kasmira came in everywhere the Marmots were
settled, with a convenient argument for the United Nations.
'We are here to protect the minority community against the
woman-worshipping oppression of the Magdalenes. They
destroyed our sacred idols wherever they found them,
oppressed the young monks who were sincere followers of
Sheikh Marmot, thrust women into the holy company of the
monasteries to worship.' Anything can sound good. Words
can follow the act easily, pulled on like a blanket, making
new shapes from hot air and the facts underneath are reborn,
re-created, perhaps changed completely.

The limousine is looping back and forth. Mr Fennel turns
to her from the front seat of the car. 'Once it was only fifteen
minutes from the airport into the city of Mesos. Now we
have to avoid the occupied portions. You see the soldiers up
there? The Marmots have built a wall wherever they could.
We placed Magdalene banners and planted trees there to hide
it.'

Anna Dorai looks at the banners: blue crowns and the Rhidus emblem, the long curling lock of hair crowned with a chaplet of tears; and young silver oaks between them, well grown in the ten years since the invasion.

'Do you see the soldiers up there?' Beards, loose trousers gathered at the ankles, shoes gleaming in the evening light with the embroidered five-petalled silver flowers of Sheikh Marmot. 'They stand at ease, casual, as if everything were simple. But as you know, those guns have nuclear missiles. They can destroy the city of Mesos at any time. What we need is a modern nuclear delivery system which will reach Kashgar, their own capital.'

'But the great powers have given you a nuclear umbrella over the Sea of Brisbane. That should be enough, surely?'

The Marmot soldiers peer at them from the top of the wall. The check-post sentry ostentatiously notes the number of their limousine. Anna Dorai moves uneasily beside Bhisham Chand, settling the blue waves of her sari firmly around her shoulders.

'It's not for us. It's only to protect their own interests. What does it matter to them if the Marmots and the Magdalenes kill each other off on the island of Rhidus? Kasmira is important because there is money from copper and marble, and a huge population. Little Rhidus does not even provide good markets for their toothpaste. We know our friends better. We need India much more than we need the great powers.'

'Our Minister of Defence Production is here.'

'We are taking him to the Palace of Delphos, where the president lives. Your prime minister will also stay there.'

'He arrives tomorrow?'

Bhisham Chand is ready now. 'At 3 pm, Madam. We must be there to receive him.'

Mr Fennel says, 'We will let you know the programme tonight. Perhaps it will be better if only the minister goes. Maybe we could take you sightseeing instead. You would surely like to see the mosaics uncovered recently by Dr Kiranos in the town of Porphyria? He plans to send a collection of mosaic panels to India as part of our exhibition.'

'When will I meet Dr Kiranos?'

'He will be at the talks tomorrow.'

'I am not attending the talks. I have no connections with missile systems and defence matters, and that's what your talks are about, surely, with the minister here?'

Bhisham Chand gestures warningly at the chauffeur, but Mr Fennel reassures him. 'Samson is part of the foreign office,' he says. 'He understands ten languages, and speaks none, he has no tongue. His reports are typed out at the end of the day and given to me.' He sees them into the hotel, politely, and arranges everything with the reception before he leaves. Anna Dorai feels safe in the efficient hands of Bashir Fennel.

Ms Anna Dorai: I like the Hotel Alinda. Looking from wide windows at the back of the room, I can see department stores and apartment blocks with clothes hung out on the balconies. No soldiers and sandbags, just an ordinary city. They said Dr Kiranos was waiting for us downstairs. We are all to have a drink in the lobby.

Bisham Chand: He wasn't supposed to be here. Now that she's met him at last, and spent the last hour with him while we all collected here, he's had eyes for no-one else. In her flowing blue sari, she could match very well with his tall, thin body and gold beard. As if Dr Kiranos and our own AD were made to go together. She is attracted by something about him. He seems to be taking charge of her. None of us dares to do that with AD, she would wither us with her scorn. The Lebanese is staying here too, at the Hotel Alinda, but she ignores him, ever since he latched on to VBS. I resent that. VBS, such as he is, belongs to me, he is my territory, to be farmed as I please. I don't want the Lebanese interfering in that.

'Sir, Ms Anna Dorai has decided not to attend our meeting tomorrow. Mr Fennel has given me the programme. We join up after the meeting, and go on to Porphyria for sightseeing and lunch. Sir, here is Mr Radhakrishnan, our ambassador in Rhidus.'

A tall thin man, dressed immaculately and stabbing at a pipe, replied, 'I am very pleased to welcome the Indian delegation. I was in the Palace of Delphos making arrangements for the minister . . . Very unexpected . . . Why did no-one inform me he was coming? Mr Vir Bahadur Singh, may I have a word with you in private? Tomorrow's meeting has been specially scheduled for you and the minister. Otherwise everything was arranged for the visit of the prime minister. The Rhidus authorities are very excited about the visit and anxious that everything should go just right.'

Bhisham Chand: His speech changes when he takes Vir Bahadur Singh off in private: a superior, gently tolerant air breathes from his pipe. VBS will be put thoroughly in his place, he will long for my submissive, totally acquiescing company.

'Why is Anna Dorai not coming to the meeting this morning?' Vir Bahadur Singh is rough and bullying, angry from his meeting with Mr Radhakrishnan. 'As part of the Indian delegation . . .'

'I say, Vir Bahadur, why is this fellow setting off with you to the meeting? Hey, Mister, who are you, getting into the car of the Indian delegation?' The ambassador's bony dark hand pulls at the plump jacket of the Lebanese.

'Mr Sayyid Ghulmahael from Lebanon.' He has drawn himself up and stands facing the ambassador with his arms spread. Casual, waiting with a steely confidence.

'Excuse me, Mr Ambassador, I have asked him to come . . . Matters connected with my ministry – defence production.' Vir Bahadur Singh gives him a small crude push into the waiting car. Mr Radhakrishnan is not satisfied and makes a stubborn move towards the car, the stiff bony shape of his spine jutting authoritatively from his suit.

Mr Fennel from the foreign office shows years of practice in the small gesture of his two hands holding back the ambassador. 'It's OK, Excellency. Don't worry about it. We know about Ghulmahael. We need him there at the meeting.'

'Just a minute, sir. Mr Vir Bahadur Singh is asking me something.'

Mr Radhakrishnan watches Bhisham Chand shove himself into Vir Bahadur Singh's car, his body slanted like the side of a bulging tent, his hands supporting him precariously. Then his head emerges from the plush interior of the limousine.

'Sorry to keep you waiting, sir. I was telling Mr Vir Bahadur Singh about Ms Anna Dorai. She has gone to the archaeological museum with Dr Kiranos, to talk about the joint exhibition. Maybe we will go there later ourselves.'

'But you have the programme surely? For your group they have arranged a special visit to Porphyria. Then swimming and lunch at the Neatani Hotel on the seaside. They seem to be taking special care of Mr Vir Bahadur Singh. I am to accompany the head of their Ministry of Defence Production, to be present for the lunch in Porphyria.' The skin on his long bony face is bunched at the forehead, as he watches Vir Bahadur Singh's limousine draw out of the gate.

Bhisham Chand gives a little bow in the direction of the departing vehicle. 'Not surprising, sir. Mr Vir Bahadur Singh is senior official of the government of India.'

Ms Anna Dorai: Dr Kiranos is waiting for me in the lobby of the archaeological museum. His tall, slightly stooped frame behind the square glasses of the entrance. Style of 200 years ago, end of the twentieth century. The glass pyramid must have been added recently. It lets light in a huge well right into the centre of the building, passing his head in a deep wave. He is director of the museum, he selected the spot to stand like that with light falling around him, bathed in it. Something is happening. His face stirs and dips inside me, reaching straight and deep like a pipe, sucking up all that lies there. Going deeper and deeper. He comes out here, to take me through the doors.

'There is a special tenderness about the way you talk of your research in Kashmir.'

'I was very happy in India. I'm not much of a believer, you know. I found evidence that Jesus Christ came to Kashmir from a record of his dialogue with a local saint, or a Pir as you call him, that Mary Magdalene had left him in Kashgar and begun a journey on the sea. It was the delight of an archaeologist, an historian, not a religious devotee. But India touched me with a deep unexpected familiarity. I felt as if perhaps I had lived there in some past birth.'

'A Magdalene talking of transmigration of the soul! Really, Dr Kiranos!' She is standing in the crook of his arm, about to begin a tour of the museum.

'Minhas. That's my name. Call me Minhas. Here, I must show you something interesting. There's no point giving you the usual spiel for intelligent foreign guests. I've looked at your degrees. You know all this already. But I want to show you a special room with stuff which I found in Nicara in the tomb of an Italian princess who came to the island, converted to the Magdalene faith, married the king's son, and stayed. Very creative person, made her own artefacts. See, this is the throne of ivory and gold she made for the king and these are the cooking pots balanced on covered tripods. Such a beautiful bed, it must have seen a lot of good times. But look here, Anna, this was in the centre of the tomb. I located it from the princess's diary which I found in an old house in Mesos which had belonged to her best friend, Mira, the chief priestess of Rhidus. The princess had planned and set out her own burial. I found this piece under the area where the head of her body was laid. The princess loved it. Her diary dates it from about the time of the arrival of Mary Magdalene in Rhidus, more than two millenia ago. Here it is.' They stand looking through glass at a scene done in terracotta. A high uneven wall encloses what is clearly a sacred area. The figures in the centre are men and women in formal poses placed around a high sacrificial stone and in the centre is the figure going up for sacrifice, a fat, misshapen man executed in great detail: thick fingers, beard, slightly bowlegged, wearing only a loincloth. Even the small indentation of his navel shows up on the huge, comic round of his belly. Clearly he will not be saved at the last minute. He is in marked contrast to the aesthetic perfection of the spectators, they are tall, stately men and women poised in almost inhuman, harmonious beauty all around, watching his progress towards the sacrificial stone where a naked priestess wearing a mask waits for him.

'Come around this way, Anna.' He takes her to the other side of the showcase. 'You see why this must have been a sacred ritual?'

Two figures, ordinary human beings, not the god-like creatures standing around within, are shown scrambling up the enclosure wall, gripping with their hands and knees, and peering over the top, their dishevelled heads thrown back in positions of startled dismay. Anna Dorai moves around to look at them more carefully. They are unusual for this period of history. She is conscious of Dr Kiranos following her, of his strong presence behind her shoulder, and his breath against her hair as he too bends to look through the glass.

Just then a cacophony bursts into the room, and both of them straighten up hastily and move back from the glass. She is in confusion, and then she is angry. They are surrounded by the rumbustious presence of VBS, his familiar spirit Bhisham Chand, and two or three hangers-on. Virtually a crowd. She is afraid for the safety of the fragile glass case, rocking slightly in the wash of their excited arrival. Then she looks carefully at VBS, forever in motion, talking, gesturing wildly, and back to the scene in the glass case. He bears a remarkable resemblance to the grotesque figure being led to sacrifice. And it is his energy, riotous and profligate, which is reflected in the two figures scrambling up the wall surrounding the scene.

Ms Anna Dorai: That's it, that's what real life's really all about. Like a herd of wild bloody elephants trampling in. What does he want?

'Oh I'm happy to see that you are still here. We were looking for you through the whole museum.' Vir Bahadur

Singh is trailed by the Lebanese and various officials from the ministry and the museum who introduce themselves in quick succession as Bhisham Chand gestures at them.

Ms Anna Dorai: The Lebanese is really established with them now and a large shadow that completely fills the large background of Mr VBS. He doesn't even look at me, or Dr Kiranos. I suppose we are irrelevant in his scheme of things.

'You know I am a collector of old coins, Dr Kiranos, my dear Dr Kiranos. I have seen the Marmots on the wall dividing your beautiful city of Mesos, it makes my heart bleed. I had heard a lot about this terrible invasion of your country. But today I have been driving through the city in daylight, and I have seen the troops in front of my eyes, standing up there with their guns held ready to shoot. My heart really goes out to you.

'This museum. Wonderful collection of old coins. There are cascades in that showcase in the other room. Do you think you could give me one coin for my collection back home? There is a very interesting one with the head of Alexander the Great. Famous conqueror, came to India.'

Dr Kiranos blushes a deep red; he does not know how to answer Vir Bahadur Singh and looks around desperately for Mr Fennel. Anna Dorai butts in. 'How can you say that? This is a museum collection, you can't just pick up a coin and walk out!'

But VBS is irrepressible, he's still looking expectantly at Dr Kiranos.

Bhisham Chand: What does a mouldy old coin matter? Mr Fennel takes VBS aside and conveys Kiranos' message. The coin is an antique, part of the national treasure. Would Kiranos give it if she asked? But AD would not ask, she's a snooty old fish, thinks she is Very Cultured Person. Maybe she looks down on all of us. But I can see the way she flatters that fancy director. Hangs on his every word.

'How did you feel when you first opened the tomb of the princess?'

'I had been excavating in that area for many years, following the track of that tomb. But it was very well hidden.'

'And especially that ritual scene!'

'Oh yes, that was special. You know that Nicara, that whole area, is now under the Marmots and, of course, they have stopped all excavations. Fifteen years of work left behind there, even my notebooks. Fortunately I happened to be in Sirocco here, in what is the Magdalene portion now, when they invaded. We were celebrating the anniversary of the monastery. It saved my life. If they'd found me in Nicara, definitely they'd have killed me. They hate me and my theories about the Magdalene, especially since I can prove them.'

'It's great that you managed to get all these objects out. It's the heart of the museum, these Nicara finds.'

'The Marmots are certainly not interested. All the important sites which are now under their control have fallen into complete neglect. It makes my heart bleed to think of all the time and effort we put into getting them going, before the invasion. No, the Marmots think that museum displays, art, archaeology, all that, are a typical weakness of the Magdalenes.'

'Madam, Mr Vir Bahadur Singh is waiting outside near the car. We are to leave for Porphyria.'

'You're coming with us?'

Bhisham Chand: She's flirting with him, she doesn't want to go without Dr Kiranos. What does she suddenly see in him, what's so special? Maybe she's just lonely. It's not normal, for a woman like that to live by herself, she's too attractive.

'Of course. I arranged the whole trip.' Then his voice drops, and Bhisham Chand has to move in closer to make sure he hears. He knows they don't notice him. There are many advantages to being nondescript.

'There's something special I want to talk to you about.' His hand on her elbow holds her back a few steps.

'We can talk now, if you like. I'm in no hurry to join the others, they can wait for ten minutes.' She wants to stay near the ritual scene, which draws her in a strange way. And also to be near Kiranos. He offers peace and quiet and beauty, far removed from the hearty marketplace of VBS's enthusiasm, which she cannot bear, for the time being.

But Kiranos shakes his head, and draws her out to the car. 'Not now, I'd rather wait till after Porphyria.'

VBS, the Lebanese, Mr Ghulmahael, and Bhisham Chand are already seated in an enormous limousine, looking out impatiently for her. It is now established without question that Mr Ghulmahael travels everywhere with VBS. He has wedged himself in the short space between him and Bhisham Chand. The others have dropped away, and hang about at an awkward distance, waiting for them to leave.

Ms Anna Dorai: VBS is snoring gently and without rhythm in a corner seat, BC supporting his head, yawning copiously himself from time to time. I must listen with great concentration to the explanation and description from our hosts. I am listening on their behalf as well, representative Indian turned towards Rhidus. Minhas and Mr Fennel. Talking about mountains, vegetation, tree plantations on the hillside, limestone quarries. This range is called 'Five Reins'. You see first a mountain like a horse and five lines of low hills coming back to a chariot at the end. They have carved a huge charioteer in the stone of the hillside. Remarkable resemblance between his profile and Minhas'. He laughs without surprise when I mention it, obviously it's been noticed before.

They point out dark green orchards planted in neat rectangles, surrounded on all sides by wind breaks of high cypress trees, and ripe, bulging oranges being plucked and packed.

'You see how the oranges are sorted mechanically? The wooden cases go by truck to Sirocco and then by ship to Europe. The Sea of Brisbane is especially warm near Rhidus, and it helps to give the best oranges in the world.' Mr Fennel is established as guide for the ordinary sights of Rhidus. Kiranos has withdrawn into the shadows of his corner. She is very aware of his lurking presence, but she must leave him alone.

'The Great Power base is still there near Sirocco? You let them stay? They didn't move a finger to keep off the Marmots during the invasion.'

'It's the call of commerce. They pay us a lot of hard currency in rent. The last government of Rhidus collapsed on the issue of foreign bases on the island. But even this government can't change this policy.' Mr Fennel is bitter. Then he gathers back his composure and becomes the polite guide once more.

'Your companions are very tired? They have been sleeping since we started this journey. Soon we will be at the place where Mary Magdalene is supposed to have landed when her boat first touched the shores of Rhidus. Shall we wake them?'

'We are not asleep, sir.' Bhisham Chand shakes Vir Bahadur Singh's shoulders. VBS then looks out of the window as if he had not been snoring for the last hour. He jumps into the conversation.

Ms Anna Dorai: Feet first and with a heavy thump. Can't he keep quiet from time to time?

Bhisham Chand: My boss is telling a long story about a colleague in the ministry who committed suicide when his wife ran away with another man, and I am providing the details whenever he looks towards me for corroboration. As with most things, I remember every detail vividly. I remember the whole incident. VBS was very upset at that time. I suspected he was interested in the wife himself, a very beautiful woman. But he can do without me at this point. He will relate incorrect facts if he forgets, just to complete the story. VBS is a man of supreme confidence.

'So simple and clear. Your wife runs away, you commit suicide. For most of us, life doesn't divide itself into such neat decisions.' Kiranos emerges from the silence of his corner. Vir Bahadur Singh resents him immediately, still sulky from the director's refusal to part with the Alexander coin from the museum.

'Not so easy, Dr Kiranos, to commit suicide. It was very sad, in fact, I was upset for days by what he did. Just to let go of life. Blow out your brains. Each one of us is very strongly attached to living. He must have been really in love with the woman, to throw away his life like that.'

She says, 'Actually, sometimes it's very difficult to go from day to day, to get up enough energy to do that. It doesn't even seem worthwhile. And to play the whole game again and to go from one life to another. At least I hope I am never reborn.'

Bhisham Chand: She has crashed into him with her slow, wonderful voice. It rests upon a cushion of pain. 'Oh . . . I have no such problems,' VBS says, 'I am a very happy man. I don't have a single enemy in the world.'

Mr Fennel puts in something about alienation from real life.

'The thing to do,' says Vir Bahadur Singh, 'is to attach yourself to life very firmly through the senses. Pick any one or more. Then wine, women, song, food, beautiful things. I am attached to reality in so many ways. I love all this. Especially beautiful women. No problems. Very difficult to shake me off.'

Bhisham Chand: I am nodding in admiration. Mr Fennel says that VBS is very lucky. AD is looking out of the window, her face stretched with irritation. The road moves closer to the sea. I can see vast stretches of blue, the Sea of Brisbane, some ships in the distance. My experience expands, one day I will travel in a luxury liner on a world cruise. VBS is my lucky mascot, I shall stick very close to him and everything will work out.

Vir Bahadur Singh is loud in his praises of the sea. 'You know, I am a land-and-mountain man. I have never been to the sea before. I am not ashamed of admitting that I am a very great sportsman. Fishing, shooting, I even play golf. The only thing I can't do is swim, though I have bought a swimming costume especially for today. Spent fifteen dollars so I must use it. Anna Dorai is smiling at the thought of Vir Bahadur Singh in a swimming costume. I assure you, Madam, I will manage very well. You can't keep a good sportsman down, no matter what the game.'

Anna Dorai turns away, following Kiranos who is pointing over the driver's shoulder, down towards the sea. 'That's supposed to be the place.'

The road descends gradually towards the beach. Huge white marble rocks of different sizes rear out of the sea, naturally placed in amazingly regular lines to form a pathway leading to the shore.

'The place where the great saint Mary Magdalene first arrived at the shore of Rhidus,' Bhisham Chand explains to Vir Bahadur Singh, who had been asleep when Dr Kiranos told them.

'But you have erected no memorial column or monument. This seems to just like an ordinary piece of the shore. Could be anywhere. We have great old temples in India, to mark events from the lives of our gods.'

Mr Fennel smiles vaguely, he does not know India at all, and has nothing to contribute. Dr Kiranos and Anna Dorai have gone on towards the water. Her feet are sinking in the sand. She takes off her sandals and walks barefoot.

Ms Anna Dorai: So this is where she arrived, her boat tossing between these pillars of the pathway. Did she rise in the boat to greet the shore, her long, travel-worn robes clinging to her body in the sharp sea-breeze? Haunted by her loss of Jesus Christ, like me, utterly alone, Ms Anna Dorai, padded and suffocated by her love for Rabin, always drowning in a pool of his spirit, always carrying his presence with me. Why does he touch all the places in my life?

'See, up there, that's her first monastery, carved from rock. She must have lifted up her eyes, and that mountain was the first thing she saw.' The voice of Dr Kiranos is behind Anna Dorai.

'But it's just caves,' she says, 'hollowed out in rock. No church, not even a cross.'

'We don't know how it was in the beginning. But all the photos and drawings through the centuries show it exactly like that. A warren of caves where they got the spirit together and descended to some secret nesting places inside.'

'Shall we go now? The other two gentlemen are already in the car.' Mr Fennel is waiting at the edge of the beach. Little pieces of mica gleam in the golden waves of sand which fall towards the sea.

'A beautiful sight. The Sea of Brisbane makes a very good photo. On my telephoto lens, very sophisticated, I even got that ship.' Vir Bahadur Singh puts away his camera with satisfaction, climbs back into the limousine. Suddenly Mr Fennel jerks with alarm. He grabs Vir Bahadur Singh's camera with its bulging telephoto lens, and focuses on a ship, still only a small dot on the horizon.

He sighs with relief. 'It's OK. For a moment, I thought the Marmots were invading us again, from the sea. We can leave now. It's not too far to Porphyria from here.'

A strange sleep overcomes Anna Dorai as soon as the car begins to move. It drops like a heavy curtain, and she cannot hear the sentences of Dr Kiranos or the resumed snoring of Vir Bahadur Singh.

Ms Anna Dorai: The boat rocks with short waves underneath. We are approaching the shore he says, there's just the wood between me and the heavy movement of water outside. My cheek is against the side of the boat, now I must rise to greet the shore, I am reaching a new country.

Bhisham Chand: She is waking now. This is the first time in our entire journey that AD has gone to sleep in the car. She's always so alert, and always on the edge of irritation. I suspect that VBS is a little scared of her. Now she seems to be coming out of a very deep sleep. She lifts her head, like a doe peering through the foliage of a jungle, her long neck turning in all directions, suddenly alert.

'Do you know that you have been asleep? We are now in

the middle of Porphyria. What shops! I find the shopping areas most interesting. You learn so much about the country just from looking at the shops. Mr Fennel, what things are worth buying in Porphyria?' Vir Bahadur Singh is wedged by the window of the limousine, peering out as they move slowly through the traffic.

'Well, you know, Porphyria is not really of . . . one doesn't think so much about the shops. It is better known for the mosaic flooring in the houses of rich bankers, uncovered in recent excavations. Aldaeus Santana, Mirtal, Sephalos, a whole series of houses. Very old. It was a very fortunate find. Dr Kiranos' department is still assessing and analysing the objects. Visitors are not really permitted here yet, not until we are ready to present these discoveries to the world. But you are our most honoured guests from India, we made a special case for you.'

'Actually, I am becoming a ruin myself from seeing so many ruins.' Vir Bahadur Singh and Bhisham Chand laugh heartily at the joke. 'You see, we have been travelling a lot during the last month and they always take us to see ruins. Quite frankly, I would prefer to see shops and cabarets, some place where there is a bit of life.'

Mr Ghulmahael agrees solidly with him. 'I can't bear to go sightseeing,' he says. 'I like my comfort too much. To relax and go through life with the minimum, that's my philosophy.'

Dr Kiranos turns to VBS with alacrity. 'Perhaps you would like to get off to the market? Mr Fennel can show you the shops. And I will take Miss Anna Dorai on to the antiquities, since she has a professional interest in these matters.'

Bhisham Chand: She is laughing, I think she is delighted to get rid of us, to go off with this tall fellow from the museum. But at least he is better than the fat fellow in the plane who has now shifted his attention to VBS. I wonder what he is up to, today? He scrambled out of the limousine and left us just as we started off. Someone clearly gave him a message.

This looks like a good shop, high glass windows with green slats, they close for lunch and siesta. The Sea of Brisbane makes people hot and lazy in the afternoon. We still have an hour to go. Gleaming crystal pieces on the shelves. VBS likes crystal, if he can get it cheap.

Kiranos is propelling her rapidly down the main street and now begins to turn and swivel through a bewildering array of side streets which get more and more narrow. The limousine is waiting at the kerb as the avid shopper, Vir Bahadur Singh, is now long out of sight.

'I want to show you something different. We won't go at all to the merchants' houses. You've seen mosaics like that before. They are contemporary with Carthage, and the stuff you see in the Musée National in Tunisia is much, much better, since they used local, naturally coloured stones. The Tunisian artisans who were imported into Rhidus from the Mediterranean by Aldaeus and Co brought some of those stones with them, but then they ran short and used local stuff.

'This is an ancient quarter of the city. See how the houses overhang the street. Layer upon layer of construction. And, being close to the sea, the ground has sunk slowly over the centuries. My theory is that the lowest layer dates right back to the time of Mary Magdalene.'

He turns into a large pleasant house only about a couple of hundred years old. Cherry trees are in bloom in the courtyard-garden and bunches of ripe red fruit overhang a central fountain. He is moving with rapid excitement. There is no-one in sight. He unlocks a heavy door with an electronic key and they descend a central staircase.

Ms Anna Dorai: I am going down through centuries, deep, deep, into the centre of the being of this island. He is a corkscrew, this Minhas, plunging straight into my heart.

'We'll be there soon. You are tired?' His body is close to hers, but his intense animal excitement is not directed towards her. He does not even wait for her to answer. 'We have almost arrived.' He takes out another key. 'This is the last door.'

She looks behind her while he unlocks it. The stairs are lost in a pale darkness. Then a light springs on in the room as the door opens, focusing on a central object, displayed like a precious museum piece. A sour feeling of disappointment invades her as she follows him to a stone box, ornamented with the now familiar cascade of Mary Magdalene's hair crowned with a halo of tears. She desperately wants him to hold her, to touch her, but he is as a holy acolyte possessed by a different excitement.

'Minhas, this is ancient Hebrew!'

'Listen, Anna, this casket holds her bones and her hair. All the indications on the box are correct, I have spent days and nights deciphering them since I discovered the box through a long series of coincidences. The inscriptions describe the relics which the box holds, and how they got there. Do you realise what this means? It is the only irrefutable proof that the Magdalene was actually in Rhidus, and did not die in Kashgar as the Marmots allege. It shakes the whole foundation of their religious beliefs, and establishes the truth of our faith. The Marmots would do anything to destroy this evidence. A sudden, surprise raid, terrorism, spies. And their tactics are tested and proven. We cannot afford to let them know of the existence of these relics and the record on the box, until they are properly protected and beyond their reach, outside the country. They have infiltrated everything here. I dare not make my discovery public. Nobody knows this box exists. Only I, and now you.'

'But what about the tomb in Sirocco? They told me that the body of Mary Magdalene was buried there.'

'No, it's empty. The Marmots and everybody else know that. If the Marmots really believed she was buried there, they would have overrun it long ago, carried off her remains. But the lapis lazuli tomb in Kashgar, which the Marmots guard as her real burial place, is also empty. This is the first piece of decisive evidence, this box, which proves that the Magdalene faith is correct, and that she came to Rhidus.'

'Why did you choose to tell me, Minhas? Why have you brought me here? What can I do in this situation?'

'I'm asking you to take this casket out of Rhidus for me. Back to India, to Kashmir. To bury it beside the bones of Jesus Christ, where it will be safe. In India, the Marmots will not be able to get to it. We trust you completely. And first, you must make it the centrepiece of your exhibition. In that way, we will announce its existence to the world. It will be a tremendous scoop for you personally, as an art historian. Your colleagues will come from all over the world to see it. Art historians, archaeologists, believers, everyone. Now you must see it yourself.'

He is lifting the lid. An ancient, sweet smell emerges from the box. She sees bones wrapped in cloth of gold which is parting at the seams. Roll upon roll of brown-gold, dusty hair.

'The Marmots want to take Mary Magdalene from us. Without her Rhidus is nothing, we are nothing.'

'And yet you want to send her away with me?

'To India. Physical proximity is not necessary, only knowledge, an awareness of truth. As I will live always by knowledge of your existence, Anna, when you leave, even if I never see you again.'

He could so easily be manipulating her. He knows her attraction to him, it is patently present between them. Her life could be at stake. Those Marmot soldiers dividing the city mean business, what is the life of an ageing Indian art historian in such a game? Then the thought disappears.

'What are the arrangements? I don't know when I will see you alone again, and we are to leave tomorrow.' Her heart sinks at the thought, and her enthusiasm leaks away.

'Don't worry. The Lebanese, Mr Gholmahael, will contact you.'

'The Lebanese! How does he come into this? I can't see myself teaming up with him!'

'He's very efficient, when he's given a job to do. I called him into Rhidus, hoping to find some use for him in getting the casket out. My plan didn't develop until I first saw you, in the hotel lobby, so radiant and beautiful. Don't worry about the Lebanese. He'll take care of everything. He'll get the casket out of the island and delivered safely to your museum in India.'

'How much have you told him? Does he understand anything about its importance to your religion?'

'It doesn't matter to him. He's doing it for the price. Actually, he thinks we're sending out a nuclear computer developed in utmost secrecy in Porphyria. In Rhidus we are familiar with the cloak and dagger game. It's our method of survival. The left hand must not know what the right hand is doing. Ghulmahael will attach himself to Mr Vir Bahadur Singh, who thinks he's working out arms sales with the Lebanese. He thinks he's an international arms dealer out to make a cut. So Ghulmahael will leave Rhidus that way, with the casket. It must get out of the country quickly. Somebody could have been watching us today.'

'Why is it so difficult? Getting it out of the country, I mean? It's your own government, at the airport, and other points of exit.'

'I daren't tell anybody. The Marmot spies are everywhere. They've worn our fabric thin, with their infiltrations. No, no, this is the only way, it must be done in utter secrecy, by the Lebanese.'

Bhisham Chand: We have been waiting on the roadside for half an hour. It is most inconsiderate to make VBS wait like this. What is she up to? He is angry now, I think I can hear him muttering. Will he shower her with rage? She appears now, deep in thought from around the corner of the road. The two of them are wrapped in silence. Have they been up to hanky-panky?

'Oh, I am so sorry, Mr Vir Bahadur Singh, to keep you waiting. Really, I am so, so sorry. We got caught up in a discussion about archaeology, the dating of a particular piece of stone. Perhaps we will have it as the centrepiece of the exhibition from Rhidus which opens in the National Museum next month. You know that's why I'm here. I was so excited when Dr Kiranos showed me the piece. But I should have remembered that you two gentlemen were waiting for us. Sorry, my fault.'

'Well, I was angry, but how can one continue to be angry when you are so charming? No, it's all right. We were just wondering what happened. We are late for lunch also, the others will be waiting: the Indian ambassador, some high official from your side. Mr Ghulmahael, the Lebanese, said he might also be here, if he finishes his work at the ministry in time. He is leaving tomorrow, with us. We're talking about some things. Such a nice man. And I've been holding these purchases. Very interesting things. Mr Fennel took us to some good shops. He has gone now to the hotel, it's a wonderful hotel, right by the sea, with its own private beach; he said I must swim after lunch.'

'Would it be wise from a health point of view, to swim after a meal?'

'Well, you know, I don't really know how to swim. And in the sea! But we can't come all the way to the island of Rhidus and not go into the sea. I have bought a swimming costume specially for the purpose. Can't spend all that money in vain. With the prime minister arriving today . . . Oh yes, he must already have arrived, it's almost 2 pm. Oh my God, these senior officials must have been waiting for ages at the hotel. Our ambassador is a very formal man, he will not like to be kept waiting, not at all. I must put my things away carefully in the back of the car, don't want the ambassador to think we got delayed because of my shopping.'

'Don't worry, I'll apologise, explain it was on my account that we are late.'

'I wish you had come with us, Anna. I bought a beautiful statue of Mary Magdalene in bright, shining colours, rising up from a boat. In fine china, I think. And a few crystal

pieces, an ashtray, a vase. I must show them to you.' He
is unwrapping them already. Light from the window goes
through the cheap, heavy glass. He is excited. 'And you
cannot imagine how cheap it was! Wonderful place for shopping. Though I am sure that you had an interesting time with
Dr Kiranos, looking at archaeological objects. You work too
hard. A young, beautiful lady like you should enjoy herself
more. Must learn to relax, like me, I am always relaxed. But
now I am very hungry, really looking forward to my lunch.
Oh, here you are, so sorry to keep you all waiting. Mr
Ghulmahael is here too, that's very nice. I'm always very
happy to see him. I'm sure you gentlemen have not missed
us very much, talking to each other, discussing interesting
things which diplomats like you always do; wonderful life,
to be an ambassador. When I get back, I'm about to ask to
be made ambassador to a small, small country, not very
important, just to taste the pleasure of flying the Indian flag
on my car, and sitting like this in the afternoon, looking out
towards a beautiful sea, and watching all those exciting
young ladies going down to the water to swim, lying on the
beach with their towels under them, their eyes closed, so
vulnerable, as if waiting for my eyes. Excuse me, Ms Anna
Dorai, you are not supposed to hear that. I am very hungry,
but yes, there is time for a gin and tonic. Can we have some
of your delicious white wine with lunch? Yesterday I tasted
one which was called "Valley of Roses" from the area near
Sirocco, I believe. My God what a fragrance! I swooned even
before I put my lips to it. Is this food typical of Rhidus, this
meat laid out, decorated with tiny stuffed birds? What are
they, partridges? I was a crack-shot in my youth, how many
partridges and quails I shot on the wing, flushed out from
the bushes by my father's dogs. Mushrooms, I love mushrooms with rice and raisins, seems a most tasty combination.'
   'Mr Vir Bahadur Singh, please come, have some of this
dessert, it is called baclava. I remember it from my youth in
Lebanon, must have been brought in to Rhidus by Lebanese
traders in the twentieth century, but I haven't eaten it since

my mother died. Modern women have no time for cooking. Maybe in India women still do some cooking. Do you have anything like this baclava in your country? It's heaven to bite into it, and have your mouth full of sweetness and crunchy with almonds and hazel nuts.'

Ms Anna Dorai: He's got his finger on the VBS pulse. Especially as he thinks it is a computer for a nuclear reactor. It's quite bulky. Poor, unsuspecting VBS, being used like this. But I cannot bear the thought of VBS in swimming-trunks, his stomach huge with food, black hairs running down the dark skin, hanging over the blue material of these thick new swimming-trunks he is pulling out of a plastic bag. My God, how ugly! Where is he going to change, everything is so unorganised. They are pressing me to go with them; he feels protected if I go, sort of safe in unfamiliar quarters, BC conveys the request, and smirks in complicity. I think he understands how much VBS irritates me. He's far more intelligent than he pretends to VBS. But really, they're going with cameras. Will he photograph the naked sun-bathers? Supposing they beat him up?

An official from the Ministry of Defence Production is waiting for them, with Mr Fennel. A quiet person, very fair, with a small moustache and bulging brown eyes. Only his diet conveys how sick he is. 'My diabetes is very, very bad. Dr Kiranos will tell you how careful I have to be. Once I hung on the lip of death.' He already has a small piece of poached fish and a pile of boiled vegetables on his plate. 'This is all that I am allowed to eat,' he says. He is an important man, the ambassador bends over him solicitously. 'Please, Excellency, let me not keep you from your lunch. You go right ahead, now that the rest of your party has arrived. The buffet is over there. It looks quite interesting.'

'Oh, we feel so greedy, eating heartily while you can eat nothing.'

Vir Bahadur Singh is shifting around restively. 'I must get back to Mesos.'

'Oh,' says Mr Ghulmahael, 'you have an appointment at what time, Mr Vir Bahadur Singh?'

'I'm not sure . . . Must make a phone call when I get back.' He is vague, pushing attention away from his statement. 'But I must go into the sea now.' He looks briefly, defiantly, towards Ms Anna Dorai, and sets off towards the changing-rooms, swinging the plastic bag which hold his brand new swimming trunks.

'Seems to me she was leaning a little close to Dr Kiranos, eh, what do you think, Bhisham Chand?'

Bhisham Chand giggles wordlessly and moves up close to the fat Lebanese who is negotiating with the management for a key to the changing-rooms.

Bhisham Chand: Best not to commit yourself to an opinion. Later the circumstances are forgotten, and only the opinion remains, like a shadow of immediate and vital interest. And you are damned for ever for taking sides. I know how to lie low and to protect myself, like a fish that swims close to the river-bed. He wants me to take a photo of him beside that marble statue of Mary Magdalene. The elegant rounded curves of her body are just visible through the flying folds of her draperies, rising from the sea, one arm holding back her long hair, the other holding a torch aloft, showing these wretched barbarians the light. What were those fellows like, at that time, thousands of years ago? Now they are these tall, fancy chaps like Ms Anna Dorai's favourite, the Museum Director. I begged to be excused from going into the sea, it frightens me. He's changed, and all resplendent in his blue costume, his belly popping over the top, the black matted hairs like a rough curtain over his skin. Maybe he's scared too, he's trying to delay going in. Anyway, there's the fat fellow, his new follower, he can take care of him, why should I bother?

'Take a picture of me, Bhisham Chand, here, beside this beautiful woman. I mean the statue, don't look so frightened, not one of the halting beauties! A bit like Beauty and the

Beast, isn't it, my standing here?' Vir Bahadur Singh's loud voice comes booming cheerfully over the golden sand.

Bhisham Chand's shoes have sunk deep in the sand. He shifts uncomfortably on small grains which have got into his socks, as he focuses the camera carefully on Vir Bahadur Singh who leans against the white marble of Mary Magdalene.

Bhisham Chand: He's a little sad, maybe feeling neglected, but I'm glad our AD is not here. She would surely laugh at him openly, she has no qualms about such things, no respect for his position.

'Will you come swimming, Mr Ambassador?' Dr Kiranos is picking at some brilliant red cherries scattered on a white plate at the end of the table.

'Well, I don't mind, I've brought my swimming things anyway. I shall use the swimming-pool. But what about Mr Ghulmahael here?'

Ms Anna Dorai: They are settling everything. Minhas takes it for granted that I will go swimming, I thought it is bad to swim after a meal. What will VBS say when he finds I've gone with Minhas because, of course, I must go with him?

'Anna, here we are, you've taken a long time to change. Where did you get that beautiful pink robe, I didn't know the hotel gave out robes?'

'It's my own, I brought it with me. Is the water cold?'

'A bit. Better to go straight in, and swim, then you warm up. Have you been in the sea before?'

Ms Anna Dorai: He can see that I hesitate, I am a swimming-pool fish. The lurch and vastness of the sea is something else – its own strong movement, which I can't control. Salt upon my lips and in my eyes, it's harsh. There's the other group. VBS, finished with his swimming, changed out of that ridiculous blue costume, BC, the faithful, carrying his camera, running along beside Mr Ghulmahael. We have to watch BC. He's a very shrewd fellow, and he watches everything. He doesn't like the Lebanese at all. But I don't think he's suspicious. Not yet. Just resentful, because he's muscling in on VBS. They're leaving, waving. Mr Fennel whispers in Minhas' ear and goes rapidly to join them. The diabetic official has disappeared already. Now it's only Minhas and me, with His Excellency the Ambassador. And the casket is right here with us, carried inside Minhas' chest, his flesh enclosing the holy, crumbling bones of Mary Magdalene. I don't have to think of the details, only of the final scene. When people walk up the central staircase of my museum, turn a corner and reach the main gallery, there will be Mary Magdalene, the pride of Rhidus, reposing in her casket, the great traveller, on her way to rest finally beside her beloved Jesus Christ, up in Srinagar.

She turns as Minhas comes up to her. Mr Radhakrishnan is out of earshot. 'Minhas, my dear, listen. Should I speak to our prime minister tomorrow? This is a highly political subject, and it's important enough to involve him. Much bigger than you and me.'

'Please, I implore you, don't mention this to anyone, to no-one at all. You cannot even imagine how dangerous it could be. All sorts of forces will be let loose. Please, trust me. Shall we walk up to the pool for a drink, the sun is hot here, high up in the afternoon?'

Ms Anna Dorai: I am seeing Minhas for the first time. A huge scar, fiercely red and corrugated, runs vertically up his chest, and, as for his feet, he has the strangest feet, almost deformed, the bones sticking out of the side like castanets. Something about his feet makes me melt. I feel tender, flowing, most tender. His feet are like misshapen babies moving softly over the hot sand. We move towards a bar built in the middle of the swimming-pool. The sun is hot, in mid-afternoon, beating upon our heads.

'How did you get it?' Anna Dorai runs her finger over the scar, softly on the bumps and knots in his skin. Her thick black hair brushes against his chest. He touches it, pushing his fingers to the scalp.

'You hair is dry already. So fast.'

She rubs her head against his palm, like a cat. 'How did you get this scar?' she says sleepily.

'I was born with a hole in my heart. They operated on me when I was ten years old. We were still somewhat backward then in Rhidus, hence this terrible scar. Nowadays they do it with lasers, no marks at all.' His skin ripples anxiously, his chest curves away from her. 'I know it looks rather dreadful. Fortunately it doesn't show most of the time. Does it bother you very much?'

'No,' she says, 'it doesn't bother me at all.'

Ms Anna Dorai: I love the scar, I want to lay my cheek against it, to lick it, to caress his long, misshapen feet, to hold them against my stomach, cradled against moist, salty flesh, gently brush away grains of sand.

The sun makes cloaks of light around them. The sound of children, balls bouncing, movement. The ambassador interrupts. 'You are not ready yet? Please hurry, we must get back. I've just been informed the whole party is to move to the Palace of Delphos, where the prime minister, and the Minister of Defence Production are staying. The minister has indicated that he wants the whole Indian delegation to be together, and our hosts have most kindly agreed. So, madam, you are to stay in the finest building of Rhidus, the palace of the president. The ceilings are painted with scenes from the long and eventful history of the island, the furniture has been imported from France and Sweden, and all the linen has been especially hand-made for the palace. As for the food, we should not even speak of it, the cuisine is the finest I have ever eaten in my whole career. I think that you are going to enjoy the rest of your stay in Rhidus, dear Ms Anna Dorai!'

'Sounds nice, Mr Ambassador. Do the others know? They left some time ago.'

'I think they'll tell them at the hotel. Don't worry about it, Mr Fennel is taking care, he's most efficient.'

But there is no sign of any of her party when she arrives at the Hotel Alinda. She goes up rapidly to pack. A boy in a

red cap, with beetling black eyebrows, smiling shyly, arrives,
unsummoned, shortly afterwards, to take her bags.

'Where is the Indian gentleman?' she asks him. But he
continues to smile, not understanding a word. He hesitates
even to take the tip she offers him in the lobby, then leaves
her with the feeling of fresh young sweetness.

Bhisham Chand: His luggage is all packed and ready, I've
done it, everything, but he should at least see it. What if I
have left something behind, deprived him of something? He
would never forgive me if I caused him material loss. But
they want to move into the Palace of Delphos. I cannot
understand why they want the change, it's comfortable
enough here. Now she's arrived too, and is asking after VBS.
He has not returned. We're supposed to reach the palace, the
ambassador will be waiting for us there. How to tell her
about Sonia from the airlines, the air hostess, he's gone with
her? I saw her from the window, a big car, and a dog on the
back seat, waiting for him. How he ran down the stairs,
really eager! But he should have been back in time for dinner.
He was excited about it. We are to have dinner with the
minister in an ethnic place, one of the restaurants with local
colour. Will they serve wine again, like this afternoon? AD
is in the lounge, ready, waiting for VBS, tapping her fingers
on the chair. She is looking at me as if I am responsible for
his absence.

'Where is Mr Vir Bahadur Singh? It is very late, even if
you have packed his things and he's ready to move. He will
have to wash, change, or something. Now there's no time
to go to the Delphos before dinner. We will just have to
leave our luggage in the car. The minister will be here any
minute, to fetch us. I must talk to Mr Fennel. Oh there's Mr
Vir Bahadur Singh, and now he's hanging over the window
of her car, talking, his camera still slung over his neck, sleeves
rolled up, patting the dog on the back seat. Why don't you
go along and tell him, Bhisham Chand, that we are moving
to the Delphos, that the minister is arriving in twenty
minutes to fetch us?'

Bhisham Chand: Well, she should have gone herself. I just stood behind him until he was ready to move anyway, how could I interrupt? She's really quite beautiful this Sonia, skin smooth as ivory, with a high-pink natural colour in the cheeks, and golden hair, real gold. VBS has the privilege. He changed very, very fast, he dares not keep the minister waiting. He thanks me – nothing left in the room, and he smells of a wonderful perfume. How did he know the name of the restaurant where we're going for dinner?

'Varia, that's what it's called. She's coming there too, the Rhidus side has invited her. You remember that gracious young lady from the airlines, Sonia, she was so kind with the bottles of champagne. I phoned her, and she took me to the president's riding estate, that's the central place where the élite goes riding, beautiful horses. She was very sad, her favourite horse, Gallant Silas, died last night, and she was in mourning for him. We went into every stable; she patted the horses, and whispered the name of Gallant Silas to all of them. They nodded their beautiful heads. How nice it was to see them. My head also nodded from side to side with them. She was quite charmed with me. We had a long, long conversation. She's very deep, very philosophical. A bit mixed up, does yoga and follows some guru, long distance. He lives in the United States, Maharishi Bandook. She swears that he gives her dreams which tell her what is going to happen. For example, two nights ago she dreamed of a huge, mad cat, all orange and black and like a large tube, dropping straight from a high ledge, down, down, dashing through a moon-splattered darkness, to shatter in a raging pool of blood on the ground far below. She woke in fear and apprehension, and rushed off to the thing that was dearest to her, her horse, Gallant Silas, housed near the Palace of Delphos, and found that he was very sick. He died in her arms, and today she is very, very sad. She says I must dance with her this evening at the Varia restaurant, it will cheer her up. How can one refuse such a charming young lady who obviously needs help? She wants to talk a lot to me, she says, about Indian

philosophy. I have suggested some books, better to be on a
guru than on drugs, though these gurus and things are such
frauds. I didn't tell her, why destroy her faith, just like that?

'She helped me in another thing. Every place I go to, I
take this camera along, which has both a telescopic and a
micro lens. To take pictures of butterflies, for my son. He is
a poet and a butterfly-watcher now, he wants to publish a
book on butterflies in different parts of the world. I'm helping
him. Today I'll phone him and tell him all the butterflies I
got in here, on the reel. The garden around Delphos is not
huge and magnificent like the Moghul Gardens near Rashtra-
pati Bhavan in Delhi, but still pretty large, full of flowers
and citrus fruits, all kinds, lemons, oranges and grapefruit.
Now, with the rains beginning, the butterflies were flocking
on the leaves, laying their eggs, like tiny seedpearls clinging
to the bottoms of the leaves and grasses. Such bright colours.
The Lime butterfly is huge, with a black and yellow mosaic
work on its wings, each with a coloured eye on it. I also got
the Mormon, which is a close cousin of the Lime butterfly,
a dark-coloured one, with large velvety black wings, a row
of creamy spots which gives the effect of a scalloped edge,
and then a red eye with a blue ring. Today I saw also a
Jezebel, but couldn't get a picture. Like a made-up woman,
with a row of blood-red spots on the outer edge of the yellow
hind wing. The main colour is white veined with jet. This
one weaved and looped in elegant spirals high amongst the
treetops, like a fatal creature from paradise. Sonia wandered
around with me in the garden, she is young, her eyes are
good, she spotted them for me.'

'So you were butterfly-watching while we waited for you
here. You're lucky the minister didn't come himself, to fetch
us.' Anna Dorai's voice is heavy with irritation.

'And what about you going off with those other fellows
to swim? You didn't come with us, why? We weren't good
enough for you, or what? Anyhow, why do you care
whether I am late or early? She cared, she wanted to be

with me, and I'm hoping she also comes to the dinner this evening.'

Ms Anna Dorai: We are climbing now, into the low wooded hills around Mesos. The trees are wild and thick, crowding close to the road. If Rabin were here with me, sitting close by, we could touch, be in the same space. He is a padding round my heart, nothing can get through. A block of deposit, like layers of limestone.

'Who are the other people at the dinner? Bhisham Chand, you would know. Our minister is invited, so their minister will be the host, that's simple protocol. Did you hear anything about the arrival of our prime minister? Everything was OK?'

Bhisham Chand: She wants to know if Dr Kiranos will be there. Now she's being very nice to VBS to make up for her irritation earlier. Nice bright place, this restaurant. I was getting tired of the trees. VBS was going on about how much he likes the natural landscape: trees, flowers, mountains, everything. There's very little he doesn't love, what an appetite! Our minister has not arrived yet, we can line up here beside their officials to greet him. She's looking out for Dr Kiranos, searching for him. She goes in. Mr Fennel is arranging everything for the dinner. They must have timed it: the music starts up as soon as our minister arrives. Did he see me, will he remember my face? I might have a favour to ask him in future. VBS is searching also, for Miss Sonia. She is at a small table near the fireplace, sitting with the fat Lebanese. His face lights up, he flounces across, getting all mixed up with the folk-dancers who have started up their act, with small musical instruments like bouzoukis and high dancing skirts. The men wear fine leggings of leather, tight and embroidered, right down to their shapely knees. I feel misshapen and ugly beside those fine bodies. No wonder she laughs at VBS when we stand beside these fine specimens. They draw the guests into their dance, mostly foreigners like us. This must be a tourist spot. A line of clumsy people hold hands and try to keep to the music. Especially VBS, he's the natural centre of such a scene, leading Sonia. The crowd is parting to make space for them. No grace, but a lot of vigour, cavorting between the other swaying bodies pressed around them. He claps and twirls, trying to copy her elegant movements. She directs this situation. The minister is watching them, everybody is watching, as VBS dances with abandon. His feet beat heavy on the floor, and the young lady twirls and jumps, her blond hair flying into masses of fine curls. The minister's face is completely impassive, no hint of a smile. I hope VBS does not fall into disfavour. At this point he does not care, but he will care later, when he feels the minister's disapproval. The minister might think he is drunk, though he has not touched the wine yet, it's only just coming in. Our host the Rhidus minister rises to cheer VBS and his partner, 'Bravo! Bravo!' Dr Kiranos and AD stand beside him, all clapping as the music ends, a superb performance. The dance floor empties. VBS holds Sonia's hand just a moment longer than is strictly necessary. She leans forward to whisper, then goes back to Mr Ghulmahael's table. He has not stirred, waiting behind a plate of food which he has been steadily demolishing. He has the right idea. Now he waves as VBS catches his eye. The Rhidus minister turns to Dr Kiranos, very respectful, introduces the head of the Department of Antiquities to our minister as if the man were a hero or a celebrity.

Ms Anna Dorai: I wanted to dance with him, but it was all that folksy stuff. To lay my head on that scar again . . . I wonder if I'll ever do that, once we leave tomorrow.

He disappears, and she travels back with VBS who is clearly pining for the beautiful Sonia, and Bhisham Chand who is quietly fitting into the shadows inside the car. There's no sign of the Lebanese. Nothing indicates that they are collaborators. The ever-attentive Mr Fennel accompanies them into the grand Palace of Delphos. 'Don't think about your luggage, it will reach your rooms.' He takes them on a short guided tour through the best suites, ornate with murals. VBS and Bhisham Chand fall back and retire to their rooms, she longs to go too, but Mr Fennel is doing his duty, pointing out all the gilt work and wonders of a lost age.

'We've put your prime minister in the Sky Suite, on this same floor. All our Indian guests are here. I'm told he's resting just now.'

Mr Radhakrishnan has caught up with them. 'It's been a long journey for him. His aeroplane had to circle the runway for an hour before they let it land. There was a strange phone call just as the pilot radioed his presence.'

'We didn't want to take any chances. Nothing should go wrong where India is concerned.'

'But what can happen?' The ambassador is an incessant interjector.

Mr Fennel is firm. 'Nothing will happen. But we have to take care.'

'I cannot tell you, Ms Anna Dorai, how wonderful it is to be the Indian ambassador here. They really look after us well. Now I must be off, but I will be here at 8 am to greet the prime minister. I will be escorting him, when he calls on the president of Rhidus, before the official talks begin.'

Mr Vir Bahadur Singh, changed and dressed in a lemon-coloured casual shirt, and fine, dark trousers, emerges from his room, trailed by a solicitous Bhisham Chand. He barely notices the ambassador, on his way to the great front door.

'Oh Mr Vir Bahadur Singh, good evening. You're going out again? You seemed tired after the Varia restaurant, but now you seem fresh and revived, ready to hit the town. Well, don't stay out too long, tomorrow's going to be a long day. Can I give you a lift into town? I'll be passing that way, on the road home.'

'No thanks, someone's picking me up. Goodnight, good-night,' he says hurriedly, as he rolls out of the front entrance, ushered by Bhisham Chand.

Mr Radhakrishnan goes off in his limousine with the Indian flag fluttering on the right-hand side.

Bhisham Chand: I would have been fine in the Hotel Alinda. Here everything is so formal and still, there's no life in this place; who wants to live in a palace? Now they are beginning to switch off the lights. It's a good thing Mr Ghulmahael arrived earlier, it was still bright when the guards came in to check if I wished to receive him, and I settled him in quite comfortably. Such an imposition, to have a foreign man dumped on me like this. Of course, this is where the palace has its plus points: these large suites. He's shut into another room, maybe he's snoring, his large belly rising and falling in sleep, peace to the Lebanese, who is to help VBS and the government in all kinds of contracts. At least I don't have to hear him, or see him, until tomorrow morning, there's even a bathroom attached to the anteroom. 'Let him in, take care of him, he's useful to us,' VBS whispered as he left, at the last minute, explaining nothing. At least he remembered to tell me, which is a wonder, he was so preoccupied with Miss Sonia in the car, the blonde goddess from the aeroplane, I wonder when he will be back? Maybe he won't come all night. Who am I to ask?

There's no way I will know when he returns, shut as I am into the darkness of this room. He's next-door, but you can't hear anything through these walls, they're thick, impenetrable, built during an era when there was still time and money for proper construction. I prefer the paper-thin walls of the Hotel Alinda. You hear even the scratching of a man's key in his suitcase, as he gets ready to unpack. But I suppose they like the style and glamour of a palace. I'm just a simple man, with simple ways. It's enough for people like our Ms Anna Dorai to be fancy and elegant. She can hold her head high wherever she goes, they will respect her, she is an honour to us Indians.

He was muttering something about his luggage, that he will have to fetch it tomorrow, since he is leaving with us on the plane. He couldn't have much luggage, such an international traveller must be going lightly. No need for him to be shopping and buying things wherever he goes. Not like us, where everybody in the family waits for the foreign traveller to open his bags when he gets home, jeans for growing boys, fashionable trainers – Adidas, Nike, Reebok – cosmetics, small electrical appliances, anything you can smuggle past customs. After all, one can't take too many risks either. If you're caught, you can lose your job. Best to be discreet, at least a little bit, don't expect too much from these foreign trips. What will Ms Anna Dorai take back? It must be quite lonely, not to have children to take things back for, though this doesn't seem to bother her very much, she never talks of children. Occasionally she asks after VBS's daughter, whom she has seen in the university. Maybe she is spending tonight saying goodbye to Dr Kiranos in her mind, unless she slipped out too, later, like VBS. But I don't think so, she's not the slipping-out kind, she would go out openly. She doesn't care too much what people think of her, certainly she does not care about my opinion. She must be lying in bed, fast asleep, her round white arms thrown wide, her thick black hair curled over the pillow, dreaming of Dr Kiranos. Here we are, in three rooms beside each other, in one straight line, and we might as well have been in three different cities, for all the connection we have with each other tonight. With VBS I don't want any more connections, the slavish attention he demands the whole day is enough, but Anna Dorai is another cup of tea altogether. She can be warm and tender. I would love to sink into her body.

The sound of her voice, screaming down the corridor, wakes everyone up. The corridor is full of life, and the sound of running feet, and loud commands being shouted in Greek. The soldiers have arrived.

Bhisham Chand opens his door cautiously. It's only because of her, she might need some help, she might lean upon him, her voice was frightened. She might be out there sobbing, surrounded by soldiers. Besides, there are too many sounds now, impossible to pretend one slept through all that. He steps out, and almost steps on VBS. He has fallen on the carpet, his limbs askew, thrown awkwardly, his turban knocked off his head. Must have fallen down drunk, there's no other way. Why doesn't he take care of such things, creating such commotion? And why did she have to shout and yell so much? If she'd just kept quiet he would have taken care of everything, dragged him into his room with the help of Mr Ghulmahael, woken the gentleman's snoring a bit. Where is he, this fat Lebanese, always sleeping peacefully? There's no sound from him.

'Can't you see, Bhisham Chand, can't you see he's dead?'

Compulsively, she has come across to him, stepping carefully around VBS. She is sobbing into his shoulder, he can feel her hot tears through the thin material of his kurta. Then she bends down and moves VBS's arm, flung across his chest. There is a gaping bullet hole, and a spreading blood stain, in the lemon-coloured cloth. How, for a man who pays such attention to detail, did he not notice this before? For example, he notices Anna Dorai's bare feet below her long white gown. Two small animals with short red nails, nestling beside his, on the carpet.

Ms Anna Dorai: Something strange is happening to me, as I stand here looking at VBS spread out on that moquette. He's dead, and suddenly I am deeply regretful. His energy is still running through me, pushing at my pain. And Rabin is moving off, loosening his terrible hold. He had enclosed my soul, wrapped it in awful claustrophobia. I could see nothing else. Then Dr Kiranos peeped in, and now VBS: his death. It is as if his dying has made me live again, feel, right to the centre of my being. I'm crying for VBS, lying there dead, with a hole gaping through his lemon shirt. And the tears are washing Rabin away. Glad to be rid of him at last, free to be here in Rhidus, or to go away. Just this soft, dead man lying here at my feet, with his fat, the black hairs running over the back of his hand, his sad, receding hairline exposed by the absent turban, everything graceful and tender as it never was before. Could we say he has died for this? For me? It only makes me cry more, standing here, clutching at BC's shoulder, the warm, clean smell of sleep coming from his clothes, it's a promise.

Two soldiers appear, dragging a screaming, protesting Sonia through the door of VBS's room. She is quiet when she sees the group collected around the fallen giant. Anna Dorai looks at her with interest. Her blonde curls are massed in disorder around a white, pinched face, its chin pointed with fear.

'We found her in his bed, hiding under the sheet.' One of the soldiers is addressing Bhisham Chand. Sonia brightens when she registers his presence.

'Please, Mr Bhisham Chand, explain to them. I have nothing to do with . . . this.' She forces herself to look at VBS, and bursts into tears.

'What happened?' he asks.

'You know I came back with him. He must have told you. Well, after some time, I had to go home. So, he went out to see if the corridor was empty. He didn't want anyone to see me leave. He was a very kind man. When he was gone a long time, I came out to see what had happened, and found him like this. I was so frightened, I just went back and got into bed. Now they think I killed him. Please, please, explain to them. I would never, never kill him.'

'You didn't mean to kill him,' Bhisham Chand says. 'You killed him by accident. You actually meant to kill our prime minister. You're working for the Marmots, those fellows standing in lines outside, at the false borders. You wanted to spoil relations between Rhidus and India, her greatest friend.'

The soldiers' grip on Sonia tightens. She stares at Bhisham Chand with round eyes, squealing with fear. 'It's not true. This man's lying because I wouldn't sleep with him, I preferred VBS. Now he's saying I killed VBS. You know me, Mr Fennel. You know I couldn't ever do this. Tell them to let me go.'

But Mr Bashir Fennel is wiping a sentimental tear from his eye. 'What can I say, my dear? I'm only thankful the prime minister is safe. We would never have recovered from such a dire blow, if anything had happened to him.'

'Anyhow, the laws of your land will protect you, if you

are innocent. Don't worry.' Bisham Chand has his arm around Ms Anna Dorai. It is a strange feeling. 'Now I must go immediately and inform the authorities about the grave danger from which our beloved prime minister has just escaped.'

Bhisham Chand: Mr Vir Bahadur Singh is dead, and they are leading Sonia away. Her breast is exposed, a great white expanse. Why doesn't she cover it up? Maybe she doesn't even notice her buttons are open, she just keeps looking back at VBS on the carpet. Perhaps she really cared for him. A big red stain is spreading around him now. I must rush off to the prime minister and inform him. It is my duty, as personal assistant to VBS, to be the first to inform him.

The corridor is now full of half-dressed people. The president's doctor, with his official black bag, is elbowing them aside, to reach the body of VBS, which is photographed before being lifted carefully towards the lobby. Bhisham Chand threads his way hurriedly between them, to fetch the prime minister.

Ms Anna Dorai: He's disappearing into the crowd. My last friend from home. I'll have to manage all this alone.

The ministers from both sides are arriving now, and the Indian ambassador hurries behind them, his glasses shining with grief. Everybody stands aside to permit the president of Rhidus to pass between them.

'I see what has happened. Mr Vir Bahadur Singh, this great Indian hero lying at our feet, died in saving his prime minister from the toils of an assassin. My security men have told me everything. They have reported that they heard a loud sound of warning from the corridor, and began to fire. But he was already dead then, and the would-be assassin had escaped after killing our gallant and most beloved officer here. Dear Mr Minister, please accept our deep sympathy for the death of your brave countryman. He died in the service of his nation, saving the life of his prime minister. If you will permit us, we will give him a great funeral here.'

'Oh no, no, that is not possible, he must return to the soil where he was born, he must be given a hero's cremation in New Delhi, but please can't you try to locate the person who killed him? We wll have numerous questions in Parliament.'

Bhisham Chand: VBS is a hero now. I've done my bit. It's the least I could do, as his personal assistant. They'll send me back on the plane with his dead body, I will have to accompany the coffin through a cheering, sombre, ceremonial crowd, and then inform his wife. The Chiefs of Staff will be lined up at the airport to receive him.

The prime minister has come at last, and Bhisham Chand is escorting him to the lobby, where VBS's body is laid out.

Bhisham Chand: He has taken the trouble to change into a dark suit. I told him that VBS died saving his life. I have never been so close to a prime minister before. The pores on his face are enlarged, full of grief. Deep tears of sorrow flow down his cheeks. What a noble leader, to be so deeply moved by the death of poor VBS lying at his feet. He kneels to touch him gently, to cross on his chest the thick dead hands of my erstwhile master, with their strong black hairs running over them; hands with which I was so familiar. This is a much better end than VBS could ever have expected, a glorious death, to have a prime minister sorrowing over him, repeating sincere, grateful words ' . . . for the sake of his nation and its government, and we honour him . . . of loss, for a great man and his shining last actions which cost him his life.'

'Nevertheless, the show must go on. We thank our dear friends from Rhidus, and especially our great friend, the president, for their kind words, in this hour of our peril. But Excellency, we Indians are made of sterner stuff. Despite the effort to deflect our attention, we can still concentrate on our bilaterial talks with your ministers and officials this morning. We must not allow our dear colleague here to die for nothing.'

The Indian ambassador is looking for Ms Anna Dorai. She is standing at the edge of the crowd, watching the scene.

'This is a really sad thing to happen,' she says, as he comes up to her. 'And he was so busy shopping, gathering things for his family, until the last minute. I feel so sad that this should happen to Mr Vir Bahadur Singh. He had such a passion for living.'

Mr Radhakrishnan is nodding his head sadly, waiting for a chance to speak. He looks curiously at her, he has never known her so simple and talkative. 'You have been deeply affected by this murder. Of course, we all are. Such a dreadful thing to happen, and just as the visit was preparing to come to a very successful note, with the high point of the talks tomorrow. But I suppose, since you were travelling in the same party, you knew him well . . . '

'I didn't know him at all outside work. But, yes, his death has affected me deeply, as if it has released me from myself.'

Now he is staring at her. The shock of the murder has temporarily turned her brain. He shouldn't really say anything serious to her yet, but later there will be no time. 'Everything will be all right, Ms Anna Dorai. Calm down, and don't let this worry you too much.' He is murmuring, hoping to soothe her with his voice, before he gets his job done. 'About the talks today. I know that you were not scheduled to attend, but now we are unfortunately one short in the Indian delegation. And we can't really take Bhisham Chand, he's only a PA.'

'But will you have the talks? How can you discuss trivial, formal details in the shadow of this?' She gestures towards the scene in front of them, which is beginning to break up. He longs to get away from her and head for home, but he follows her gaze. He still has his responsibilities for the day ahead.

'You heard what our prime minister said. 'The show must go on.' We must steel ourselves to this pain, and continue. We must have you in the talks,' he says firmly. 'We must present a united front, especially at this time.'

The body of Mr VBS has been draped in the Indian tri-colour flag – he is a hero now – and placed on a stretcher. He is carried aloft in ceremonial splendour towards a long, black Mercedes, a hearse, which waits in the porch. The prime minister of India, the president of Rhidus, and their ministers have left already. The crowd, in phalanx around the body, is now beginning to disperse. The Indian ambassador is seen slipping through the wide portals of the Palace of Delphos, constructed grandly for precisely such occasions of state. There's no point in waiting any longer. She turns towards her room. Mr Ghulmahael, the fat Lebanese with hooded eyes, Dr Kiranos' emissary in the secret project of Mary Magdalene's bones, is at her elbow. Minhas has entrusted her with a vital mission. The fate of the whole religious battle between the Marmots and the Magdalenes hangs upon getting the casket out, with the help of the Lebanese whom she suddenly finds she dislikes intensely. The whole flux of her feelings for him now comes together in that one point. But she must work with him for the sake of Minhas and his deep spiritual attachment to the safety of the casket. The bones of Mary Magdalene must be preserved, with Mr Ghulmahael's help. Seeing him, the new burden is back on her shoulders. The death of VBS made her forget for a while. Dawn is brightening outside, soon the dangerous events of the day will be set in motion. Today the holy casket of Mary Magdalene must leave Rhidus secretly, bound for the safety of her museum.

'Can I speak with you for a moment?' he says. She was not expecting a direct contact so soon. A shiver of fear passes through her body. His earlier bantering tone of light flirtation has vanished. The voice is cold and serious. They move behind a large, ornamental Chinaman in brilliantly coloured porcelain. Green fronds from a pot he holds on his back fall over Mr Ghulmahael's head.

'You know about the computer-casket?'

She smiles briefly.

'It must leave Rhidus today with the coffin of Mr Vir Bahadur Singh. You must say it contains his 'effects'. It is too large to go any other way, they would spot it immediately. But now, in the confusion of this . . . death . . . it will get through easily. In such a delicate situation, nobody will ask questions.'

Suddenly she understands. 'You did this? You killed VBS?'

A deep sorrow rises to overwhelm her. She and Minhas were part of the death of VBS . . . They had killed him, just as much as the Lebanese.

He shrugs. 'The casket has to get out. By any means.'

'All this, for the bones of Mary Magdalene? They're not worth his death, anybody's death. Just to win a crown from the Marmots? How could Minhas be so blind, to trust someone like you? You're evil. You're a fat, poisonous slug crawling over the casket with your sticky juice.'

'I don't know what you're talking about. I've been given an assignment, and I intend to fulfil it. It's no use getting emotional about VBS. You never liked him very much, anyhow, so why are you getting so worked up now? Besides, he's expendable, and he's got himself a hero's funeral. We can have much advantage by his death. I want only a little bit of help from you. Since you are a member of the official delegation, nobody will suspect you.'

'You'll get the help. I'm bound to give it to you.'

Her body feels like a rock as she turns from him and goes towards her room, placing one foot carefully before the other. If she goes any faster, she will be sick right there, in the corridor.

Bhisham Chand is in her room, sitting on her bed. 'Why . . . ?' she says. 'What do you want? I feel absolutely exhausted, I must lie down. Otherwise I'll fall.'

'Sure, sure.' He moves hurriedly to a chair.

'You implicated that girl, Sonia. You know she didn't kill Mr Vir Bahadur Singh. And you're the one that created all that drama, about killing the prime minister. I don't care about the speeches and the flag. If Mr VBS can get a bit of glory, it's all right with me. But that girl must not suffer. You must make sure you save her.'

'Oh, don't worry, she'll get off eventually, even if she has to spend some time in jail. I know she didn't kill VBS. Why don't you just come here and sit by me for a while?' He has moved to the bed, and is tucking his feet under the blankets. He pats the place by him. In normal times, he would never have dared to take such a step, but under the shelter of VBS's death, anything was possible. Even a short liaison with Anna Dorai, queen of his dreams, the unimaginable, precious gift for a needy clerk.

She is still distracted, moving around the room, picking up objects, an ashtray, a nightie, a grey suitcase, putting them down. 'I'm going to leave behind a testimony that Sonia was with me, all the time. That apart, Bhisham Chand, who do you think really killed him?' It's important to find out how much the shrewd fellow has guessed, she must protect him. No more deaths in the name of Mary Magdalene. The Lebanese was now a force of nature, without good or evil, no compassion. He has been unleashed, now he moves inexorably to his end. VBS has paid a price. Been blown out, just so casually. 'Who do you think killed him?'

'The Lebanese of course. He came in to spend the night in my room, so he was right there, on the scene. In fact, it was poor Mr VBS who got me to smuggle him in. The Lebanese had disappeared when I went in from the corridor. But I can't understand his motivation. What did he hope to gain by his death? What did anybody hope to gain?'

Swimming

She comes in quietly and seats herself in a corner, smooths down her yellow cotton salwar-kameez decorated with tiny white polka dots, the yards of chiffon around her neck. 'Will you have some tea, or something cold? Whichever you prefer?'

Hari Sharan Kukreja breaks away from a conversation with her husband, and looks through tinted glasses. One of his eyes points in a distinctly different direction from the other. His white hair, swept firmly back, glows in the overhead light. 'Yes. Some tea please. But please, do not bother yet. Just keep sitting. We are coming from home.'

'But that was a long time ago. Chandigarh is far from here. Forty kilometres? Makran is forty kilometres from Chandigarh? And it must have taken you some time to find the house. It is the first time. I wish that you had brought Mrs Kukreja. The pleasure of meeting her would have been great.'

'She was not so well today. But I brought my daughter-in-law Madhu, my son, my grandson Suresh. What a fine boy, see how he listens! I love him very much. I said to them, 'Come with me to meet Mr Garkal, you will see some interesting paintings. And then, perhaps, he will give also some explanation. I have brought Suresh's horoscope. Perhaps Garkal Sahib will have some time to read it, afterwards.'

She gets up abruptly, her clothes falling in straight lines around her slim body. 'I'll get some some tea,' she whispers. Her voice knocks in her ears. But the visitor and his family have already turned away from her. She passes her hand over

Suresh's head on her way to the door. His hair is springy and fresh under her fingers. Their white Maruti car, laden with dust from their journey, is clearly visible in the early evening light, just beyond a mosquito-screen door. For only a short while, darkness comes early these days. Soon the car will disappear, and then the visitors. She and Surinder Singh Garkal, left in this narrow, box-like house, spending the evening, then the night, and then the next day alone. The anniversary of Ranjit's death. (They picked a fine time to arrive.) Killed while swimming. His head hit the edge of the pool. Knocked out cold, sank like a stone to the bottom.

She arranges everything in the house, cooking and cleaning, washing and ironing. The small squares of the rooms are perfectly prepared, as bases for the departure of pawns. Every day it is the same chess game, her husband's game.

'My wife does everything. She even stitched the curtains.'

His high-pitched voice comes through the thin walls. He is sitting on the sofa, his quiet head shaded by a white beard and a cool, grey turban, held at an angle, his eyes fixed on some point on the wall as he talks.

She goes past cane chairs near the ironing board. A brilliant red Toshiba iron stands ready for the next round of clothes. A present from her younger son Surjit. Her only son. His wedding photograph is in the drawing-room, quite close to her husband's favourite chair. Shining silver garlands draped over his turban, smiling at Smt Meera Garkal, Customs Officer. Surjit married a colleague, they are very happy. He couldn't even wait until a year had passed since his brother's death.

She reaches the kitchen, a long, narrow corridor which runs the entire length of the house, and faces the sun. In summer it is an oven. Even now, though windows stand open at either end, and cool evening breezes should be blowing in from the forest area, the heat courses through from one end to another like a rippling stream, and she is riding on it with no control. This morning she encountered the security forces, in the forests at the edge of Makran.

'Bibi, you should not have come so far, alone. Who knows what might have happened to you? Do you come here often?'

'No, this is the first time. I have never come before, I don't know this place at all.'

Trees growing close to each other, and a narrow path between them. She tried to keep close to the path, but continued eyeing a huge, open, sunlit ground to the left, a natural clearing. They came upon her suddenly, turning the corner of the road, coursing along the path: two young men in uniform, the one at the back carrying a gun chained to his shoulder. The sound of their scooter reverberated through the forest. They were grinning at her through the early morning light.

'What would people think, a lady emerging from the trees, in this lonely place? They would certainly ask questions,' said the first young man.

'Why?' she said, 'I'm just walking.'

'But here? You know this area, and the times in which we live. Very dangerous. So close to the state capital, and yet not as well protected. We have instructions to stop and search everyone who passes through, on account of the terrorists.'

She looked at them for the first time. Their faces were like spread-out puddings, rolling over the edges of their bones, very young. And their eyes like small bits of brown glass glinting in the sunlight, alive with curiosity and a mocking hilarity.

'Where do you live?' the other one asked her, from the back of the scooter, fingering his gun. 'In Makran? The address please?' But he made no move to write it down only repeating, 'Mrs Garkal. Wife of a retired DIG of Police. Madam, does your husband know that you are here, wandering in the jungle by yourself?'

For the first time, she was afraid. They might turn up at her house and tell Surinder.

'Soldiers came here about you. Two jawans from the CRPF – the Central Reserve Police Force. They're supposed to be looking for terrorists and they find my wife instead.

Wandering alone in the forest. I told you not to do that. Still crying and mourning for Ranjit? I told you, that's over.' She knew the look of pity which would pass over his face, but underneath, always, there was anger, impatience, frustration. He wanted to shake the memory of Ranjit from her, as if it were a rotting fruit.

'You're a married woman. You have children, madam?'

'Two sons. But this is no business of yours. I'm not doing anything wrong. You are after terrorists, people who throw bombs, and kill innocent passengers in buses. I'm going home, leave me alone.'

But they were barring her way. When she turned, they were still in front of her, and now they were openly laughing.

'Well, you know, you're still young.'

'We could well ask, what you are doing here alone. Where's the fellow? Have you just risen from the grass?'

'And look at the way your nipples jut out of your kameez.'

His two hands reached across, waving in the air, his feet settled more firmly on either side of the scooter, and he plucked hard at her nipples, through the thin cotton, pulling them like ripe cherries, then rubbing his palms over them, slowly. They had all the time in the world, for ever. The other one clambered off, still holding his gun, and came right up, nothing between them. He slipped his hand into her salwar, and his fingers went like a knife into the soft flesh between her thighs.

She wrenched away and ran screaming down the path. These days soldiers could do anything, in the name of security. The sound of their laughter swelled in her ears. If Ranjit had been there he would have killed them. How dare they touch her, hurt her, raise all these phantoms in her body? Even Surinder was not allowed, not since Ranjit died. Let him keep to his paintings and his religion. He is explaining them to the guests. The house is so small, you can hear everything right across. The picture of Kabir reaching for his god, longing and yearning for him. Kabir-the-weaver pictured as a loom and the god as a flame across a wide field of snow; pure and cold. Her flesh is still mourning the death of her son. What can she do about it?

'We must accept the will of God,' he is saying. 'Only in that is our peace and happiness.'

Her nipples still hurt from the morning, the patches around them are like purple flowers.

She lifts down boxes and tins well stocked with home-made snacks. One should always have some things ready, even a cake. She slices it carefully and arranges everything. Bright black raisins stare up at her. A flat glass bowl with six separate divisions, each filled up, peanuts, fried squares, sweet round balls of yellow sweets. The kettle is boiling – too much – a volcano preparing inside a mountain, huge flows of lava gurgling to the top. The tea will not taste so good.

They turn towards her as she enters, and the young lady jumps up to help with her heavy tray. She gestures to her son to pass the snacks around.

'You have taken so much trouble!' the boy's father murmurs from the sofa beside Surinder.

She tries to smile reassuringly at him, but the teapot is hot in her hands, burning her skin. She wraps her dupatta around its ceramic handle and resumes pouring perfect streams of pale brown liquid.

'I am very happy that you have come all the way from Chandigarh to see us. We do not get many visitors.'

Mr Hari Sharan Kukreja's head is leonine, thrown back, his glasses catch the light in gentle waves. 'It would be worth coming a long way, just to listen to Mr Garkal's explanations of his paintings. They are so full of spiritual meaning. And in addition, he is so expert in reading horoscopes! Surinderji, tell these young people about that famous case of Justice Chhabra.'

Surinder is ready, his sentences follow each other in peaceful progress, he does not need to look at his guests, all this has been said before, several times.

'It was such a long time ago. There are more recent instances. But Justice Chhabra's is a well-known case.

'I was still in service at that time, just coming up for promotion to DIG of Police. Posted in Chandigarh, and building this house in Makran. So, I was shuttling back and forth between the two places, in my jeep. It was easier in those days, still perfectly safe, because it was before the terrorist trouble started. I was extremely busy, but, when Justice Chhabra called me, naturally I reported to his house straightaway. He was hoping to be appointed Judge of the Supreme Court, and to move to Delhi, and he couldn't bear to wait for the news. He wanted me to read his horoscope, and tell him immediately what would happen about his appointment. I looked at it carefully, and then I looked again and again. There was no mistake about what I saw, but I didn't know how to tell him. But I am not afraid of these things, I take the name of God and tell the truth, whatever it is, and I did just that.'

'I said to him, 'Judge Sahib, you will never enjoy the fruits of your labours in the Court'. This made him very uneasy, and he insisted on knowing more. No astrologer wishes to predict death, but it is a fact of life, and, since he was pressing me,·I told him he would die a most painful death. He sent me away immediately, almost threw me out of his house. The Inspector General called me and he was furious. 'What have you told Justice Chhabra?' he said. 'The man's mad with you, he's throwing all our cases out of court. And don't you know, your case for promotion is coming up next week, are you a fool?'

'I kept quiet and did nothing. The truth is the truth, and no-one can quarrel with what God has written in your destiny. That's what I keep telling Parvati. Anyway, Justice Chhabra went on tour to Amritsar, and he was killed in the first wave of terrorist violence which hit the city. A most painful death. He was shot in two places before they finally killed him. And he died on the very day that the appointment to the Supreme Court was announced.'

The girl is getting restless, Madhu, the young mother. She holds the narrow book of her son's horoscope between her hands, pressing the edges from one palm to the next. 'I want to ask some questions,' she says, 'about Suresh.'

Mr Kukreja frowns briefly at his daughter-in-law. 'We'll come to that soon. First I want these people to hear about your paintings, Garkal Sahib. That one, for example, which you explained so well last time. There, above your head.'

'I have a new one as well. Finished only yesterday. But first I'll read Suresh's horoscope.'

The boy's father asks the usual questions, she has heard them from several parents. What profession will he follow? What will be his education? Will Suresh go into politics? Parvati hands around the snacks once more, offers each one a second cup of tea. She looks at Madhu, waiting for her question.

'Will Suresh love . . . ? What will be his relationship with his mother?'

'Oh, good. He'll love his mother like any dutiful son. Not very deeply or obsessively. Not like our son, Ranjit. He was devoted to my wife.'

Parvati smiles briefly, and looks above the girl's head. Ranjit's photograph is on the mantelpiece, smiling out of a broad silver frame inscribed with the badge and motto of the sporting club to which he had belonged. The inscription thanks him, on behalf of the staff and members, and commemorates his activities in a blood donation camp, held a month before his death.

'Surinder, why don't you tell them about Ranjit's death? If you can speak about Justice Chhabra's. This one is far more interesting.' They are silent, watching her. Surinder's voice continues to flow smoothly. 'Our son Ranjit,' he says, 'killed while swimming.' He is still bent over the boy's horoscope, laid out on the table in front of him, his body leaning forward lumpily in the cane chair.

'We know,' Mr Kukreja murmurs sympathetically.

Surinder's finger traces the charts of the horoscope. He

changes his glasses to peer at tiny numbers inscribed inside each compartment.

'The boy's mother has dark moods from time to time, in which black clouds of depression descend upon her, but they pass. That's all I can tell about her, from this horoscope. As for the boy's relationship, it's all right. Nothing special with her. Regarding his future, it is very good. His father will be proud of him. He will do all the things his father and grandfather could not do. Like enter politics. Maybe one day he will be prime minister, if the country survives in one piece. Nothing, for example, like Parvati's with our son Ranjit, who died.'

'Tell them about it,' she says, 'about the way Ranjit died. Tomorrow is the anniversary of his death.'

'Maybe we shouldn't have come today,' Madhu says, 'we're intruding. You must be sad.' She comes up to Parvati and sits beside her, reaching to touch the soft yellow material which covers her knee. 'Suresh, why don't you go outside and walk around? See the neighbourhood.'

'No, no.' Mr Kukreja's voice is sharp, with a hint of fear. 'It is dark already, and this house is rather isolated. You know that this is an area for terrorists. They have been very active lately.'

Madhu's husband smiles and puts his arm around the boy's shoulder. He is happy and contented with the prediction regarding his son's future. They go out towards the front porch, fussing around with something in the dust-laden Maruti. She follows their passage briefly, then turns back to Parvati.

Surinder Singh Garkal is folding up the long charts from Suresh's horoscope, very carefully, putting edge to edge. 'This is all I have,' he says, 'this small house you see in front of you. No other property. No income apart from my pension, and my wife does everything here, herself. No servant. We don't keep a servant, though Surjit, my son, is in the Customs Service. You see his picture there, his wedding picture.' He leans across to move a vase full of flowers out of the way, so that they can all see his happy smiling face beside Meera's. 'He has tried to persuade me. 'I'll pay for it,' he said. But I did not agree. One should be content with what one has. I have my books and my painting, and I try to help people, if I can. Kukreja Sahib, did you know that I am practising a bit of homeopathy? Quite successful.'

'It's you who killed him,' she says, 'seeing things that were written. You made them happen.'

A small gasp from Madhu, and her father-in-law leans across in deep embarrassment, to take his grandson's horoscope. But Surinder smiles the small smile of martyrdom.

'How many times I have told you, Parvati? Be content with what God has done. Our lives are in his hands. I only saw what was already written. Death by water at an early age. I warned him, don't go swimming, avoid water. But he insisted.'

'He was proud of the power in his body. These are his cups, he won them all in the water, there was no reason for him to die.' She darts across the room with the speed of a young girl, and pulls out gleaming, polished cups, clanking in her arms as she arranges them in neat rows in front of her husband.

'God does not give reasons,' he says. 'We must accept. I was always afraid when he went into the water. And that time, I knew. We phoned Chandigarh, at my sister's house. He had gone there for something quite different. An interview for a banking job. Shaila said, Ranjit has just left for the club, with some friends. Swimming, I think. Parvati and I took a taxi, straightaway, but we arrived too late. He had struck his head against the edge of the pool, and drowned immediately, without a sound. Nobody had a chance to save him.'

'You could have saved him. But you did nothing, you accepted. Everything.'

'What could I do? It was God's will. I've told you, don't mourn. Be happy.'

'Never. Why accept? Accept?' Her voice has risen, it is

powerful, like a man's. Her body is shaking with anger. She holds her hand against the cups, and they fall over. The crash breaks her voice. She rushes from the room.

The fellows are back from the porch, and Madhu gathers up her son. 'We should leave now,' she murmurs.

But Mr Kukreja is still involved with his friend Garkal. His voice is kind and soothing, attempting to fill the gap left by Parvati's departure. 'Garkal Sahib, you haven't told us about your pictures yet. I want Suresh to hear. He will learn from you. I admire you, your great spiritual strength.'

Garkal does not need comforting. His heart is like a lion's. He draws his strength from God. His back is straight and confident; it doesn't even touch the cushions in the sofa.

'We can begin with this one here on the wall. It is one of my favourites. There you see the icy mountains of the Himalayas, with Mount Kailash in the distance, the sacred mountain. This bird is the Arctic tern, flying between them. It comes from Siberia, flying over thousands and thousands of miles, to arrive here, in the Indian peninsula. It goes back the same way once the snows of winter have melted. I read about it in a book in the Chandigarh library. I sit there for hours doing my research – keep myself busy. And here, below, I have written a verse from the Guru Granth Sahib, our Holy Book, my son, written hundreds of years ago, ages before people had discovered and recorded these scientific facts of nature.'

He points to lines of black, untidy writing at the bottom of the picture. It says, 'If the Holy One can guide a bird over thousands of miles to its home, why don't you trust him, with your life?'

'You know, I do, Kukreja Sahib. I have given my life to God. He holds it in his hands. That's what I've tried to show in my last painting, the best I have done. I intend to conse-crate it tomorrow. I plan to hang it in my prayer room before I begin the Akhand Path, the twenty-four-hour reading of the Guru Granth Sahib which Parvati will share with me, to mark one year from Ranjit's death. That's why she's so upset, she is remembering, but don't worry, she will be OK.'

Madhu hopes he is right. She wonders if he even sees his wife. He hasn't looked at any of his guests as he talked in his slow, firm teacher's voice. His eyes go slowly over the wall above their heads.

'But why am I sitting here talking? I'll bring the painting in to show you before you go.'

His feet fumble for his slippers and he leaves the room slowly. One leg droops somewhat as he walks, from accustomed disability.

Madhu reaches across to put the plate of snacks back on its tray, bringing off a line of red ants which has begun to invade the fried sweet things, and moves around with haste, collecting cups and plates. They must leave soon. No more accidents. Her father-in-law said the road to Chandigarh was dangerous in the dark. They can't be too careful. A young child in the car makes them especially vulnerable.

'Oh, how could you do this? What was it? Why didn't you talk?'

The sound of Mr Garkal's voice cuts across everything in Madhu's head. She rushes to the next room, looking for them, and then into a bedroom. Parvati is sprawled on the bed, surrounded by bits and pieces of painted canvas, ripped and torn with a knife. Her eyes are wide open, and she lies absolutely still on the coverlet watching her husband. He is jumping jerkily up and down, on his shortened leg, moving around the bed, his gestures harsh and angry as he collects the pieces.

'What was the point? I can't understand. Why did you do this? My best painting. Completely destroyed! Do you see, it was a picture of the longing of a human soul for his God? To be received in the bliss of his enlightenment. This here was a symbol of the Nirgun Bhagwan, God without attributes, a wide stretch of open snow, with a red throbbing centre. And on the other side with the stanzas from Saint Kabir, adapted in my own words, I don't even have a copy,

I can never do this again, the Sagun Bhagwan, God with attributes, a busy place of worship, a temple with a street outside and a river flowing by, boats and commerce, and the details of everyday life. Everything about my life was in this picture, and you cut it up. Tomorrow I planned to give it to God, for Ranjit. How could you do this?'

He has collected all the pieces, and by now is oblivious of his guests, crowded at the door. Madhu pulls Suresh away. Her husband gently nudges his father towards the car.

'They'll be OK after a while,' Mr Kukreja says. 'Settle down. It's the grief from the death of their son.' He embraces Suresh. 'Come and sit in the back of the car with me, what a bright future Mr Garkal predicted for you!'

The Face of Dadarao

His face haunted me. I saw it first in the office of the Mahila Samiti, which was still in Ranjana's garage at that time.

'Come and find out what it's like, Ujjala. Maybe you'll join us. It is important work.'

Why did Ranjana want me there anyway? I am a reed, all split up, only attached to one small point, and the wind blowing through the long fragments.

'I don't need to see more people in pain, Ranjana. Try being a physician in a general hospital, especially now, in the harvesting season. They come in from distant villages, with mangled arms wrapped in rags, caught by open threshers. Yesterday a woman came with her baby who had crawled into the machine while she worked.'

'This is different. Besides you don't have to keep coming if it bores you,' she said. 'Give it a try.'

Her face shone with sincerity and affection, I could not run away from it. I was clinging to her at that time, anyway, wanting to be near her, though she couldn't tell me much. Her situation was so different, she had not had a choice. Ashok had left her and the boys. Then she had reconstructed her life with dignity and even a kind of passion, her body loosening and growing larger and larger as it flowed into hard work, organisation, setting up a women's resource centre. The shadow of a moustache developed on her upper lip, lines cut into her small mouth which was tough and kind, her smooth cheeks ballooned out. Her eyes shone with a glow that I trusted.

'Which is more difficult? Having a choice, or not having one?'

She was impatient, she didn't like abstract questions. 'What's the stretch of your freedom? Don't leave him, Ujjala. Marriages like this are not made every day. He is a fine man, and he loves you. You are free to work, to meet your friends. What else do you want? You should see how some men are. And there's Noni to think of.'

Noni, with her pigtails and rosebud mouth, anxious to have her ears pierced, exquisite, and so easily injured. It sounded simple to stay, when Ranjana spoke of it.

'Besides, what's your choice really? There is no other man, Arun Narayan has left already. For whom are you leaving Ranjit?'

'I'm not leaving, Ranjana.' But it was not the whole truth, and she knew that. She said, 'It's not easy to live alone, I can tell you that. It's horribly lonely, even if you don't have to worry about money.'

I didn't want to talk about it, I merely wanted the comfort of being with her, so I went to the Samiti office that morning. Dadarao and I entered together, although he stopped short, at the gate, with his son. Dadarao and Guddi were to sign an agreement. She was going back to him. Guddi was already inside, talking to Ranjana, perfectly at ease. She fitted into the room much more smoothly than I did.

Ranjana was teasingly censorious. 'Well, Guddi, are you really going back, or will you change your mind again?'

Guddi giggled a little, delighted at the attention. A placid, pretty woman, her large, shining eyes seemed much older than the designation she announced for the agreement. 'Guddi, w/o Dadarao, age twenty-seven years.'

'No, it's all right,' she said, 'he's waiting outside. I'm willing to sign. He's very keen. Maybe they told him it would help him get out of the police case against him. It's for this,' she explained, drawing me into the discussion.

She touched a knobbly, healed scar on her temple with a finger which was still tender and speculative.

'I think he really wants you back,' Ranjana said.

'Yes, maybe,' and she giggled again. Then she was shrewd, wanting to please Ranjana. 'All because of you and the Mahila Samiti. He thought, how long will she stay with her parents, then where will she go? She will come back to me. Sure enough, I had to leave my parents after two or three months. But I came here instead, began working. He saw that I would not go back until I wanted to. You had put me with Nafeeza. He began hanging around outside her room near the railway station, waiting to speak to me when I came out. Then the hearings in the case started, and he kept staring at me in the sub-judge's court.

' "Our quarter in Saket is empty," he said. "It comes to bite me with its emptiness when I get home from work. Now, if you and Sonu were there . . . "

'Slowly, one by one, he began selling or breaking all the things we had bought since our marriage. "Today I cut up the big basket in which you stored the onions", he would say.

' "Why are you doing this?" I said. 'Be in peace. You've done what you had to do, already." Really, you should have seen me, how I was that day when he knifed me.' Again she touched her scar. 'A heap of blood. That day I thought I would die.

' "What does it matter about the things," he said, "if you're not there?" '

'Anything special you want to put in the agreement?' Ranjana could see Dadarao getting impatient outside, taking short steps towards the garage, then going back to Sonu.

'Well, I don't know. He should change his ways. Not get angry and depressed without a cause. Not stop me from going out. I don't know. You talk to him about it.'

It was his eyes, mainly, that held me. They glittered with pain. A freakish intensity hung about the lashes, separating them out as if the sun were shining through. The bones of his face were jagged, crazily determined, holding up a fair, faintly scarred skin, a sparse black beard. I was surprised that

Guddi, who had lived with Dadarao's face, was so spread out, so calm. But she was not living with him then, she was torturing him with her absence.

Dadarao also did not know what he wanted to put into the agreement, and he didn't seem to care much about that. 'Anything you like,' he told Ranjana. 'You know the whole case so well, I only want her to come back.'

But Ranjana wanted to put it down in black and white, she knew it was better that way, so they went over all the weary steps. He would not drink, he would not smoke too much.

'When I went to the quarter the other day,' Guddi said, her voice full of self-righteous, housewifely assertion, 'there were piles of bidis, those dirty things he smokes, in every corner. I don't know what he has been doing while I was away.'

He would let her go out from time to time. 'I don't know what she finds in her parents' house,' Dadarao said. 'Especially with that stepmother. Did I tell you that she was offering me her own daughter as a second wife, even after all this? So I can't be such a bad chap after all. The company pays me six hundred rupees, which is more than most guards get, and we own the quarter we live in.'

'I want to sell it and go somewhere else,' Guddi replied. 'I don't want my children growing up there. It is filthy, nobody cleans the drains, and rubbish piles up in the narrow streets. Also, there's no school for Sonu. And there's nowhere I can go to work nearby.'

'She's not really interested in working, only in getting out of the house. There's lots to do at home, if she paid any attention to that. I earn enough. But she can go out to work if she wants to. I'm not stopping her.'

'And I must come to Samiti meetings once a week. On no account will I miss that. After all they have done for me. They saved my life.'

Ranjana had been writing busily, trying somehow to put their spongy fears and pains into the formal language of the agreement. Now she wanted to stop, to leave enough place at the bottom for their signatures. She looked up and smiled at Guddi. 'But when you tell him you come here, you must really come here, not go anywhere else.'

A loud sound came from Dadarao, a sudden burst of emotion, as if he were looking at something inside himself.

'It is coming to Delhi which spoiled her. In Pahari Dhiraj, in our village, all this would never have happened. The two families and the other villagers would just come together and settled everything. I have lived in Delhi–Faridabad all my life, but when it came to marrying, I went back to the village to fetch a wife. Her uncle arranged it. She had always lived with her uncle's family, her parents were in Delhi like myself. The village is full of mango trees. It lies in the Ratnagiri district. The best mangoes in the world. You know Ratnagiri mangoes? They are bright yellow inside.'

'Dadarao,' Ranjana said, 'what about the knife? Why did you do that?'

He didn't look at her. In fact he didn't look at anybody, least of all at Guddi. The blazing eyes were still turned inside. They slipped over our surface like a forest fire.

'Only she talks about the knife. It's her story. Who knows who did what.'

'What do you mean?' Ranjana was stern. She held Guddi's head between her hands, thrusting the scarred temple towards him. 'She was gashed and bleeding. The police have photographs. In the Central Delhi Hospital, she was given seventeen stitches, and still the wound wouldn't hold. Kept opening up. She could have lost her life. Or at least have been blinded. There's no doubt about the knife. Why do you still deny it?'

'Whose knife, what happened, only she knows. There are no witnesses. Not a single man from the neighbourhood will stand up in court and say what happened that day.'

Ranjana was sceptical, but friendly again. 'Dadarao, forget about witnesses and police cases and all that. We know you can get a man to say anything in court, or not to say it, provided you pay him enough. That's not the point. But such a thing must not happen again.'

'If she says I did this with the knife, then it must be so. But I will never lift a hand to her, I swear that, you can write it down. Forget about the knife, and about the police case. That can't be helped, it will go on, and I will fight it, but she must come back, that's all.'

'What happened?' They both turned at my question. I had to ask about the knife. Maybe it was a way to reach the ravages in Dadarao's face.

Ranjana nodded towards me. 'This is my dear friend Ujjala. She will be working here regularly now. You can talk to her if you have any problem after this.'

The Samiti was still spreading its quiet mantle around Guddi. She handed each of them separate copies of the agreement.

Guddi gave hers to me. 'Keep it for me here,' she said.

Then she talked, quite easily and naturally, oblivious of Dadarao's presence in the room. 'He's right, not a person in that whole locality of the city centre stirred to help me when it happened. I lay there bleeding on the ground. I thought I would die any moment. I didn't even have the strength to hate him for it, or to feel the pain.

'A big crowd had collected. I hoped that somebody would tell my brother. I gave the address, my father's house was just around the corner. 'Or call the police,' I said. But he told them that I had run away from home, that I had been missing for two years, and he had just found me. He had drink inside him and he sat on his cycle flourishing his bloody knife, but they still believed him. They clucked their tongues and muttered that I was evil. No-one moved to help me. As if I had deserved it. My brother found me on the road an hour later. Someone passing on the road outside their house had yelled out that I was lying there.'

Dadarao gave a short laugh. It felt in my ears like the sound of the devil rocking in a hot place. I looked at him. I haven't seen his face since then, but it's been with me all the time, a filter blocking out the sun.

After that only Guddi came to the Samiti office. Dadarao did not come again. Maybe he was too busy managing his all-night job, and putting in appearances in court during the day. The court was far away, on the other side of the Jamuna, in Shahdara. The case kept getting adjourned and then the judge hearing evidence fell sick.

Or maybe the agreement was going well. Guddi seemed to have no complaints. She came even more regularly when we shifted to the new Samiti office. Its woodwork was shining but hollow. Already the tap in the bathroom dripped continuously. Nevertheless, being awarded formal premises under the Sheetal Colony flyover was official recognition and good for the Samiti.

It made us all somehow more business-like in our approach to cases, and pleased my professional soul. Only sometimes I missed the peace of Ranjana's garage, and cool breezes which had come in from the public garden in front of her house.

Here the roof and furniture, even the large posters of revolutionary women which hang on the walls, shake and rattle each time a bus passes on the bridge overhead. I spend a lot of time at the window. It looks out on the road below. Still sheltered by the curving bridge, a line of rag-pickers' shanties has sprung up on the other side of the railway line: just pieces of tin and gunny sacking and some stolen bricks patched into heaps of grimy waste. Children play amongst them in the middle of fast through-traffic and the numerous feet which come to the food and tea stalls all day. Children always worry me. I fear for their safety and happiness. Take Noni: the way she ran out on to the road after her father, her body shaking, screaming to him to come back, not to go away, I almost died watching her small body spread-eagled against the darkness.

The view from the window just takes in, from the left

corner, a small glimpse of a copse of trees planted along the edge of the road which runs under the flyover. In a few years, people walking from where I stand now will see the tops of silver oak trees, the white underside of their leaves flashing against heavy, russet-brown bunches of flowers, and elegant waving spirals of eucalyptus trees. I make a detour to park my car there under one of the trees, as if shade from the branches will hold it safely, like a child, while I am upstairs. I can see it too, from the window, square and orange, still covered with dust, strongly solid and reassuring, as if, any time, I can move off in it. Though I am not thinking of running away from the Samiti office yet.

Guddi fixed upon me in her casual, smiling fashion, as if Ranjana's reference during the agreement interview had passed her irretrievably into my orbit. I tried to dislodge her quick, sharp sentences, back to Ranjana's care, but she was undeterred. 'Guddi. That's the name I gave myself, a little before my marriage to Dadarao. It's from a movie, you know. The one with Jaya Bhaduri. I loved seeing movies. They built a new cinema in Nirath, which is only a few miles from Pahari Dhiraj. My uncle used to take us there at least once a week. I was very excited about marrying Dadarao just like Amitabh Bachan and Jaya Bhaduri in *First Love*. And I loved the idea of coming to Delhi. It seemed like a magic city, full of freedom. My parents had refused to let me live here before I was married. All those years I was shut up in Pahari Dhiraj, roaming like a stupid thing under the mango trees. And then he wanted to shut me up again, here in this wonderful city of Delhi.

'I wouldn't have got into this other mess, if he hadn't been so harsh with me. Always angry, and I never knew why, always suspecting me of looking at other men. 'You're so pretty,' he said, 'they must be dreaming of you at night. And they can hardly keep their hands off you.' I don't know what he thought, that he had got himself a personal film star. I liked the idea of their dreaming of me. But still, there was nothing happening at that time. So funny. When there was really nothing, he drove me out of my wits with jealousy and suspicion. And when there was something going on, he thought I was safely in my parents' house.'

'You mean Samanth? Dadarao didn't know about him?' The face was not that of a man who merely suspected. It was one whose life was cut away by knowledge, like a knife going between the banana leaves, cutting flesh from bone, hot sap dripping on the ground below. Ranjana had told me he had even been at the Maurya Clinic, lurking as a shadow in the sordid corridors outside, when Guddi went there to have Samanth's child aborted.

'Oh no,' Guddi said, 'he never knew about him. And please, don't mention it, even by mistake, when you come to the meeting in my house next week. You know about the meeting? Savitri, Fatima and the others are coming there instead, this place is a bit far for us. We're hoping to start a local Samiti. Ranjana didi is very pleased.

'No, Dadarao didn't know about Samanth. Well, maybe he suspected. Samanth was his friend, actually, and he came to the house a lot. Dadarao didn't mind because he helped us with money and things when Dadarao was without a job. Spent more than two thousand rupees on us. I wondered if he would ask for them back when I told him I was cutting off from him, going back to Dadarao.'

'When you made the agreement?'

'Yes. But still, I told Samanth I was going back only for a year, to try it out. Why cut him out completely? I have no intention of going to him again. But let him live with uncertainty. After all, he kept me dangling for so long. You see, he's much older. His wife died long ago. He's waiting to marry off his last two daughters. Then he says he will live with me. I believe him, but what's the use of his taking me then? He will be close to sunset. Maybe a few years, and that's all. Much better with Dadarao. At least he's young. And if he behaves himself . . . In any case, I went to Samanth only because he sympathised with me, showed me a bit of understanding and tenderness when Dadarao was hard and cruel to me in front of him.'

I preferred to think of love and passionate intensity, of irrational movements of bodies, a conflagration. Ranjana said these were bourgeois notions, but she could not give me accurate information of how it usually was with Guddi and Samanth or how much of what Guddi now said was lies. After all, the underside of facts soon steps away. The only thing which returns steadily to me, like the harsh breathing of air, is the face of Dadarao.

I wish Guddi had not brought her decision to me for discussion. I tried to put her back with Ranjana. She would be the best person, so much experience. She wouldn't fall into these traps of vague doubts and ambiguities, tears and passions suspended tenuously from facts. 'She will move you straight to the point of action, whether you should go with Dadarao on his posting to Jammu, or stay on in Delhi, in your quarter in Saket with Sonu, to keep on with your job. Of course, board and lodging is free in Jammu for him, if he goes alone, but there are other things to think of.'

So many other things, like the fringes of a dark funeral shawl, waving and jingling as you walk. I was the wrong person for Guddi to ask. I could feel a man's pulse, prescribe a series of tests, analyse X-rays. Come to a reasonable diagnosis, then proceed to erase pain, like the slate of the body being wiped clean. All this was easy. But to help Guddi take a decision, with the face of Dadarao hanging inside me like a cruel, heavy curtain, was cutting into my heart.

'Discuss this with Ranjana,' I said.

'No, with you.'

Some instinct for torment made her insist upon laying it out before me like a pack of cards, each with its face down. How could I pick one and say, this is the right one for you, when I myself knew no sense of right and wrong, only the terrible beauty of love, and felt inside, bursting again and again, only a sudden, soundless time-bomb, the passion for destruction.

It was Arun who first felt the impending sense of doom. The pain did not touch me until later. At that time, I felt only a mountain stream rushing in my blood, the thunder of a certainty and delight I had never felt before, not with Ranjit, not with my work, not with the unfolding miracles of the world, even as a child. Even Noni, heart of my heart, whose shining magic I must protect, did not touch me as Arun did. As he still does.

Arun felt the doom from the time I began to speak of leaving Ranjit. The rest was a traditional situation. Ranjit Grewal, journalist, comes back unexpectedly from a foreign trip and finds his beloved wife, whom he trusted and adored with long-standing passion, in the arms of his best friend. Well, not quite in his arms. But he stood at the door and heard me tell Arun that I loved him. I can guess how it sounded, because I know how it felt saying it, as if my whole life were in the words, and there was no place for anything else. Maybe it was worse than finding me in his arms.

Ranjit is a large man, six feet four, and broad. The sound of his body thrashing out of the house began the avalanche. Noni came running out of her room, both of us dashed after him into the twilight, calling to him to come back. He stopped his long strides for a moment, the wind blew out his mane of soft black hair. He snatched her up and held her tightly.

'You know what your mother's doing?' he yelled, his voice going into every house that ever existed. 'She's sleeping with another man.' Then he dropped her and went on, his huge figure fracturing the gathering darkness of Green Park.

She ran after him in terror, not knowing what he meant. 'She won't do it again. You'll promise, you won't do it again? Mummy will promise. But come back. What will I do?'

What did promises mean in all this? And agreements? What do they ever mean?

He reached the main road and waited there, the evening traffic roaring past him in oblivious confusion. He was like a blind, bewildered monster on a TV screen, thrusting his huge head this way and that.

'You work there, don't you?' he said, pointing down the road. Lights of the All-India Institute of Medical Sciences glittered in smooth grey buildings which sheltered the night agonies of my patients.

Then he turned and walked fast in the opposite direction. I picked up Noni and stumbled after him, petrified that a passing car would knock one of them down.

He had reached the Kutab Minar, and was like a caged animal looking for a gap to go through, when we caught up with him.

I saw him there in concentrated awareness, like a swords-man, completely alert, the mind of somebody facing death. From the corner of my eye I saw the crowd gather, loitering rickshaw wallahs, scooterists, bus-drivers waiting to go home, even a belated foreign tourist in search of handicrafts. The chowkidar was not yet certain that he was directly involved. He paced before the entry gate with hesitant steps, watching, ready to guard his territory, to defend the ancient tower if called upon to do so, as if this lost, fumbling crea-ture, now in complete despair, could threaten it. I did not know who he was. Ranjit Grewal, my husband, a man I had injured, a man in pain, a man? I knew only the face of Dadarao. It drew me in like a whirlpool, swallowing my breath. I had to get him back into the house.

Then suddenly it was over. After a long time, after no time, immediately, or when hundreds of days had passed. There was no way of telling. A taut string broke. It hung ugly and limp, without life. He picked up Noni. She was a black crab clinging to his shoulder. He gathered me up and I was a sleepwalker. We went home.

It seems like a simple picture, the end of a story. But stories never end, they go on. How could I cut into a talking voice, produce for Guddi the arbitrary silence of a decision?

Decisions are funny things. Like black rocks in the middle of a running stream. Water breaks up against them white and frothy, utterly disturbed. It flows over and around with greater force, for a moment, because of the great hole in its heart. Then it is covered, water comes together again. Water is not plagued.

Arun Narayan made a decision. Made from materials which Ranjit and I provided for him, from our lives. A happy family, father, mother, child, a husband who loves me. He decided to leave it like that.

'Better for all of you,' he said. 'You'll see, in the long run, this will give you happiness.'

I did not argue the point with him. He had presumed already on the nature of my happiness. 'And your happiness?' I said. 'What about that?'

'For a short while I dreamed of it. Now it's over.'

'Can't I change that?' I wanted to scream at him, to pit the whole strength of my being against the passing water, to leap out and hold it in my arms, I could see it passing. But I was circumscribed. Time, place, and principally, the decision of Arun Narayan. I was wrapped, held down, suffocated by an enormous helplessness.

'Ask Ranjana,' I told Guddi, 'discuss it with her, whether you should go to Jammu with Dadarao or not.' I could not bear to ask her about Samanth. She had decided already about leaving him.

I should have seen the decision in Arun's face, it was closed in upon itself, separated out already, the eyes were two dark tunnels going into the mountain. I was waiting to pick him up after his press conference. I had parked anonymously outside the Indian Airlines building on Barakhamba Road. He had walked down rapidly from the Press Club, and patches of sweat were large under his arms. I knew the faint, gentle smell of sweat on his dark skin. I had licked it, put my face in it, fractured his separateness in the warm ease of my flesh. I was delighted to see him. But this time, somehow, his clothes kept him in from me, as if the white khadi of his kurta-pyjama were a stiff prison wall he had slung around himself. I should have seen his decision in that, though there are no real points to be had in a warning. Just understood the nature of decisions, how they close you away, shut you in. Then I could have helped Guddi, maybe even helped myself.

In short, I was not prepared for what he had to say. 'You're thinking only of Ranjit,' I accused, still childish and close, hoping to dispel this new, heavy cloud of locusts. Maybe they wouldn't settle, they would pass. Just a minor crisis. Arun and I would return to how it was before Ranjit found out.

'I don't want to injure him. And there is Noni, whom I love. You too. It's for your good. You see, I'm a politician and you know my kind of politics. It means going to jail, living a hard life, being ill, being in disgrace, etc, etc. Currently my work is in Delhi, but it won't be so for long. Soon I'll go back to the South, and you don't know my villages at all.'

His voice was kind, I would vote for such a voice in the next elections. But just now I was still fighting to make it particular, to keep it loving one-to-one, to keep the sounds of it from spreading into general goodwill for the people.

'I will take care of you,' I said, 'when you are ill. After all, I'm a doctor.' Only I laughed at this. I could not even take care of the face of Dadarao. It overflowed and swamped me, made morality ridiculous, dissolved the commands which Arun had released into the air.

But one thing is clear, that which he made solid in the flux. If I leave Ranjit now, there's no going back to Arun. He's still in Delhi but that's not the point. Does it matter to Guddi that Samanth is here? What does going to Jammu mean to her? An irrelevant extension on this large stretch of boredom, waiting to die? If I leave Ranjit, it will not be to start anything.

There was no sign of Dadarao at the next meeting, in Guddi's house. I did not ask her if he was in Jammu, and whether she intended to join him there. I sat with the others on a durree in the middle of the tiny room. All the 'regulars' were there: Ranjana, Fatima, Nafisa, Moti, and a few women from the basti, the locality itself, whom Guddi had persuaded to attend. Her position in the basti was just like before – slightly superior – as she disdained the filth running in the gutter outside, and the dirty, illiterate children with whom Sonu was playing, with rousing glee. Now a meeting of the well-known Mahila Samiti was being held in her house. Soon, perhaps at the next meeting, a health worker would arrive, to induce the basti women to follow elementary practices of hygiene and sanitation. But, more important than that, Guddi had gone back to Dadarao, the circle was complete once more, he still loved her and cared for her. A new mantle of strong respectability hung over the young flower of the Hindi movies, Guddi, placid and benign, who had once giggled with sudden delight.

The room was neat, recently whitewashed, even though harsh acrid smells from outside, of shit and rotting vegetables, stale tobacco, moving animals, percolated through easily, obviously Dadarao had reacquired his discarded belongings. A string cot, rolls of bedding, some stacked tin trunks, had been pushed against the walls to make way for the alien invasion in the centre of the room.

'The kitchen is separate.' Guddi took me proudly to an alcove which led off to the left of the room. What else could she want?

Still, there is a curious restlessness. As if she is going away all the time and never quite leaving, and the grief which comes from that.

I won't mention it to Ranjana. There are some things she does not understand. For example, the face of Dadarao. That it is my face as well, whether I stay with Ranjit, or go away.

Fur Boots

We are travelling over land covered with snow. Suddenly Mediterranean countryside, also in the heart of winter, is left behind, and here everything looks up from a distant, immaculate white layer: small black trees, thin ribbons of roads, clusters of houses. Then the buildings get larger, became factories and office-blocks; we are approaching the capital of Malgary.

I am the leader of the delegation. Leela and Mr Kumar are with me: we have been invited to visit the country.

'Come to Pludova,' she said. 'We will see you there in six months' time.' Her arms were full of flowers; we had arranged a farewell reception for their team at the end of long talks in New Delhi.

'Oh yes,' I said, not believing I would go. 'I would love to see your beautiful country. I'm sure I'll come there some time.' The usual diplomatic talk.

'No, no, I'll make sure you are invited, you must come. Even if it's for two days, on your way back from some other visit. You travel a lot, don't you, in this job?'

'Yes,' I said. 'These days it is important to negotiate many things for one's country. You know that.'

She nodded and smiled. One of her front teeth is pale chocolate in colour, it makes her mouth perfectly charming.

'Our minister will come here to sign the agreement. But you must come for a few days, just to tie up loose ends. We must make sure everything goes well. This agreement is very important to us.'

I knew then that I would be going to Malgary. Marta is a

powerful woman. She was easily the youngest person in
their delegation though bullying the others, accepting or not
accepting our terms, as she thought best. That's how we
tell the position of someone in Malgary, where posts and
designations are empty words for us, until we see the power
and the body which fills them out.

Looking from the window to the snow spread out far, far
below, it is safe now. The sense of confusion, of lines crossed,
of going back and forth to catch the truth of the matter, is
gone. Athens Airport is already three hours behind us.

We were there for hours, sitting in the plane, getting out
to identify our luggage, going back and forth in the aisles,
talking to people, just being there, emptily, suspended, not
knowing what was happening. And then an air hostess told
me about it, only because we had VIP tags on our luggage,
and they had received special instructions about the official
delegation travelling to Pludova from Athens by Malgar Airlines. As there is only one plane every other day, Marta must
have told them of our group. The girl had a very white face,
and a line of large pimples running along her chin. She was
fully a head taller than I, the pimples ran off in a line from
my nose. She was tall and angular, very bony. Were all
woman from Malgary like that? I knew only Marta. She
stood there, uneasy, making small movements, wanting to
get away, but since I had asked, she replied, 'Oh. Yes sir.
We have a problem. You see, three passengers have checked
in and disappeared. We can't find them on the plane. But we
must find their luggage. Who knows what is in their luggage?
These days, we can't take any chances.'

If the plane should explode, move in a series of shattering
projectiles, each little piece of steel breaking away from the
others, moving out in terrible radiating lines, rays of the sun,
from the central, bursting, shimmering point of terrorist's
bomb, hidden away to cause our deaths, vacuous, unselected,
and without hatred, tucked into the centre of a suitcase, I
could understand what she was saying.

There were no further explanations. The tall girl gave me

nothing else, or did she see me merely as a short man with an expanding belly, clad in a suit, my overcoat poised on my knee, a scarf? How shall I wrap it so that the wind rising from the snow of the airport does not crucify me? It was three hours of going back and forth wrapped in the slightly sour smell of fear, before the tall girl with pimples, stewards, an elegant German hostess with strictly permed blond hair, moved to the doors, bolted them, did all the preparations of departure. Then we took off. Has Marta been waiting at the airport of Pludova all this time?

The ground is rapidly coming closer. We are directly over the city now, everyone knows that, it is not my special secret. Pludova is below us, the plane is full of movement, the bustle of bags, hand luggage being collected, we have fastened our seat-belts. Our seats were right up in front; I am first in line to disembark. I should have expected the wind. My feet slip on the steps going down – thin leather shoes, not quite the thing for snow-covered Pludova. The temperature is minus three: I can see her now, hurrying across the tarmac in a small cluster of people.

This is the face of fantasy; Pludova is a flower opening out in Marta's face. Her eyebrows are fine, thin lines which meet in the centre, over the bridge of her nose, her eyes are large, green and completely opaque, heavy under a layer of distinct eyeshadow; eyes which are completely in control, they will draw my two days in Pludova straight into the centre of their efficient care. Why has she chosen to give me her special attention? Her hair has been cut short, it folds around her face in layers of burnished copper. The colour is different. Last time I saw her hair, it was black.

'You've changed your hairstyle. This suits you very well.'

She takes off her black skin gloves to shake my hand, then she turns to welcome Leela and Mr Kumar. A man behind her even taller than she is, with caved-in cheeks and dusty eyes, presents Leela with a bunch of magnificent magenta carnations.

'Every six months I cut it, or change it, or grow it. Some-

times people find it difficult to recognise me. On behalf of
the government of Malgary, I have great pleasure in welcom-
ing you to Pludova, I hope that you will enjoy your stay
here.'

'In your care, I am sure we will. Thank you very much
for inviting us.' Leela is young and charming, perfectly
enthusiastic. Marta pays her very little attention. 'Oh, but it
is so cold here. My feet froze, walking across the tarmac.'

'My dear, this is the heart of winter, we have to expect
the cold. Minus three, and it will go much lower. If you're
dressed warmly, it's all right.' She glances briefly at Leela's
feet, open black sandals with nylon socks, already flecked
with stains of drying ice. 'In Pludova, you have to wear
boots.'

Of course we all look at Marta's boots. We are sitting on
a ring of velvet sofas, waiting for her minions to fetch our
baggage, and suddenly her boots are the centre-piece. Only
the cadaverous man, who has been introduced as an architect
and deputy chairman in the Ministry of Culture, and who
knows no English (Why is he here?) hovers mystified at the
edge of the circle looking at the boots. They are magnificent:
pale maroon suede with square high heels.

'Oh yes, yours are just the right thing. And they are
beautiful.'

'With fur inside. I have had them made specially for me,
I know a man with a factory just outside Pludova. You see,
I have rather strange feet, very broad, the normal sizes don't
fit me. Sometimes I bring the leather in from abroad. He
made a pair of evening shoes for me from snakeskin I brought
from India.'

Do we know at any one moment what happens? It's only
afterwards. I know I am in love with Marta, I am tremen-
dously excited, I see broad white feet, smooth and fat, nestling in maroon leather, safe and protected from the cold of
Pludova winter. I feel an enormous tenderness about those
feet, a blessing on the leather, the shoemaker who protects
her, though God knows she is strong, she can take care. Am

I in love with her feet, her boots or what? Who knows? And can one separate these things? I bend down to touch my shoes, my hand seems so short and ugly, the fingers stubby and end-stopped, graceless. How could anyone sleep with a man whose hands looked like that? I long for an artist's hands, the fingers long and going on for ever, caressing her feet, her instep, the soft, wrinkly skin between her toes.

'My shoes are from Japan, some kind of processed leather. You don't have to polish them, I just wipe them in the morning. They were fine for Athens, but here they will be utterly useless.'

She looks at them kindly. 'Well, it's only two days, we won't let you suffer much. There will be cars, you will not have to walk, unless you want to.'

I want to walk up and down the snow-covered mountains with her, turn her face to the grey sky and wait for the sun to shine on it, shake the branches of a pine tree over her crisp, dyed hair. Her neck is a thick white column above her black fur collar, everyone is getting into their coats. They are waiting for me, the luggage has arrived, piloted by two nondescript young men in trench coats, our air hostess with the pimples hovering anxiously behind them.

'We can't find your bag, perhaps it got left behind in Athens, in all the confusion with the luggage.'

'But I identified it, you remember, it has a blue stripe across it.' She moves her shoulders helplessly. 'I don't know what happened. We've sent a message to Athens. Pehaps it will come by the flight tomorrow evening.'

Marta's voice is icy and cold, fierce. 'By which time our guest will be ready to leave. How could you do this? How will he manage here?' And she shifts to their own language, it is quite clear from the tone what she is saying; the girl's skin pales under her pimples. I interrupt, 'Oh please, please, don't worry, I'll manage with my other bag, it's got all my toilet stuff, I just won't change my clothes.' I can't bear Marta's terrible tone of voice. Is she threatening the girl?

'Tomorrow, sir, tomorrow definitely, before you leave,

we will get the bag back, don't worry.' She seeks my protection and her voice clings to me imploringly.

Marta lifts off her, lets her go. 'We can leave now. Indeed, I am sorry that you are being inconvenienced.' The deputy chairman shakes my hand comfortingly, and leads the way out of the VIP lounge.

'We have put you in a small hotel in the centre of town, more convenient that way, you will not have to travel much to get to your appointments. It is the Hotel Mira, in the square which contains the statue of General Sendova, who is known as the Saviour of Malgary. On the other side is the Pludova Church, which gives the city its name. It is where the city began, hundreds of years ago. Beside it is the large Kriesky Church, it is an active church, for the Orthodox religion. Some people go there, although you know we have no religion in this country. You can walk across to see the church if you like.'

It is not far from the airport to the city, already we are approaching the outskirts.

Leela is a young woman, fond of the good life; in Athens she was out in the tavernas all night with young friends from the city. There is a note of disappointment in her voice, she is arguing, 'We don't have to travel very far anyway, Pludova is a small city, is it not, Madame Brutonov? I am told there is a fine hotel on the other side of town, a modern Japanese hotel.'

But Marta is not taking suggestions. 'Yes. They built it, now it belongs to us. Perhaps we will take you there this evening, to an official banquet. Let us see. There, you see, the gilded dome with a cross. That's the Kriesky Church.'

Marta is very efficient, she has everything planned. She clusters us in the lobby of the Mira Hotel. 'One minute please, before you go up. I must tell you today's programme, it is rather rushed, you see, as you are here for such a short time. We would very much like you to stay longer, but you are important government officials, very short of time. This morning, you are to meet my husband, who is Minister of Science and Technology, and then we will have lunch together in the Sheraton Hotel. In the evening is a meeting with the Deputy Minister for Defence Production. After that you will be free to decide what you want to do. Perhaps visit the Kriesky Church, it has a most interesting crypt, or attend the official banquet. This afternoon, after lunch, we will visit the National Gallery of Malgar History. Tomorrow we will visit the National Gallery of Pludova, you could lay a wreath on the tomb of Madame Shilkova, who was Minister of Defence until last year when she passed away suddenly at a conference in Peru. Then I have arranged a lunch for you with Boris Levertov, who is Poet of the Royal Academy of Malgary, and President of the Writers' Union.'

'Oh, it is a very busy programme.'

I knew, of course, that Marta was married, but I had not thought of her husband. He is a minister; is this where her power comes from?

'Then we must get ready for the first appointment.'

'You are very late for that already, because your plane was delayed for three hours. But I warned him, and he is still waiting for you.' The husband of Marta. We shall meet him soon.

It is difficult to get Mr Kumar away from the reception desk. His bulky figure leans anxiously over the counter as he asks for our passports. 'Surely they don't need to keep our passports? Why does the hotel need our passports?'

'Oh come on, Mr Kumar, don't worry so much. We will get them back before we go, nothing can happen to our passports, we are state guests. I don't know about the others, but we're safe.' Leela is impatient. She is whispering to him, but her voice is sharp and clear, it reaches us on the sofas and Marta's head snaps back to glare at her. The green eyes are full of fire, and I love it. Then she shuts it off. 'I'll wait for you here,' she says.

'Have you seen the rooms? They're poky little holes. Oh yours is a little bigger.' Leela flounces into my room within

fifteen minutes, ready to leave, trying on the light switches.
'At least you have an overhead light, I have two little lamps in
my room, the only place that's properly lit is the bathroom.'

'Well, maybe my room is bigger, but look at the furniture.'
It is big and heavy, and stands around the room like family
occupants, large brown sofas which cast thick shadows
against the walls. I want to get away soon, to Marta in the
lobby. I am the first to descend.

She is standing at the reception, with our passports in her
hands, her long white fingers are closed around them like
lily leaves. 'Here they are, your companions were so worried.
According to hotel regulations, they're supposed to keep
passports until the guests leave.'

'Well, let them keep them, it doesn't matter.'

'No, no, don't worry, I've spoken to them. You were
very quick, coming down.'

'Well, there's not much preparation one can do, with one
bag. I have only the clothes I'm standing up in.' I rub the
tingle of cologne in my cheeks; can she smell it?

Marta is anxious to collect us and move off to the meeting.
She says nothing, but I feel her waiting; then Mr Kumar
comes down. She looks quickly behind him to see if Leela is
following, then goes to the internal telephone. 'You are
coming down? We are all waiting for you. Soon we must
leave.'

I can hear Leela's voice at the other end, and she is down
soon, obviously bathed and changed, a little flustered, the
shadow of Marta's disapproval on her face. 'Well, you know
we were very tired from the plane, we spent three hours just
sitting around waiting for that bomb scare to be sorted out.'
Does Marta register the explanation? Where is she – already
in the meeting with her husband? Her husband, the minister.

'It is a Sunday, we have opened this office only for you,
nothing's organised.' But there is a girl in the anteroom to
take our coats, and then tea in large, white translucent cups,
the glow of hot liquid coming through to the flowers printed
on the outside.

The minister is at least twenty years older than Marta. He greets us at the door. You can tell his age from the folds in his neck, but his face is youthful and smiling, plenty of hair cut boyishly across his forehead, and large, wide-open blue eyes, very intelligent.

What does one talk about to the Minister of Science and Technology? That subject is not my charge, I am here to talk about the agreement, if there are any problems. We are to supply large-scale orders of boots and revolver holsters for their soldiers, co-operation in the future between our two governments, it is just the beginning. We discuss the theory of conferences, he goes to a lot of those. Does Marta travel with him, zooming from one capital to another, buying snakeskin here, a piece of silk there, building up bit by bit this charming personality with which I am in love? I want to look at her all the time, but I am leader of the delegation, I must talk to the minister. He is a nuclear physicist of international repute, I am a small-time poet and government servant. What will connect us? Just this vague network of official obligation, the powers that we represent, something beyond ourselves, and Marta who sits between us. His English is not so good. She follows his words eagerly, supplying them when he misses a portion of a sentence, and translating quick-fire for the deputy chairman who sits cadaverously in an armchair on the side.

'This is my new office. I moved in only a few days ago. You know that today is a holiday, I would normally not be here. But my wife wanted me to meet you today and whatever she wants, I do. Oh I think I must tell you how we first encountered each other. I was Dean of the Science Faculty in Pludova, Marta was taking care of a delegation of eminent scientists from your country. There was one man whom I particularly remember. Very old, very venerable-looking, with a long, thin, white beard.'

'Professor Malgaonkar.' Mr Kumar doesn't talk much, and only when it is absolutely useful.

'Yes, yes, that's the name.' Already Marta is smiling shyly, of course, she knows the story, perhaps it is true, and it has been told before. His voice is gliding so comfortably, so amiably through the sentences.

'Then Madam was already in service before you got married?'

'Oh yes, she is very young but very good at her work, everybody says so. She is a senior official now in the Ministry of Defence. In fact, it is very difficult to get her to travel with me, she goes off on her own missions, you know how it is with working women.' He is generous and indulgent with Leela and her question, as men are with pretty young women, and Marta doesn't like it much, she hastens to get back to the story and begins, 'Well, you know, I was supposed to reach the dean's office at a certain time, with the scientists, but the old gentleman had a problem at the last minute, there was something he absolutely insisted on buying, so we were twenty minutes late.'

'I was angry about their being late. It meant my next appointment would be postponed and I am very particular about punctuality,' her husband says.

'I asked her in a frosty voice, 'Which university did you receive your degree from?' '

'I said, 'Blenkein University', and he said, 'Well, they should have taught you to be punctual.' I could have died. I didn't know what would happen, and it wasn't really my fault, being late. But we were terrified of this dean. And we knew he was a very powerful man. Maybe he would put me in prison.'

'Well, we were married within a month. Who can resist Marta?'

Her husband is smiling tenderly at her. They must have related this story together hundreds of times. I could kill him now, a rage of possession fills me. How ridiculous; is she even looking at me? This is all very mysterious, and very sweet, I am so happy, just being near her.

'Well, my friends, Marta tells me that we are meeting for

lunch at the best room in the Sheraton Hotel. It is at the top of the hotel, you will have a magnificent view of the city of Pludova, covered in snow. I hope you are not finding our city too cold? We are used to it, but you come from a warmer climate. What about you, Madam, you do not feel cold in your beautiful silk sari?'

'Well, not really,' Leela replies. 'Except when we walk outside. I envy your wife's beautiful boots.'

'Those? Oh yes, they have fur inside, her feet are snug and warm, I had those boots made specially for her. But you can buy a pair of boots here, if you like.'

'Oh no, what will I do with them in my country? It never gets that cold where I live. Besides, you know, boots with a sari! It wouldn't look right.'

We have half an hour before lunch. Her husband, the minister, is to meet us at the hotel. She drives us through the city. It is so small that soon we begin to recognise the buildings from passing them again and again: large, neo-classical, the Party Headquarters, Tomb of the First President, the War Museum.

'I don't suppose shops are open today, Madam?'

'Well, you know it's Sunday. But there are some special shops, and some art galleries. Would you like those?' She is asking me, as if Leela the questioner did not exist. Does she feel my adoration going out to her? She is soft and warm sitting next to me in the car, her black silky coat nestles against my arm.

'Anything you say, Marta, whatever you suggest. We are entirely in your hands.'

'Besides, there is not much time. About fifteen minutes, then we must reach the hotel, the minister said one thirty.' Mr Kumar's high-domed forehead is wrinkling in anxiety, he has registered the story about punctuality, but I refuse to take responsibility, it is up to Marta now.

'We have time for one art gallery,' she decides, 'it is nearby.

In the afternoon we will see the National Museum of Malgar History. Are you tired?'

'Oh no. Let's go to the art gallery.'

It is full of pictures, what else are art galleries for? She is telling us about the position of the arts in Malgary, her voice is strong and confident, it goes in and out of facts in measured tones. I trail after her like an obedient calf wanting only to nuzzle against her large, full body; the others are listening, at least when Mr Kumar keeps pace with us, and Leela, of course, Leela asks questions. She is our pride, holder of our banner, I leave it to her.

'Our artists are a spoiled lot. There is no such thing as a starving artist in Malgary. They all become members of the artists' union if they have had two shows. They pay their regular dues, and also a certain percentage of each painting sold. In return the union takes care of them when they are not painting, or not selling anything. It pays for gallery space, fixes the prices on paintings etc and arranges for the government to buy paintings for public buildings. So they earn well. Oh, I must sit down.'

She collapses on a bench against the wall. Above her head are two beautiful, calm landscapes and between them, a view of Blenkein, the oldest city in Malgary, with Gothic buildings which seem to be leaning crazily over each other, toppling as if someone had pulled at a string which held them together. I am kneeling at her feet, all this chaos is above our heads, 'What is the matter? What has happened to you, Marta?'

But she isn't saying anything, just pulling off her boots hastily. 'What's happened, can I help?'

She is crying with pain, then moaning softly, rubbing at her feet. They sit there in front of her: large, white, the nails painted a bright red, gleaming through the transparent nylon of her stockings. I long to fondle them, to rub them where they hurt, to hold them against my breast, hide them away for myself. 'What is the matter?' Why doesn't she tell me?

'I don't know. I suddenly felt stabs of pain, as if knives

were going through my feet, I just had to take my boots off. Forgive me.'

Soon her social graces would be back, my heart was dropping rapidly, like a stone going through water.

'Let me see, inside the boots, what is the matter.'

My hand sinks into the secret fur inside, goes through all the spaces still warm from the impression made by her foot. I feel and touch, a deep thrill goes over my body, but there is nothing here, only the flat feel of the leather through the fur, the small indentations where her toes had established their positions inside the boot. I look up and see her face, something has happened to her, the skin of her face, the glassy green lake of her eyes, are cracked and broken up with fear, she doesn't know why. Then I see Leela's face. She is standing over Marta staring at me with total amazement. I see my picture there: a plump, ageing man, utterly respectable until a moment ago, in a brown cashmere sweater and tweed coat, crouching at the feet of a large white goddess, feeling the insides of her fur boots. Suddenly it is a question of my country's dignity. How quickly things formalise into these large questions, so irrelevant to the heart of the matter. What is the heart? I am ravenously and utterly infatuated with Marta, I love every inch of her feet and fur boots, and the spreading spider-web of fear on her face makes me love her more. I stand up hurriedly, maybe it was just the light from the pictures, a reflection of the chaos of the town of Blenkein from above her head, her face is now smooth and smiling, undisturbed in its total confidence.

'I am sorry to have troubled you all. These fur boots are usually so comfortable, that's why I like to wear them, but sometimes they trouble me, I don't know what it is. Maybe the foot twists, it's like knives cutting at the skin.' She turns her head, and, for a moment, the shadow of mystery catches it again (Or am I imagining it?) like openings in her being through which I will crawl inside, wriggle right to the depths of her being, curl up there like her sacred creature, nibbling at her sweetness. 'But we can go now. Oh dear, we'd better hurry, we will be late.'

Mr Kumar is already in the car, waiting for us. The beefy chauffeur switches off his radio, puts on his peak cap, and opens the door for us.

The minister is already there, in the lobby of the hotel, waiting for us, a small pile of cigarette butts before him. He stubs out his latest cigarette and rises to greet us. The look he throws at Marta is full of helpless resentment, a kind of fire; she does not respond to it.

'I'm sorry, sir, that we're late,' Mr Kumar says. Leela is wandering around the beautiful, glittering shops which circle the lobby: dollar shops; light glances off the Cartier watches and French perfumes, displayed in the windows. The sound of a violin comes up behind us.

'I arranged for music,' the minister says, gesturing towards the violinist, a tall man who bows and scrapes, his long, greasy hair falling over his instrument. 'Marta told me that you were very fond of music.'

'For him they will do anything.' Marta is building up her husband. Does he need her support like I do? Maybe she is asking forgiveness for being late. 'Musicians are chosen through a central board which doles out the jobs. The Ministry of Science and Technology has a member on every board in the country. My husband is a very important man.'

'Oh, I am sure he is. Look how everyone rises to greet him. They all seem to know him here.' What has happened to Mr Kumar? We have travelled often on government delegations before, I have never heard him talk so much. Perhaps he feels a gap in the position of leader where I once stood, and is rising to fill it.

'Maybe, sir, we can talk a little bit about scholarships. Training is part of my charge, in my own country. I have a friend who is a laser technologist, he wants to come to Malgary for a year's training, maybe you can help him.'

'Of course. You know in what high esteem we hold our friendship with your country.'

He is walking us along beside the huge plate-glass windows which surround the restaurant. We are on the topmost of the hotel's twenty storeys. The city of Pludova stretches all around, far, far below. If someone should fall from here, he would go straight into the snow, dip into it, disappear for ever; the white would close over his head. A few buildings, black in their stark contrast, rise here and there, and, of course, the enormous Centre of Culture, with its formidable opaque façade, and high bronze piece of abstract sculpture in front. Otherwise, everywhere, lies the terrible, furry whiteness of snow. I am relieved that the table he has chosen for us is well away from the windows.

The others are talking, that's fine with me. I don't want to say anything, just to watch Marta. But the minister must not notice. His eyes go everywhere, those luminous, intelligent globes of blue. Better to concentrate on the food. It is the national dishes that they are feeding us. First a pale, slightly sour goat's cheese from the hills, served with green peppercorns, and a clear white wine.

'Our red wines are better, they have more body, you will get some with the main course.' She leans across to talk to me, always she has a special attention for me. I flower and glow in her circle of warmth, the front of her dress moves slightly away from her body, green and blue stripes on a thick, soft material. I can see the tops of her breasts, the same colour as the goat's cheese, pale, white, not quite smooth. I wonder what they taste like. Will she let me nibble at them, lick, more gradually into the space between? What are they like, released from cloth and bras? Will they spring upwards, rush into my mouth? The violinist has been joined by two juniors, they are becoming an obsessive presence. The others in the room are turning to look at us, we must be special to merit so much official patronage. Today I do not like the music, it interferes with the image of Marta which fills my mind and excites my flesh.

We have a choice in the main course. A trolley with steaming brown pots has drawn up beside us. A formidable steward bends respectfully over them, lifting off the small lids, explaining the contents, and Marta translates, 'Will you have lamb? It is cooked with carrots and peas. Or veal? And the third is a fine, wild roast pork. Take your choice.'

My stomach turns slowly at the sight of the enormous portions still bubbling in the brown pots; each gets one. What happens with the food which remains? Surely we are not expected to eat such huge quantities? Little pieces of vegetables on my plate, small slices of bread with fresh, wholesome butter, that's all I want, but I dare not ask for it. I don't want to introduce anything more into this solid globe of friendship forming within the afternoon conversation. I serve myself small helpings from the pot, and carefully put the lid back on, covering up the boiling cauldron, not letting them see the huge chunks of stuff inside. I play around with the food on my plate. The wine is good. Now soft and full in my mouth, it creeps in through all the cracks in my being, settles in small pools and recesses, spreads like massaging fingers through the hard knots in my back. I am happy just to be here with Marta. So what if she has a husband, an important minister, I have no choice in the matter of desiring her.

'I'm afraid I must leave you now. I have to go up to Miranda, in the north of the country. A huge exhibition on nuclear technology is opening there this evening, lots of international dignitaries, we have to look after them carefully. The prime minister has asked me to inaugurate the exhibition. I shall be back tomorrow morning, so perhaps I shall see you before you leave. You have a lunch with the President of the Writers' Union, our famous poet and my good friend, Boris Levertov, maybe I'll see you there. Meanwhile my wife will take good care of you. But in case we don't meet again, goodbye.'

'Goodbye, excellency. Maybe you will pay a visit to my country? Then we will have the pleasure of looking after you there?' I am delighted that he is going. Suddenly Pludova seems the most beautiful, open and free place in the world, soon it will contain Marta and me together.

We go on to Tarkova and the Battle of Tarkova Pass, a subject represented everywhere in the National Museum of Malgar History.

'We took the palace of our last king to house the museum, it was opened only about ten years ago.'

The cold grips us, although we are standing in the pale afternoon sunlight of the street outside, looking up at the museum. For some unknown reason, the car has dropped us at the end of a long street and disappeared. My feet feel as if they are bare, touching the snow underneath. Leela is hunched in her thin woollen coat, and Mr Kumar is busy covering up the gap between his fur cap and the top of his coat. Only Marta is resplendent and perfectly comfortable in her black fur coat and maroon fur boots. If only I could be in there with her, wrapped up in that coat, sneaking into her fur boots!

'There's a sculpture garden just beside the museum. Would you like to see that first? Of course, now it's under snow, but it's very beautiful in summer, when the grass and flowers are out.'

'Shall I take a photo of you, Marta, there, beside the nymph?'

We have all taken out our cameras. She looks at me briefly, and walks across the snow. The nymph is a black, thin figure curled in strips of clothing. My camera lens sees only Marta, a stark patch of face above the fur coat.

'They are expecting us, at the museum. I said we would be here after lunch. Just one moment, please.'

She comes back from the museum office with a slim young girl in a pink sweater. 'This is Miss Sheila Pinata. She will show us around the exhibits.'

The young lady is very conscious of her grasp of the English language, her sentences come out in carefully constructed wholes, which cannot sustain interruption, and Marta constantly interrupts her, superimposing her own explanations of the objects on display. We go rapidly through the older exhibits. Gold masks and laurel wreaths, stone vases, a throne in granite from an ancient king of Malgary, a wonderful collection of painted ceramic ware, its colours still glowing like new, hundreds of years later.

'And now we are approaching the modern period of our history. Our long war of independence, and the freedom movement as a whole. Also, of course, you will now see many references to the Battle of Tarkova.' Miss Pinata's steps go faster as we leave the Gallery of the Alphabet. I would have liked to stay longer there, it is nice to think that Marta's people invented a method of communication, the gallery is full of enormous stone replicas of the first letters.

Marta says, 'You know about our freedom movement? We were colonised by one nation after the other, constantly throwing out invaders, only to have a new set come in. It lasted two hundred years, and we lost many brave partisans in the struggle.'

The young girl's voice is sharp and reproving. 'I am to tell them all that, Madam. It is part of the tour of the modern galleries.'

Marta is surprised, she is not used to being ticked off, and Leela is openly amused by the exchange.

Then Tarkova begins: a huge picture facing us, a scene up on the mountainside, the Tarkova Pass, with dead and dying partisans scattered all around, and a few brave ones, still able to move, hurling the bodies of their dead companions down over the edge of the mountain on to the heads of the enemy below. You can see the tension of waiting in their backs, hope on their faces, any time now reinforcements will arrive, and disgust at what they are doing, all in a good cause. Blood of people they know is upon their hands.

'It was a very important battle.' Miss Sheila Pinata is at the beginning of her discourse, her voice has an opening cadence. 'It marks the end of five hundred years of Turkish occupation.'

'Five hundred years! But the city of Pludova and the people

of Malgary do not show the slightest trace of Turkish influence!'

'Yes, we pride ourselves on that, Madam, that we lived five hundred years under a foreign ruler, and kept our cultural identity absolutely intact.' Miss Pinata is smiling, the guide and the real person interchange occasionally. 'Please notice the costumes of the partisans. And here is another painting by a modern artist, the royal painter of our last king. On this painted scroll is a long poem about Tarkova Pass, written by Yuri Gorbachev, the great hero of the battle. He and three other leaders were hanged by the Turks before they left the country.'

'It is, of course, in your language. Can you translate it for us?'

'Of course. This is what it says, I will do the translation . . . '

'Oh, that will take too long, we don't have the time this afternoon. I will give you later an anthology of our poetry in translation, you can read this poem there. I know of your interest in poetry, you are a poet yourself, are you not?'

'Who told you that?'

'Well, you know, I have my ways of finding out. I bought a copy of your book when I was in your country eight months ago. But come here, I must show you these pictures, of Yuri Gorbachev and the others, but especially of him, he has such a fine face.'

Enlarged photo-portraits of the four men, done in the sepia tones of the last century, look out at us from the wall. 'This is Yuri Gorbachev. He was so young when they killed him!' It is the hard, stretched face of a man under great stress. Below a great, curling partisan's moustache, his mouth is open, fresh and vulnerable. She likes it. Where does he touch her, this dead Yuri Gorbachev in the picture?

Miss Pinata has been holding back too long, now it is too much for her, the words come in small stones, shattering as they hit against each other. 'If you had very little time, you should have told me, you should have said, we have this much time, and that would have been enough for me, I would have adjusted the tour. It is perfectly possible to do it in different times, we are trained for all this. Why do you interfere constantly, the gentleman wanted a translation? All right now, Madam, you show them the rest of the museum.' She turns and walks off, her thin back straight and fierce under the fine wool of her sweater. None of us dare to look at Marta's face, and what she does with it, before she calls us from the door, her voice untroubled and flat.

'Perhaps Sheila — was that her name? — has other work. We will walk quickly through the rest, you must be tired. We have forgotten that you made an air journey this morning. Perhaps just these brocade national costumes, and we leave.'

She makes only a short visit to the office before we leave, and the director of the museum comes out to see us off, his face strongly shadowed with concern. 'I am sorry, there has been some trouble, I must apologise. We will make sure it does not happen again.'

'What will he do?' Leela whispers to me, as we walk down the road, temporarily out of earshot of the others. We know that Marta has set in motion some wheels of destruction. Sheila Pinata will not survive them.

Marta says, 'I'll pick you up for the church this evening, the crypt is interesting, and tomorrow you may not have the time. They tell me there is a service at six pm; you can hear the choir.'

Leela and Mr Kumar prefer the official reception at the Japanese hotel, she needs the bright lights, she says. It is only Marta and I for the church, just as I want it.

It is completely dark when we get out into the square outside the hotel, and all the street lights are on, they reflect and wink in the thick, slushy snow outside; passing traffic throws little cold flecks of it on our hands and faces. We are walking across the square, a huge, neon clock at the top of the building indicates alternately the time and the temperature, −2°C. Right in front of us General Sendova's statue is clothed in reflected light, the shoulders pale, ghostly and laden with snow, the face turned away into the shadows of a greatcoat.

'He is known as the Liberator of Pludova, he took over all operations after the Battle of Tarkova Pass, and marched into Pludova at the head of the Liberation Army. That's why they put his statue here, in the Central Square.'

'But he arrived too late to save Yuri Gorbachev and the other heroes?'

'Yes, they had been hanged already. There's a very beautiful painting in the National Museum which that woman should have shown you this afternoon. I couldn't locate it. I don't know the museum so well. It shows the hanging of the four martyrs. Yuri is going up first, to gallows on top of a small hill, his face turned to the setting sun, and mourners are hunched all around.'

The cold is all around us; Marta looks at me, there is a feeling of being alone in the snow. The steps of the church are slippery with melted ice, I lurch against her.

'Careful! You can break your bones if you fall! We can see the crypt later, it is the oldest part – what is left of the original church. This one is later, built over the crypt. Lots of tourists come here.'

We slip past heavy, sodden drapes at the door, hung in many layers to keep out the cold air, go past a little kiosk selling holy pictures and records, and finally enter the church. The ceiling and walls are heavy with colourful, gilt-laden paintings of scenes from the Bible: Christ on the Cross and weeping women around him, huge figures of the prophets, gory pictures of the martyrdom of the saints. The imagination of Malgary is laden with death and destruction. There is more gold and rich splendour, huge, gilded chandeliers with wrought branches hanging from the ceiling or pushing up from ornamented pillars, robes of the priests in blue and maroon, fringed with brocade, painted statues of saints, and of course, the choir, which is hidden away in one of the upper balconies. It begins as the service opens, their voices soaring in sweet lamentation. Preaching is at a minimum, just a few words, no discourse, no sermon, only the rituals of consecration, which is when I notice the congregation, in tired street clothes, bundled into shabby woollen coats, their faces still pinched and pale with cold. Marta is like a magnificent goddess amongst them, a church and spire all by herself, a chapel where I worship, her high-heeled boots and black fur coat raising her above their anxious faces. They turn to look at her covertly, in fact nobody stands too close. Though there is a fairly large congregation, a space seems to melt around her wherever we move, as she takes me around the church.

'Would you like to take photographs?' she says.

'Is it allowed?'

'Well, not really, but nobody will dare to stop you while I am here with you.'

'Let it be, Marta, it is not important.' The memory of Sheila Pinata is still too close. I comfort Marta, holding her away from the rejection of those around her, though she does not feel it. She is already halfway down the stairs towards the crypt.

I miss something. There is a queer, unusual feeling, and I realise it is the silence. She is not talking at all, not explaining, not giving me the history of the icons, and there is no one in the crypt except the keepers, who merge into their dark chairs in various corners. We wander, strange and awkward, from one narrow wall to another, each square inch laden with rich icons, beautiful, two-dimensional pictures of ancient Malgary faith, the same faces with round, calm eyes, the Virgin Mary, the princes from the East, Christ as a baby but with full-grown adult features, framed in glowing haloes. A smell of incense comes from the heavy stone walls. It is a long tour, my shoulders are aching, I long to hold her, we turn the last corner and move out, still in silence. Outside, she wanders away, it is quite clear that I am to walk across the square to my hotel alone, and I go.

When the bell of my room rings much later at night, I

know immediately that it is her. I have been lying in the
darkness of the room waiting for her without knowing it,
with the huge Pludova moon glowing through the window
like one of the haloes from the crypt, which has seduced her
and bound her to my heart. In the narrow passageway to the
room, I take her in my arms and hold her, there are no words
now. At last I feel her body against mine, as if it belonged
there, round thighs, small, firm breasts, and a wealth of
softness, like a sweet wave on which the song of the choir
had floated in the church. My head, my blood, my flesh is
full of her. We make love through the night, waking again
and again to reach for each other, as if going back, back,
back, through years and years of Malgary history to reach a
time before the continents split asunder, when we were
joined and inseparable, those whom God hath united, let no
man split asunder. The inside of her body is a corridor of
power, a welcome where the outlines of my flesh fade and
disappear, and bliss is my complete nameless existence, from
here I have no need to go anywhere. When we sleep in the
early hours of the morning, I float in a dream of Yuri Gorbachev and the Tarkova Pass, hurling over the edge of the
mountain all the dead creatures I was before I came to Malgary and became nothing in the arms of Marta. I wake in
the morning and find her gone, and this is a most cruel thing.
I sit down to write.

Tarkova Pass: Haiku
Point of great lament, a painted
holy place from which
we fall over.

I am visitor to snow, the girl
stands firm and warm
in her fur boots.

Mountain is a peril, we know
nothing, pass the message
of freedom.

She brings me in a suit of sunshine
to this fierce battle,
where can we go?

Who can we wait for? Even
our own approaching soldiers
bring the death.

I know only this moment of snow,
when Tarkova
is my triumph.

In her borrowed warmth,
we merge in the edge of loss,
she must go now.

Receive my body when they hurl it
from the Pass,
I am your dead flesh.

I am in the bathroom when the phone rings, and I leap across the space, dripping water like a submarine. The sun is high outside the window, my love poem must have taken a long time.

'Hullo.' Her voice is different, soft, intimate, like something speaking from my heart, and disembodied. I am drawn straight into it, now undistracted by her physical presence. 'Marta. When do I see you?'

'It must be with the others, my darling. Oh dear, I hope the hotel people are not listening.' She sounds confused, no longer in control, all the winds of heaven are flowing through her, through me; we stand together in the warm sunshine.

'Marta, when do we meet? Marta.'

'Soon. In half an hour? Will you and the two others be ready? I will come to fetch you.'

'I'll go anywhere with you. Where do you take me now?'

'To the tomb of Yuri Gorbachev.' She is laughing, and teasing. 'You remember, I told you about him yesterday? The hero of Tarkova Pass, who was hanged later by the Turks, he is our national hero.'

'I am jealous of him, you looked at his fine features with great admiration. I don't want you to like anyone but me.'

Her laughter is like temple bells in the morning, cutting through the early light, a young girl's laugh. What are we doing, talking on the telephone? 'Yes, I like him. A visit to his tomb, laying a wreath, is obligatory for our important foreign visitors. That's the only part of the programme that doesn't bore me, I like going to Yuri's tomb.'

'OK. Anyway, he's dead. Come soon.'

Her face greets me openly, maybe she is not aware of how exposed and obvious it is. Do Leela and Mr Kumar know? Can they see it in the way she shakes my hand?

This morning is created especially for Marta, for me, a cup of blue sky, sunshine, a crisp, cold glitter of snow, and General Sendova in the square before us, riding straight up into the heavens, the most benign and beautiful statue in the world. There is no place in this to ask her, surely she feels just like this? Something in me is pulling her deep into the innermost happiness which is here, I know it, this morning I know happiness, the feel and flavour of it. Just temporarily it has to do with sex. My body tingles when she brushes against me. I feel deep excitements in considering her nipples nestling against my chest, my finger, oh yes other parts of me, exploring the warm recesses between her legs. But sex is only part of it, I am not exactly a virgin presented with Marta as a Christmas present, that's not it at all. I have just never been alive before, and this morning, as if Malgary had been my creator, the Marta of Malgary, this morning I am alive, never before have I been like this. I don't even need really to touch her, she is the compendium of the most beautiful things inside, how does one say it? All this is just happening, a benign principle working towards heaven, like General Sendova riding in front of us.

Well, we have to move, to go on to the cemetery. She has a wreath in the car, all the flower shops are open today, it is Monday in the city of Pludova, and the car winds through snowy streets to the tomb of Yuri Gorbachev. You can tell right away that it is the tomb of the national hero, made in shining black marble right in the centre of the cemetery. Did they displace some other dead bodies to give him that position? And someone has swept the polished surface clean of snow this morning. But we are the first today with flowers, perhaps there are no other foreign visitors just now in Pludova.

We wait for the chauffeur to park the car, and to lumber towards us with the wreath. The trees in the cemetery are small, black and bare, and the other tombs are irregular heaps of snow, with dark corners, some crosses, a few angels, and, here and there, low statues and busts of those who have been buried there, keeping the flesh in stone, when even the bones have probably crumbled below.

Yuri Gorbachev's tomb has a bust too, the same determined face with curling moustaches and sharp eyes which Marta liked so much in the museum portrait. 'Is it copied from the picture?' But when I turn, she is not there, I can't see her, I am lost, a poor figure in snow and trees of the cemetery 'Marta? Marta!'

'There.' Leela touches me lightly on the shoulder, turning me. I see Marta kneeling in the snow, her black coat spread out in the snow below her, laying a small bunch of flowers on a tomb about three lanes of graves away. Then a moment of silence; we are waiting for Marta, for the wreath; a wind blows now. I catch sight of a different car, a small car with dark glass at the windows. It fits neatly into the narrow lanes between the trees, stopping right beside Marta, its black, shiny surface is just beyond her coat. A door opens. Two men are lifting her off the snow, she is resisting, struggling, her white face snaps over her shoulder, calling to me, 'Help me! Oh please, help me! They are taking me away.'

One of the men puts his hand over her mouth, they almost lift her off the ground, and push her into the car, bundling her coat behind her, exposing her legs and the long maroon fur boots. The boots hit against the edge of the car, and one of them comes off. It stands by itself for a moment, upright and alone, deep red against the snow, cooling rapidly. Then someone leans out of the car and pulls it in. And me, her tender white foot exposed to brutality, I burst across the stretch of snow to the car, but Leela and Mr Kumar are behind me, instantly, fleet as panthers. They are holding my arms, I am stopped and straining. The car pulls away rapidly; the figures in the back seat are a dark blur; I no longer even know which is Marta.

'It's no use, there's nothing you can do.' Leela's voice, who wants this softness? It has nothing to do with me. Marta has gone in that car.

'This is their country, you can't mess with them, and she belongs with them. Anything you do now will only get us into further trouble.'

'But I love her, I must get to her.'

The white cemetery and trees, the car which had smashed through normal time, close in round my statement, dragging in their surprise. Even if they had known, why should I say it, openly, like this? It is not necessary.

'What's the use? They have taken her away, there's no reaching her now, and today we are leaving.'

'I'm not leaving.'

Leela passes over my words. 'I hope they let us leave in peace. Please, you must remember, this is an official delegation, we cannot make a diplomatic incident.'

'I will speak to our ambassador.'

'What will he do? It must be happening all the time.'

'But not to Marta, not to me.'

'Excuse me, but I don't think you come into it at all.'

'Not at all.' The chauffeur speaks English, we never knew

that, he is standing behind us with the wreath, urging us towards the tomb. And beside him, materialised from nowhere, the Deputy Chairman of the Board of Culture, the architect with caved-in cheeks who had greeted us at the airport. Did he come in that small black car which has carried Marta away to destruction if not death? What will they do with her? They are holding out the wreath. I have to take it, a solid phalanx is moving me towards the tomb. I march between them like a prisoner taken to the hanging. It is here, the edge of the tomb, black beside my feet. I sink into the snow, I am Marta on the snow. I put my head down on the tomb, and her loss and sudden departure go through me like a knife cutting at my insides.

I don't know how long I have been there but Leela is tapping on my shoulder, whispering into my ear.

'We must go now. These men are waiting for us. Please. You must do this for us, for our country, somehow we have to leave this evening and with a semblance of dignity.'

'Dignity?' The word is foreign, the sounds of it stand up in high black columns pressing in on me. 'Dignity?' We move down the narrow lanes with the solemn footsteps of a funeral hearse, flanked by its two guardians of death. They stay with us as a constant presence, we are their precious parcel, they must deliver us to the plane.

Mr Kumar has doubts about that. He displays his passport with minor triumph, he is voluble. 'I am so glad I got our passports back from that chap at the reception. Can you imagine if he still had them? Why, they could have done anything with us, and who would have known? We could sink like stones into this deep sea of Malgary, disappear for ever, like this woman Marta.'

Suddenly he is on first name terms with her, now that she has gone. My fist shoots out and catches him on the jaw, his face breaks up in surprise and pain.

Leela holds him back, quietens me. 'Hush, hush. This is just what they want, that we should fight with each other.' Our two stalwarts have come in from the front of the hotel

to see what the disturbance is about. They stare at us impass-
ively. What am I doing, a beady-eyed balding man in middle-
age, hitting a colleague on the jaw? What's happening to me?
I must return, somehow squeeze back into the mould, poet
– bureaucrat, what a combination! Where is Marta, every bit
of me turns in all directions, looking for her.

'Now we have to take you for lunch,' the chauffeur says.
'You remember, with the President of the Writers' Union?'

'Is that still on, even though Madam is not here? Couldn't
we just stay here in the hotel quietly until it is time to leave
for the airport?'

The chauffeur translates Leela's request to the deputy chairman, and then his reply. 'Madam being here or not makes
no difference, you are guests of the Malgary government,
and your programme has been already arranged, the deputy
chairman will take you there.' He looks at me with total,
evil delight, such a feeling taking complete possession of him.
'The Minister for Science and Technology will be there.'

Leels has not understood. 'But he was supposed to be up
north somewhere, in Miranda, opening an exhibition.'

'Oh yes, madam, he was, but last night, he came back
unexpectedly.' He is enjoying himself. 'Your lunch will be
at the Merton Hotel. It is one of the finest hotels in Pludova.'
He has heard Marta often, he is repeating her cadences, or
do all the intonations of guides for foreign visitors to Pludova
sound the same? Only his voice is different, harsh and quiver-
ing with relished drama.

'We will leave right now,' I say. All the games must be
played, though something else holds my real life.

We sit in the lobby of the Merton waiting for Boris and
his group to come in for lunch. We are ten minutes early,
the modern splendours of the Merton rear away from us,
glassy tablelamps, polished marble surfaces, the inscrutable
sameness of five-star furnishing. The deputy chairman sits
with us in total silence, never taking his eyes from us, all
movement is in his bushy, fluttering eyebrows which crawl

across his face. Leela asks, 'Does the president, he is a poet, isn't he, does he speak English?'

His cheeks creak into acknowledgment that she has spoken. Her question hangs in the air, waiting for the group to turn down the space of the lobby, we are informed that they have arrived. Boris Levertov is leading them. He is a huge figure with faded auburn hair standing around his head, his suit stretched tightly across his chest, as if he is not used to wearing one. A quiet, frail woman, with ravaged face and long strands of black hair hanging down her back, walks behind him. 'My wife. She is painter, you understand, artist. My English not so good, but we will translate.'

And, of course, he is there, her husband, the Minister for Science and Technology, right beside his friend Boris. His enormous eyes are blue and shining this morning, an incredible blue. Marta and I have been lost in those blue eyes. But Boris is looking around. 'Where is Marta? She is with you?'

'Marta has gone away for a while, on work. I will translate today,' the Minister says.

'Oh, do not worry, we have also official translator, Anna Serena, she is arriving in few moments. Oh, here is Anna, we were just talking.'

Anna is a modern Malgary woman: urban, sophisticated, with a fine hairstyle and subtle make-up. She likes me, she is smiling at me. I want only Marta. I want to kill her husband but I dare not make a single move towards him; he is here only to torture me with his presence.

More people join, they are expected, the table in the dining-room is a large one. They are introduced, their names and designations fade into a blur with the Christmas decorations, even a tree in one corner. Surely they should take off this faded glory? Everywhere else in the world the Christmas decorations have been taken down by this time.

'First I will tell little bit about Writers' Union.' The wine has begun, the first course, a heap of cheeses and salamis, I can see tucked away on the stewards trolley for the next round some familiar, brown-topped dishes steaming up the air above them. Have I been punished in Malgary because I did not eat enough of their national food? Remember how they said it: 'If you waste your food, the witch will come and get you.' His blue eyes are watching me, he is quite unembarrassed about staring at a guest, as is the artist-wife of our host. Do I give her inspiration? Will she draw me soon, rush back from here to get it all down, with my brown skin and slanting unhappy eyes, my plump, ageing cheeks? I will never love another woman. How will I leave Malgary today? I know they will never let me come back here.

Anna Serena is translating, Boris is giving me a long history, how the union was formed, what it does for the writers. No-one starves in Malgary, not writers, not artists, what happens to the others? Then some history of Malgary, and, of course, Tarkova.

'He wishes to make you a presentation now. We have been told that you are a writer, a poet in fact. We make you, therefore, honorary member of the Writers' Union, of the Golden Order. Mr Levertov will pin this golden badge on your chest and present you with an anthology of poetry which contains work from the best poets of our land.'

The ceremony takes place; I present the face of a zombie to the photographers. Can Boris feel the total absence of life in the hand which I offer him, as he gives me a book bound in beautiful black leather?

The minister now makes his contribution to the gathering. 'Dear sir, in this anthology you will find poems also from our friend Boris Levertov. You must now request him to recite for you his poem on Tarkova. No-one says it as well as he does himself, it is a very famous poem, many songs have been made from it, and some part of our national anthem is also taken from it.'

'He says he will recite if you also will recite from your poetry, afterwards.' I feel the edges of the paper in my pocket, I had meant to give it to Marta this morning, years have passed since then. Anna Serena is accustomed to translating Boris's poems; we go very fast, her gravelly voice with

a slightly American accent coming quickly after his booming,
slow roll of words.

The Brave Defenders of Tarkova Pass.

We had marks of bondage, the dark stain
of slavery, but now these are gone,
Tarkova gives us liberty.
Fear was our companion, and shame,
we slept with the cattle in hunger and pity,
now Tarkova has redeemed us.

Our great gleaming symbol, the symbol of glory.

Tree trunks and boulders are splattered with blood,
Yuri Gorbachev is here with his shining eyes,
leading our brave deaths,
'Hold out, hold out, Tarkova is your history!'

Where is the help? No sign of our brother eagles –
soon the peak will go, we'll lose the battle –
Where are the partisans? But we will fight to the death.
Suddenly there's a roar, our people arrive. . . .
Success did not come too late for some
of us, but those others
whom we hurled from the mountain heights,
our dead companions, brothers of our soul,
are buried for ever in the snow. The invader
will not dare to step again across
Tarkova Pass, entrance to our beating hearts.

When there is storm in the mountains, think
of a bleak peak and boulder-strewn wastes,
Tarkova sends its glory
from valley to valley, from age to age.

Oh yes, we all clap, there is applause. 'Wonderful! Wonderful!' Mr Kumar wakes from a dream of chicken and chunks of pineapple, his voice is louder than the rest, it muffles my faint tones, but still they will not let me be.

'Now sir, everybody insists, it is your turn.'

'Well, it is also a poem on Tarkova, written last night, or really early this morning.' I look into the blue eyes, and I am not afraid, words do not need human beings behind them, my poem stands alone, it is for Marta, I will never give her a wreath, and no-one will paint her picture for the National Museum, she must have the poem.

Anna Serena has trouble translating my haiku. I explain the form, units of seventeen syllables, objective verse. Like any schoolmaster, I set it out; now I do not even feel the blue eyes upon me. Marta and I were together last night, I do not think we will be separate again.

Boris, especially, is bewildered. I watch him grappling and trying with the words, he wants to get to them. Then he gives up and relaxes.

'Oh marvellous. Your poem is splendid, sir, absolutely splendid. And we are honoured that foreign visitor, so distinguished, should write about Tarkova, that this great national battle has moved you to write poem about it. We will publish in Writers' Union Journal. Please give us text, here, right now, we will publish your poem.'

'Oh no, I must revise it, I will send it to you, Mr Levertov, not now. You understand this was just a first draft. I will have to polish and clean the verse.' I cannot put Marta into their book. Boris means well, I cannot fool him. Marta I must carry with me.

'It is very late already. Perhaps we should go directly to the airport from here?' Leela has caught the fear of Mr Kumar. Neither of them wishes to go back to the hotel, in case they never get to the airport at all.

'Well, you know, you have only one small case. Is it possible?' Mr Kumar's tones are insistent, I nod.

The English-speaking chauffeur and the deputy chairman

have materialised in the dining-room; Boris tells them to fetch our luggage. He has had a lot of wine, he wants to talk, we settle down with Anna Serena in the lobby, the other guests have left. I am floating on what could be a sea of pain. There is a desperate, underlying tug, pulling me down, down, into the knowledge that soon I must leave, and never see Marta again. The deputy chairman comes strolling back and settles his long-legged form into a sofa beside Boris.

'The luggage of your party has arrived, sir, and is in the car outside; you may leave whenever you are ready.' Maybe Anna Serena has a lover, she has to go somewhere else, she keeps looking at her watch, but I am too exhausted to help anyone. I wait helplessly for Leela and Mr Kumar to arrange our departure, they do it with a great deal of zest. I am protected from Boris by the language barrier, he has from me only translations of faded emotions, of gratitude and leave-taking. I am saying goodbye to Malgary, he cannot know that I am saying goodbye to Marta.

'But your poem on Tarkova, we must have your poem as soon as you have revised it.'

Oh yes, the poem. He sees me into the car, shaking my hand.

'We have to get back your suitcase. Don't you remember, yesterday the air hostess said you would get it when you were leaving, it would have come from Athens today?' Leela bustles around, asking, but no-one seems to have heard about my suitcase, and the deputy chairman has long since retreated into wordlessness. Then she spots the air hostess we remember, having a coffee at the bar. I watch the two women, Leela is gesticulating strongly, the air hostess shrugs her shoulders and throws up her hands. It is quite clear she is not going to help, now that the protection of Marta, of the Malgary government, has been taken away. They want only to put us on the plane, to have us leave.

The chauffeur comes in, carrying a large cardboard box

tied in brown paper. 'For you,' he says, 'from the Minister of Science and Technology.'

It sits on the long table in front of us. 'Aren't you going to open it?' Leela says.

An enormous lethargy sits upon me, I cannot seem to be able to move any single part of my body. 'You open it. Please.'

She is curious, she slips off the twine with ease. It is roughly and hurriedly tied; she opens the box. Marta's clothes are inside, what she was wearing this morning. I take the box on to my lap, lifting out the articles one by one, shaking them out. At the bottom, in a plastic bag, are Marta's boots, her fur boots. There is still some dried mud caked along the edges.

Sanctuary

Places sometimes generate their own people. They arrive without explanation, squeezed out by the pores of the earth. As if they had no before or after, and in a short story it is possible to catch them like that, still suffused with the pangs of birth, sometimes still carrying the faces they had before they were born. I cannot name them, they are like my dead father, just a partition between being and non-being. Who will tell this story? It must tell itself. I have shown you already the pipes and sanitary fittings, placed the innards of the story out there for you. And time, what happens to time? Can it be a sequence?

The journey here is not very complicated. If you're coming from Connaught Place, which is the centre of New Delhi, you must take the ring road until you come to Hyatt Regency Hotel. Turn left here, go straight through at the next crossing, and then you are at another circling road, facing a clay shop with the pots laid out in neat rows, mouth downwards, all the distance to the main road. You cannot afford to be untidy with pots: they develop cracks, water seeps through, and then, of course, what's the use of a pot which cannot hold water? You can tell right away if it is defective. It rings false when you strike it, not the clear, smooth tones of a good pot, but halting and flat, as if the tongue of sound dissipated through the crack. You will also find a furniture shop there which shows the raw, bare wood of the frames, before the painting and polishing, before the beautiful tapestries are fixed. Pots and furniture, baking in the sun. Turn right for a short distance, and then left at Munirka. This road is different. It is already entering the place. A burnt-out hotel rises on one side, and, on the other, far behind scrub and thorn trees, behind a huge electric power station whose clear grey pinions rise in a thick jungle above a low wall, are the quarters of the university hostels. If you see them from the road, they seem deserted, but can any buildings be so, in such a busy metropolis, Delhi, where the rents are very high? The road has been cut through steep walls of rock, and if you turn right at the T-junction, you are among the new housing, shells of buildings which are slowly being filled in by the estate-developers. Buy the co-operative housing, pay the prices for adulterated cement and faulty construction, hope only that your luck is good, that the roof does not develop cracks and fall in upon your children. Can you remember, are the mango orchards on this side, or on the left? Is it possible to see them, thick, leafy, old, dusty, a most venerable source of income, laden with *dussheri* mangoes during the season? The land is good for fruit, it all depends on the nature of the pocket you have bought. It might be better for wheat, or corn, or mustard seeds, it's somewhat a question of trying the land out, to see which way it will go.

But I am certain you pass Rangpura village having just left the great city of New Delhi behind, before you come to the last turning of all, the one which takes you into the heart of the matter of this birth. The village is a series of small shops and houses on either side of the road. Most of the produce is out on the pavement: vegetables, small pitiful piles for people with small coffers and flat purses; rows of ribbons and striped cotton material to be stitched into underwear, hanging out on lines, so you can see at a glance if you want to buy. Count your money before you go in, everybody here knows the approximate cost.

The new turning is the last one before you reach the tomb of the Fakir. It evolved by the passage of feet and trucks when they began to construct the Rangpura housing complex.

The wall for the park, with pointed iron stakes on top,

was made first. It arches out in a bulge from the housing complex on the opposite side from the path; you can't see whether grass has been planted, flower-beds laid, or pits dug for trees. Soon the monsoon will arrive, the season for planting trees, ashok, gulmohor, champa. Eucalyptus is no good for this area, the water-level is too low here, you have to take tube-wells far, far down, to eighty or ninety feet, before you hit water, which then glistens in a distant, black, receding film at the end of a long tunnel. The housing complex comprises blocks of flats in three storeys, irregularly bunched for some obscure aesthetic reason, or to leave place for paths and garages, parking for cars and scooters. Who knows what the plans are, if there are any? Meanwhile the walls are ready, but the roof of the last block has not been completed, light fills the empty shells through gaping spaces which are doors and windows, and the tall sky comes in huge gulps into the top storey. There is no sign of building activity this morning, no trucks standing by with material, no people, no bags of cement you open and pour into an iron basin, to be made wet, and plastered over the naked red bricks. Where are the workers? Has something happened? No girders or secret iron rods to strengthen the roof have been fixed today, no trowels, no equipment, no women breaking stones, no children playing, their naked bottoms smothered in dust. It is impossible to know when all this stopped, because I will not tell you, I cannot look beyond one moment at a time. It is not, you know, a matter of patience; it is a matter of being so utterly drawn into one moment, you have not the energy, even if you close your eyes and pray very hard, to look beyond it.

N comes down the turning off the main road, past a board which says, with an arrow, Rangpura Housing Complex, still new, its lettering still black and fresh. Why speculate how long it will be before these flats are complete, and if this board will still be legible then, or defaced beyond recognition by the passage of time? Why open the womb of time? It does not nurse a foetus, it is not a happy mother, time.

Breathless with waiting, its foetus comes out as soon as it is conceived, phat, delivered upon life each moment, raw and fresh, you just have to learn to look at it, treasure it. To accept everything that happens, not to fight too hard, but know also what opposes you, know it so utterly that it disappears, merging with the general common enemy, so subtle and fragrant, it changes as the current changes, as in sword-fighting, until death occurs, yours or your opponent's; there's not so much difference between the two.

N detaches a cloth bag from her shoulder where it has made a wet patch, blows at the sweat, and rolls up the windows of her Maruti jeep. It looks like a dusty road, the dust will rise through all the windows, coat her hair and eyelashes, settle carefully and secretively on the hairs in her nose. There is no time now to close up the back of the jeep against the dust, she must proceed as she is, drawbacks and all. The jeep is light and new, for a moment she forgets the colour and opens the door to check and to confirm, electric blue, N has chosen the seat covers, grey, with a thin black line along the edges.

The jeep starts up, light and swift, held in gear: her own animal, her blue coursing chariot. She surveys the dust path riven by the twisting tracks of heavy trucks, its bumps and hollows, small pyramids of 'malba' which must be carefully avoided. A traffic barrier, a check-post, a question mark at the top of a small incline. Its long bamboo pole stands almost straight up in the air, weighted by a stone at the other end. A rope to pull it down, to bar the way of trucks and electric-blue Maruti Gypsies, dangles uselessly from the other end. A small sentry-box beside the barrier is deserted. She peers in, and finds that its erstwhile occupant has left behind the pictures of his gods: Hanuman carrying the mountain with the sacred medicinal herb; many-armed goddess Lakshmi, gold coins falling in a steady glittering shower from fist to fist, and Saraswati the goddess of learning, a vina balanced delicately on her lap and on the tender, indulgent swan whom she rides, her feet nestling in his purple down. All cut out and stuck on the bare walls, left unworshipped in the hot, windowless space.

She can see a long distance from here, the land is flat, and rolls out in all directions, cut into plots and farms by wire fencing and iron staves, one-roomed shacks on almost each one. Conical black chimneys, spewing smoke, rise into a distant sky from sloping brick kilns. Here there is clay, soft, yellowish-coloured clay which comes off moist and sticky in your hand, very good for bricks. Small hardy horses with woven rope panniers roam the land, grazing, wait for bricks to bake, and carry them off. The tower of Kutab Minar is way off to the right, only the absence of smoke separates it from the factory chimneys. Here the water is deep below the surface, the whirr of motors from tube-well pumps is carried on the wind. In some places the wheat crop is still standing, dry and yellow, waiting to be cut. She has been told that on this farm the wheat is now fully harvested.

The sound of water is suddenly strong in the air, somebody has opened a tap full force and a steady gush free-falls through to a slab three feet below. N is absorbed utterly by the sound of water in the hot afternoon air. She locates the tap, out in the open between two blocks of flats. Did the woman sit under the tap for her bath? She is dried off now, wrapped in a clean sari. N can sense the smell of soap and clean things in the way the woman tucks the end of her sari, a much deeper blue, a deep, deep blue, around her waist. Then she bends over to comb out her wet hair. It is not the long black cascade of the movies, wet hair being combed out beside a village stream, pricking out electric ions of desire in the air of the cinema hall. This hair is harsh and thick, so full of rugged curls that the comb moves with great difficulty, in short spurts and snatches. N cannot go on until the woman has finished, she is watching also two dark, thin men. They too are looking at the woman. She finishes combing her hair, and straightens up, pushing it back, tying it in a thick bunch behind her. Her thin, blue body, with its huge mass and crown of hair, is now ready, N goes on down the path, her jeep pushing up silent billows of dust on either side.

The farms she passes, each carefully fenced in, to make sure no-one makes mistakes about possession and boundaries, share another quality, of dusty leaves, and sparse crops, and desertion. Perhaps it is the time of afternoon when people are hidden behind shelter and silence of suspended time, long before they will break into the sudden activity of early evening and the sparse movements of a hot night.

A small army detachment had camped just opposite, you could tell from the uniforms hanging out to dry, from lines strung between two neem trees. The men used to appear in striped underpants and vests, dodging between low barracks of corrugated iron sheets and the line of makeshift latrines at the opposite side of the plot. Sometimes a water-tanker stood up at the front, hitched to a line of taps where the men bathed and washed their clothes. Today the camp is lifted. No men, no water-tanker, no underwear. The doors of the latrines hang open. Most of the sturdy iron sheeting has been lifted off the barracks, they are in various stages of ravage, open to the sky.

The path ends in a mass of tyre-tracks going off in all directions across the plain which stretches in front of her. She drives the blue Maruti Gypsy carefully to the left. Here it is difficult to remember, with no fencing, not even a dust track. One tuft of old grass looks quite like another, you cannot plan a path here. She picks her trajectory from some memory which resides in her stomach. If asked to indicate a path, this knowledge would never rise to the area where maps show thin black lines. If examined it will disappear, melt into nothingness.

Once she spots their shed, it is all right, her jeep points and readjusts itself automatically.

'Shekhar! Shekhar!' She sticks her head out of the window, so that the sound of her voice reaches farther, above the heavy sound of the tube-well motor, to wherever he is. He has fixed barbed wire across the entrance to the farm.

The motor is switched off, a moment of unceasing silence, and he appears from behind the brick shelter which houses the electricity connections. One of his eyes is swollen, half-closed, the hump is a black animal in the bony countryside of his face; the other eye trusts her. He is wearing the same nylon bush shirt she has always seen — ageless and undying. Its cream-coloured flap hangs like a flag from his gaunt shoulders, his bare waist drops thinly into his trousers.

'Where is your companion?'

'Sathi is in hospital. The police took him there, they said he was badly hurt. Babu came, after I telephoned you. He registered a case with the police. I said I would look after Sathi, but they took him off anyway.'

'What happened?'

'They came to steal onions. You know the crop is almost ready. And look, the wheat is cut, and waiting to be threshed, how did we know what they wanted? Kallu out there began to bark, we switched on the searchlight. Then they attacked us. Came on our land and attacked us.'

She looks out towards the wheat. It lies in soft, golden piles in the fields, gathered close to where it has been cut. 'You will have to tie it up, bring it together at one place. Then we must get a thresher. How long will Sathi be in hospital?'

'Why don't you get him back today? His wounds will heal very fast, once you bring him here.'

'You know that these things are not so simple.'

He is putting some tomatoes and a pile of aubergines into the back of the jeep. 'What happened to the okra? I see no sign of okra, and we planted so many seeds.'

'It just did not grow, I can't understand what happened. The seeds sprouted, plants came up about six inches. Then they all withered. You want to see them? The stumps are still standing in the field.'

But she is already backing the jeep. 'Wait, wait, there are some early guavas, on the trees at the far edge of the land. If you wait five minutes, I will run and fetch them for you.'

'No, no, I have to go now.' The edge of the jeep's tyre climbs a pipe which runs from the tube-well. Shekhar runs to draw it away. He stands with his arms hanging loosely at his sides.

The road to the Fakir's tomb is even more difficult. There is no trace of a path which she can pick up, none of the trucks go in that direction, only grazing cattle and hobbled ponies from the brick kilns. The knots of dry grass are hard and virgin, unattacked, they rise up as firm obstacles under the jeep. Dust is more abundant. She shakes it out of her hair and clothes when she finally stops, as close as she can reach to the broken line of fencing round the Makbara, the tomb. She gets out and carefully locks up the jeep, pulling down the shades, protecting the vegetables at the back from thieves.

She looks for places where the cows have crossed over, and the fencing is pushed down, the barbed wire trampled and twisted into the ground, and steps neatly across. She locates the place immediately, almost in the shadow of the high wall of the tomb, a small rosette of stone, perfectly circular, with eight pillars holding up a high, domed roof, and all the spaces between them open to wind and light. Who sat there, out in the grounds? Was this where the Fakir meditated? Many know the story of his life. He was the son of the Sultan of Delhi, his only son, who turned from the splendours and power of the throne into the dim caves of a hermit existence. They must have tried to prise him out of it, to get him back to his material duties, but he was stubborn, wandering the open spaces of Delhi in utter quietude, until his sister Razia Sultan, who had been pushing all the time for the trammels of power, was permitted to climb the throne. Did she allocate land from the precious acres of Delhi? Pay for the heavy red stones which made the construction? Select craftsmen for the flattened Arab domes which adorned the high building?

There is no sign of him, the space under the outhouse is empty except for waiting blocks of stone. Her entry startles a wave of parrots nesting high up in the cornices. They fly out, dropping small downy green feathers, sticks, pieces of grass, dried droppings, a flash of red beaks, the sound of screaming birds. She settles on the stones, among the swollen, floating paraphernalia of random nests. The sun is still high and white, but it appears to be moving visibly downwards towards the long, flat horizon.

The keys of the Maruti are formidable, long, brisk and efficient, with a large, ornamented piece of linked metal attached to the ring. She tucks them deep into her shoulder bag, and moves out towards the main building. No point in waiting here.

The entrance must be on the other side, here there is just high wall, even the dome disappears as she gets closer. She follows the wall around.

A long flight of shallow steps leads up to the wide-open entrance, the watchman is standing right there, at the head of the steps. He has been watching her arrive.

'Take your shoes off here.'

'Is there someone to look after them?'

'Oh yes, they are perfectly safe. Don't you see the other shoes?'

There are indeed some other shoes, all jumbled up, abandoned, as if they have been there a long time. Has M arrived? Once again the questioning and anxiety starts, the waiting. She looks up and sees the watchman, as if for the first time. He has a small moustache on his upper lip, and ragged eyes which seem to slice the air wherever he looks. He pushes away a small, netted cap which was once white, and scratches his head through a ruffle of hair. It is not possible to ask if M is here.

The stones are still hot from the afternoon sun, they burn her bare feet until the soles get used to the heat.

'Oh, you have some construction work going on?' A jungle of scaffolding covers the opposite wall which itself stretches, in cut, pointed fennels in the splendours of a fort, all around the high platform.

'Just some repair work. But it has stopped now.'

'Why don't they take away all that stuff?' There is no sign of him. Will he be late again, one hour, two hours? How the past, and the later past, come rushing in, just having found a crack in the wall. No defences work, maybe it's better not to have walls at all, to be so completely open and vulnerable that winning and losing is the same thing.

The watchman is at her elbow, hovering and curious, uncomfortably close. Best to talk to him, occupy them both while she waits for M.

'What year did the Fakir, Razia Sultan's brother die? Did she have this beautiful tomb made right away?'

'Oh I don't know any of these fancy things, history and all that. I'm just an employee of the department, posted here to make sure that no one damages the monument.'

'Is the Pir here today? At least you know that?'

'Yes he's here, downstairs, praying. You want to go down there?'

She casts a quick glance around. M is not standing in any corners hidden by scaffolding, or a bend in the wall, her eyes empty out all the possibilities. The staircase into the room below is cut off by darkness, a few steps from the top. She nods, and the watchman gathers up his lamp, to show her down.

This is where the body was actually buried, a small hump in the ground, everything else is just layers of shell after shell.

The Pir is the saint who arrives to worship at the Fakir's Makbara, and stays as long as he wishes. Nothing indicates the day of his arrival or departure. She is lucky to find him here, the air is blessed with his presence. He sits with his back to her, absolutely straight, his face shrouded in the folds of his robes. A candle burns in a corner of the dank, steamy place which smells unpleasantly of bats. Soon the candle will have burned itself down. The Pir does not notice her, his prayers are thick around him, crowding the room.

'Does he meet people?'

'We have a lot of traffic here, no-one around knows how long the Pir will stay, or when he will come next, so they turn up to see him whenever they get the chance. Once a week there is a mela, a fully fledged fair, below the walls of the tomb. But the Pir greets nobody. They beg for his bless-ings, but he does not notice. Occasionally he nods at one or the other, but being noticed does not really matter. It is said that he is a rich man, he does not need their offerings.'

M is there. She sees him immediately as her head rises above the flat, square entrance of the tomb. He is leaning against the gateway, his bare toes tracing the lintel. 'Where were you? I've been waiting for you,' he says accusingly.

'You're late, as usual. Can't you be on time for once? Especially when I need you.'

'Don't you always need me?'

She senses a grin in the air beside her. The watchman of the Fakir's tomb is right there, still holding his candle, leering at them, watching every development like a hound with his nose to the wind.

'No use standing here. Shall we go down to that other place outside? Where we were supposed to meet.'

'Come with me,' he says, 'it's better here, we can look out from the ramparts.'

'You will have to leave the place soon.' The guard is intrus-ive. 'I close this place as soon as the sun sets. Department orders.'

'But the sun hasn't begun to set.' M points to a low red ball, still visible in the sky above the ramparts. The guard reluctantly watches them walk off.

'You can see everything from here. Even as far as the Kutab Minar. It could be another factory chimney. Smoke-less.'

'Oh no, you can tell the difference right away.'

The wandering horses have been galvanised and loaded, a line of them, carrying bricks from the kiln, is picking its way across dry land. A small boy – does he seem smaller because of the distance – is directing them from the tail-end, almost as if by an effort of will. Then she spots Shekhar, on his bright red bicycle. 'How will he bring Sathi back on that?' she says abstractedly.

'You called me. Now tell me, what is upsetting you?'

'Everything. You, me, my husband.'

'Don't call him that. That speaks of families and possession. Call him by his name.'

She puts her hand out to touch him lightly in thanks.

'Listen. I have to tell you. Whom else can I tell? You are my dearest friend.'

'Well, yes, you must talk to me. What is it?' He caresses her head softly. She feels the guard's eyes on her. 'The Pir is here today,' she says. 'He's praying down below, near the real tomb.'

'Don't worry.' M hasn't turned from the ramparts at all.

'Yesterday, last night, Sunita and her child came over for dinner. You know the house is being painted? Everything is in a terrible mess, the living-room is full of furniture from the other rooms, the ironing-table, dust, pieces of distemper. But she was lonely, so I asked her. It got late, and she couldn't go back alone. Usually he would drop her home. This time he lay back in his chair and said, 'If you love me as you say you do, you will drop Sunita home. I don't feel like moving right now.'' '

' ''It's OK, I'll go on my own,'' Sunita volunteered.

' ''Oh no, that's perfectly all right,'' I said, ''no problem at all. Of course I'll drop you.'' And I did.

'The gate outside had been left open. I suppose the servants expected me back quite soon, so I didn't have to press the horn, I drove straight in, and you know this Maruti jeep of mine is quite soundless. I opened the door at the bottom of the stairs, and I heard his voice in the living-room. I was surprised, I thought that the servants had left already, and the children were asleep. Without another thought in my head, I went into the living-room. He was rising hastily from the stool beside the telephone. It was on the tip of my tongue to ask whom he had been telephoning at this hour of the night. Then I saw his face. I tell you, I will never forget his face, seen across the legs of upright beds draped with protective covering, stacks of books, dust-laden suitcases. His face. I can't describe it. I knew immediately he had been telephoning a woman, his woman. And I could not bring myself to ask, or to comment at all. I just smiled at him.

'He came after me, into the bedroom, very aggressive, I could feel the physical presence of his body looming against me. He almost shouted at me: "What is the meaning of that terrible smile?"

' "What smile?" I said, still hoping that the moment would pass without violence.

' "You still have it on your face. It's sarcastic, accusing, mocking. What does it mean?"

'I was not even aware that I was still smiling, I had lost touch with my body, and now I was afraid. I consciously straightened my face. Besides I had no right to accuse him, no moral right, only this acute subversion of faith. He had always said he loved me, and he had pursued me with dogged devotion, all through these last years of my affair with you.

'So I replied, 'No, I am not smiling at all. Really, you're imagining things. There's nothing, I'm not accusing you of anything.'

'Then he went away, and I felt as if a great danger had passed temporarily. But everything inside me was in a shambles.'

'Well, you did right. You had no moral right to ask him, or to accuse him, considering that you yourself are unfaithful to him.'

'Is that all you can say?'

'What else? You know that I have never promised you anything. So if you think that at this point I will say, leave him and come and live with me, I love you, I can't live without you etc etc . . . '

'That's exactly what I want you to say.'

' . . . just because you discovered last night that your hus-

band was having an affair with another woman, well, I'm
not going to say it.'

'Oh, no, you're right, you never promised me anything.
All you said, from time to time, very occasionally, was that
you loved me.'

She can feel the guard beginning to move towards them
from the gateway. 'The sun has set now,' she says. It is a
fiery glowing mass, already half below the horizon, picking
out the distant tower of the Kutab Minar in aching colours.
'We should go.'

> Walking in a monument,
> you turned to leave
> its loneliness, my gift.
>
> I travelled long to reach here.
> Did we miss each other
> on the journey?

She walks across to her Maruti jeep. It is a mass of black
shadows now. She opens up the back, and gathers the vegetables into a bag which she slings over her shoulder. Then
she fits the key carefully into the ignition, shuts the door,
and walks away. The jeep is an abandoned hump as she goes,
then she can no longer see it, and it gathers up its own life.

The water-tap is closed now, no sound comes from the
shells of the new constructions. She coughs loudly through
the darkening air, calls out, asks if anyone is there. She does
not really expect an answer, this is just part of the protocol
of abandoned places. Then she moves up to the first floor.
At some time in the future they will put banisters on the
stairs, smooth them out, make them safe for children. Rooms
open out in clusters from a main entrance. She moves at
random, searching blindly, then settles into one at the end
of a corridor, a gaping hole for a window looks out towards
a moon coming up in the sky. The malba has been cleared
out of the rooms, but a little bit of concrete and brick still

remains on the floor. She brushes it away from a small space near the wall, and lies down.

The sound of Shekhar's voice wakes her, calling her name from far, far below. It is already dawn outside, pale pieces of cloud spread across the grey. She settles her bag in the corner and goes down. The woman in the blue sari, still rough and coiled, also emerges, rubbing her eyes. Bunches of her hair have broken loose from a long red thread which had bound them, hanging over her shoulder. She needs a bath. Where are the two men who had watched her yesterday? N smiles and nods at her, then turns towards Shekhar.

'What is it?' she says.

'This morning I was coming back from the hospital with Sathi sitting on the back of my bicycle. We had to pass the Fakir's tomb, a large crowd was gathered outside. I don't know how to tell you. The Pir, the Baba, he comes here sometimes, a very holy man. He was murdered last night. They say he had a lot of gold, and it's disappeared. So has the watchman. People say they heard loud cries during the night, but they couldn't tell whether it was a man's voice or a woman's. Some say a thin figure in a blue sari ran under the lights on the main road. But nobody's come forward to report the story. Who wants to be involved in a police case? They found your jeep parked just outside the edge of the Fakir's tomb. The engine was still running. I knew you would be somewhere nearby, I thought I'd come to warn you. Maybe you should leave. What did they do with your jeep?'

'I don't know. Maybe somebody used it.'

'The engine was still running. Shall I . . . take you on my bicycle? I managed quite well with Sathi.'

'No,' she said, 'I'm staying here now. The Pir's given me a place. She's left, the other woman in the blue sari.'

The Man Who Seeks Enlightenment

He has chosen the way of pilgrimage, to go to Kailash-Mansarovar, the sacred mountain and the holy lake. Each circling of the mountain, each dip in the icy waters of Mansarovar, wipes out the sins of one life, according to the Vedas and other scriptures. But that is an account to be kept in the celestial books. Enlightenment must be something else. Girish Dhume is certain he would know about it, afterwards, but for the present, he cannot describe or even imagine how it will be.

He has tried, for Chitra's sake. She has been asking him, from the first day when they met in the offices in Delhi, as the pilgrimage group was getting together and completing the official formalities of departure. It was the first time he tried to think, 'What is enlightenment?' He had always taken it for granted, that he and everybody else knew. In India it was accepted, that you searched for enlightenment. He had never encountered this insistent questioning before. She was restless and demanding, as if she could not sit still, wanting to know everything. Maybe urged on by the private sorrow of her father's illness. She had mentioned that she could not bear to see his pain.

'What are you searching for, all this spiritual stuff, enlightenment?'

'Why are you going, yourself?' he countered.

'Oh, for me it's a job. I work for Starship, the travel agency which arranged your pilgrimage. They needed a volunteer to lead your group, and I offered.'

'It was my good luck,' he smiled at her. 'I had the chance to meet you.' The pain in her heart bothers him. Though she has spoken only once of her father's impending death, it is a patent presence whenever her fears bubble up.

Getting up early in the morning, nothing unusual about that; in the last many days, he has grown accustomed to leaving camp between four and five o'clock. They are at Navidhang, the last camp on the Indian side of the border. As they cluster around the tent-kitchen near the flagpole, sipping tea from steaming glasses, the sky clears and the hill on the opposite side of the valley leaps into sight. They had heard so much about it, but the clouds had wrapped it in a thick pall ever since they arrived the previous day. Now, suddenly, the hill is so amazingly close that a crow flying straight across would surely bump into it. On the almost-straight, high face of the mountain, just as had been promised, is this amazing sign, a distinct 'Om'. It is the letter whose sound, if properly intoned, puts you in touch with your inner being, the mantra or holy chant with which you begin each religious undertaking. It is complete down to the smallest curve, laid out in finely banked white edges of snow and ice on the black rock. Surely an auspicious sign for the crossing into Tibet this morning?

The first horses leave soon after. The sun is not out yet, just this faint light in the sky, and the amazing 'Om' bidding them farewell from across the valley. Some of the pilgrims have gone with the horses: Alok Sen, a dark, wiry figure with a small blue pack bobbing from fragile supports on his back; the sturdy Bhilwara brothers, their square bodies making a separate unit; and Chitra Sinha, walking, practically running, beside the patrol commander, Sher Singh Alawat, who will see them safely over the border into the hands of the Chinese guides. His long legs move amazingly fast over the ground. The commander, accustomed to this terrain, his breath comes in steady gusts, will make the height quite well.

What about the others, the pilgrims, Mrs Karnik, Sharda Behn, mounted on horses, and Madhu Rani Gupta, her horse clutched between her legs in anger, although the day has just begun? What has she found to anger her already?

Girish Dhume neatly skirts the small knot of three women and goes on ahead. The horses want to rub up against each other. Madhu Rani Gupta is pulling hers away. She wants always be be apart; she suspects deep, dark designs upon her person even in animal minds, or does she think that man and beast are equal in this respect?

Sher Singh Alawat towers above Chitra. The two are clearly visible on the hillside in front of him, talking, or at least Chitra is talking, he can tell from the sharp movements of her hand. She turns to look for her horse, it is way behind them. Ram Bagh, who leads her horse, got up late this morning. He murmurs as he passes, hastening to catch up with them.

Girish Dhume settles his pack more comfortably on his back. A horse would make life much easier up the slopes, but it is not good to take a horse. Enlightenment is not an easy thing, it may cost you everything. What's the trouble of travelling without a horse compared to losing everything? They say you must be prepared to lose your life if you must win it. A horse costs too much money, he can't afford it. As for Chitra, is she watching the sunrise, and the slope before her? She is a thin woman, the bones around her neck are fine and fragile. She is like a goddess to the waist, small pointed breasts, slim arms, long fingers. But below her waist it is something else, those hips are quite disturbing.

Alawat's woman was quite different. At first it was difficult to tell which was his woman exactly. There appeared to be three of them.

'Come with me to the village,' he said to Chitra. She was the official leader of the group; he wanted to entertain her. 'I will show you the life of the élite up here in the mountains. It's nothing like what you know down there in the cities, but still, it has a charm of its own.'

She took Girish Dhume with her. Alawat did not seem to notice him at all.

The doctor tagged along too, and they became a party of four. They spread like a miasma over the evening: every house opened to watch them pass, though not a single villager was actually visible, save those drinking near the tea-shop. The only noise that came out to the path was the disembodied sound of 'gur-gur' tea, being churned with salt and butter in long wooden receptacles.

'She has sent word,' Sher Singh Alawat said. 'They are not ready yet. We can go to the temple, meanwhile. It's one of the local sights. I suppose they are preparing some things for you. I said make something special.'

'Oh, you shouldn't have bothered them.'

'No, the reason is that they hardly ever receive guests. They enjoy it. Besides, I promised I would show you all the good things of the village.'

The doctor was a large man, his arms hung loosely at his sides. 'Today I'm fasting, I must go and say my prayers. Call me from my room when you are leaving.'

'Take a good look at the trees, you won't see trees for a long time, after this.' She looked puzzled. 'You haven't seen pictures of Tibet? There are no trees there. Everything is rock and bright colours, barren. Nothing grows except sheep and prayers.'

'These are fruit trees?' The village was left behind. They were getting into orchard land, and, beyond that, a gradually thickening jungle.

'Apples. It's a pretty rich area. The families you are about to visit are landowners. These girls, my friends, study down on the plains, in Lucknow. They are here now, for the summer holidays. So, here's the temple. But, be prepared, it's a temple of Durga,' he said. They stood at a stone doorway.

'Oh God,' she said, 'someone's made a sacrifice here.' A mangled cock lay at the feet of the goddess, its blood smeared all over the stone.

Girish Dhume looked carefully at the small, crooked trees on the way back, though it was difficult to see much in the gathering darkness. The tall ones were deep in the jungle. Alawat was explaining the land system. 'One doesn't get much chance to talk up here. Especially to educated people. There's me, and the doctor. And, in the holidays, the girls from Lucknow. One of them, the one I like most, has a brother in the navy, who is very jealous and protective. Last month he was here on leave, and we had another person to talk to.'

The girls were waiting, the doctor was there already. Alawat looked at him briefly. 'They called me,' he said.

The room was tiny, a window stood open above a large iron trunk, covered with a carpet which served as a sofa. Alawat made a place for Chitra in the centre, stationed directly over a pattern of dusky-pink roses worked into the wool. Girish Dhume trailed off into a chair in the corner. Two small green apples, their leaves still clinging to them, lay on a table, displayed like museum pieces in a fine brass bowl. He had not seen fruit since leaving Delhi ten days ago. Slowly, the three girls filed in.

'Why don't you say something?' Alawat said, after a while, not looking at anyone in particular.

'We are waiting to bring in the things.' They disappeared down a short, steep staircase and returned with plates, samosas, tea, and small flat cakes.

'Where are the apples from?' Girish Dhume asked.

'From our land outside the village. You want? They are not so sweet yet.' The one who spoke was a little older than the others. He decided from the way she looked at Alawat, and from the slight deference which the girls showed her, that this was Alawat's woman, the one with the brother in the navy.

'You girls have not worn your traditional costumes, your jewellery. Our visitors are from Delhi, they have never seen such special things before. This lady is an important professor in the university. Madam, Shalini is studying in a girls' college in Lucknow.'

Shalini smiled. Her wavy hair was drawn back into a thick plait. Smudgy shadows of kohl lay over eyes which were clear and appraising as they surveyed Chitra, who had worn small turquoise earrings for the evening's festivities. 'We are collecting the costumes. Some of the stuff is at Madhu's place. You will go there.'

'Maybe you can take pictures. I saw yesterday that you have a flash on your camera,' Alawat said.

Shalini pressed the two green apples into Girish Dhume's hands as he exited.

They were stopped on the way to Madhu's house by a man lying in wait for them outside his door.

'You must come to my poor house.'

'On another occasion, Ram Phal. We do not have much time today.'

'Five minutes, sir, just for some tea. This poor house has nothing else to offer you today.'

'He gives us horses for the border patrol, one of the contractors. We'll spend just five minutes, then.'

There was no sign of the girls when they emerged, so they walked down narrow alleys, with the houses rising into two storeys on either side, and turned down a sudden, sharp corner. This house had an open space in front where an old lady was working on a loom.

'Beautiful carpets,' Alawat said, smiling at her. 'How are you today, Aunty?'

She nodded cheerfully. 'Very well, thank you. The girls are inside. Call me if you need anything.' She put away her loom, gathering up the lamps beside her. Shadows felt dark around them. They headed up the now familiar steep wooden staircase, repeated in every house, towards light on the upper floor. His feet glanced off the narrow planks.

The girls entered from a side room, preening in the glow of lamps. They were transformed by long, woven head coverings, silver chains and belts. Their lips were bright with lipstick. Each had an intricate turquoise, coral and silver necklace, which fell splendidly to her waist, and smooth ancient turquoises in her ears.

'We shall wear these clothes and jewellery when we get married,' she said slowly, offering butter tea.

'Please, please, if you do not want tea, ask Aunty for the drink. Maya's mother makes a beautiful white rice liquor.'

'For me, tea is fine.' What would Sen and Dr Karnik say if he went back with his mouth smelling of liquor? Besides he never drank, even in Bombay, it was one of the things he had given up in the last two years, ever since he had begun the search.

'Madam will try some,' Alawat said, gesturing to Shalini, 'now it is dark and cold, the right time for rice liquor.'

The girls went off together to make more preparations. 'I will be getting married soon,' Alawat said, 'as soon as I can get one month's leave to go home. My mother has chosen the girl, she's quite nice.'

'Will you bring her here?'

'Oh no, this is no place for a delicate girl from the plains. Madam, will you take a picture of the girls, when they come back?'

He wanted to ask if Shalini knew that Alawat was getting married but he felt he could not intrude.

'You should see the pictures up on Alawat's walls,' the doctor said. 'Really sexy ones.'

They could smell liquor being decanted in the womb of the house. Maya carried in small glasses.

Chitra arranged them for the photos, Shalini in the centre, the other two girls on either side. At the last minute, when she had adjusted the flash, Alawat darted in and stood behind Shalini, his tall young body sheltering hers. She looked up at him for a second, and then back to the camera.

'You also, Madam, join us for the next one. Mr Dhume will take the photograph. But you must wear local dress. The girls will help you.'

He could barely see the group through the lens of the

camera. Light from the kerosene lamps flickered and dashed on to the faces, all of them had bent lower, clustered around Chitra who was kneeling on the floor. 'I can't have my trousers showing below this beautiful dress,' she said, tucking her feet away under the hem of the robe. 'Oh, this jewellery is so beautiful.' Her face was deeply suntanned, her eyes huge and luminous in a thin face. Her hair hung in dark, unwashed curls about her cheeks, escaping strongly from the tent-like folds the girls had draped over her head.

The flash-bulb exploded into their faces.

Girish Dhume carries the light of the flash-bulb with him this morning, and for ever. Nothing is lost on the way, and yet nothing is the same, subtly and constantly transformed. Chitra is still talking to the commander and looking back for her horse. When it catches up with her, she sheds a couple of layers of clothing, and slings them over the saddle.

He too feels the heat of walking. Everyone has dressed extra warmly this morning. The doctor and Alawat briefed them, with dire threats and warnings, about the weather at Lipu Lekh Pass. The air was warm in the briefing tent late last night from the breath of more than twenty people gathered there. Rain fell slow and cold in the pitch darkness outside.

Alawat began the speeches. 'Please, I have to brief the whole group formally, and the doctor wishes to give you medicines. Tomorrow you will cross the border. For a few days we will hear daily reports on the wireless. After that even the news will stop. So it is very important that you should be in good health.'

'Good health of the plains means nothing here,' the doctor said. 'Everything is different in these parts. Those who do not live up in the mountains have no idea how it is; the thinness of the air, the height, it changes everything. This is why I examined you all very carefully yesterday. Apart from one or two cases, which I have been watching, everyone was OK and fit to go. You have come a long way to reach here,

I would not stop you unless I knew that the risk was great. Miss Madhu Rani Gupta, how do you feel today? You had a fever yesterday, and I advised you to rest. You know that I sent back Mr Praful Sharma, he had severe breathing problems. I could have sent you back too, but I thought maybe your fever would even out. After this present meeting, I will examine you again.'

Madhu Rani Gupta was standing at the mouth of the tent, her body wedged into the opening, as if at any moment she would leave and be alone again. Girish Dhume was nearest her, crushed at the edge of what must be the doctor's camp bed. Chitra was far away; seated beside Alawat, she was the leader of the group of pilgrims. He felt a terrible wave of disturbance, suddenly hot and hostile. It flowed out of Madhu Rani Gupta's solid body close to his, from her square legs, and from the small glittering eyes behind her glasses; maybe she still had the fever. Her voice was hard, the words came out like stones thrown across the space. Chitra turned her face slightly away from the impact, because Madhu Rani Gupta was pointing and gesticulating towards her. 'It is Chitra Sinha, she's the one who is conspiring against me. The doctor does what she says, all of them do as she wants. Look at her sitting there like a queen beside the camp commander! Who does she think she is? She wants to get rid of me just because they appointed her leader, since I'm the only one who presents her with any opposition, any resistance. But I'm a tigress, I will show her what it means to be a real woman. Somehow or other, I will go on this trip.'

'But my dear Miss Gupta, I didn't say you were not to go, I asked only if you had a fever.' The doctor was trying valiantly to make peace.

'It's the same thing. You were implying I should not go. I know all you men, I know how you work. There's only one thing you are interested in.'

'I will make sure that you don't go, I will not even wait for the doctor's verdict, and I have full authority to decide here. There is no court of appeal.' Alawat's voice moved in a shelter around Chitra, she sat there a stricken creature, angry and helpless.

'The woman's mad,' Dr Karnik murmured beside him, 'or she's suffering from menopause.'

Girish Dhume looked hastily towards the entrance of the tent, hoping she had not heard – there would be another explosion – but Madhu Rani Gupta had gone already, the thongs of the flap moved wetly against the canvas. The others withdrew reluctantly from the spectacle and waited for more instructions.

'The water in Lake Mansarovar is icy cold, don't go in at once, but in stages. Wear dark glasses in the snow at all times, don't let your shoes get wet . . . '

He feels hot too. The sun is beginning to rise now, the sky gets paler and paler, and the mountains are high dark crags against it. Maybe he should take off this shiny yellow raincoat, air will move through the pores in the sweater below, touch the pale configurations of his skin. But then he would have to carry the hot heavy bundle of the raincoat, which would cling in a mass to his shoulder, his arm. The muscles in his body refuse to get warmed up, they move slowly, creakingly, resisting his movement. It's such a short distance to Lipu Lekh Pass, eight kilometres, but straight up, they said. The climb will begin soon, there is no way to command his body.

Chitra's horse has returned to the path. The horseman stands at Girish Dhume's elbow. 'Madam said, if you wanted to ride, please use her horse.'

He looks up for her, but the two figures have gone over the ridge. Her clothes have been bundled up behind the saddle, he adds his own raincoat, and climbs on to the horse.

But once the ice starts, it gets difficult to ride. The path becomes a narrow, curving thing which clings to the edge of the mountain. Ice comes down in straight, casual sheets over the sides, split by small streams of water as it melts rapidly in the rising sun. Deep streaks of mud across its virgin surface, and the marks of horses' hooves fill quickly with slush. He gets off the horse.

The horseman sends him on ahead. 'Once the horse has passed, you would find it difficult to walk, the ground gets slippery and wet.'

Far ahead he spots the blue plastic backpack of Alok Sen and, below, a cluster of horses. Mrs Karnik, Sharda Behn and Madhu Rani Gupta are still attempting to ride, clinging to their saddles as the horses veer around the bend.

'Where are the Bhilwara brothers?' he asks the horseman.

'Oh far ahead, Sahib, they went ahead of the camp commander, Sahib.'

The Bhilwara brothers, scions of a cow-herding community in Gujarat, had made their bodies solid and vigorous with years and years of a pure, strong, vegetarian diet, milk and ghee and curds. They carry their bulk with amazing ease over the hillsides. Each evening they open packages of dry gujias and pre-cooked chapatis heavy with sugar and ghee, to supplement the thin lentils, rice and potatoes which the rest houses provide to the pilgrims.

No sign of Chitra and Alawat.

'Maybe she needs her horse now,' he tells the horseman, who hurries on ahead and is soon out of sight; his speed and energy is magical. The doctor catches up with Girish Dhume, panting with effort. He slows and they walk together.

The doctor's horse is right behind them. He gestures to it. 'I try and ride wherever I can. All this walking! Alawat is like a goat on the mountainside, but he is a much younger man. Who is this crank you've brought along with you, this Madhu Rani Gupta?'

'I don't know. I think she's come from Delhi, and I'm from Bombay. But even the Delhi people don't know her, where she works or lives, she refuses to divulge any information about herself because, she says, people tend to turn up and contact her later and make a nuisance of themselves.'

'She is bound to make problems for the group, better

watch out for her when you are in Tibet. At least until now you have been in your own country.'

'Well, it's up to Chitra Sinha, she's leader.'

'You saw the performance last night.'

The climb has got steeper. Vegetation is a short, springy yellow grass still wet from the night; ice lies in the shadow of overhanging rocks, where the sun cannot reach.

'How much further is it?'

'Another four kilometres. You're only halfway there.'

He stops to drink water. The weather is beginning to change, clouds have come over the sky. It has been an extraordinary bright blue, so clear and heavy, and amazingly homogenous. Now it is beginning to lighten into grey, as clouds with rough edges grow at the tops of mountains: proliferating, magical creatures.

'Is it going to rain?'

'Maybe.'

All vegetation falls away, the path begins to go through rock and boulders and then ice, which is still in patches, with stretches of black rock showing up between. Higher up, a glacier starts, the patch lies across it. The doctor gestures to a twist of glacier which goes around the mountain, Lipu Lekh Pass is on the other side. The surface of the glacier is still virgin and white, unmarked by passage. Alawat is supervising the pitching of a small tent at its base.

Chitra is seated on a nearby rock, her sun-hat pushed back on her forehead, fiddling with her camera. Slowly the horses gather and the pilgrims appear in straggles.

'How will we all fit in the tent?' One of the Bhilwara brothers, stopped short in his brave upward ascent, stands at the edge of the tent eyeing its proportions.

Chitra laughs. 'AK, if you were to go into that tent, there would be room for exactly two others!'

'It's for an emergency, and as a central meeting point. You're not all supposed to get in right away.' Alawat comes sauntering up.

'Well, I hope there are no emergencies.'

Girish Dhume likes to think about Kailash, the sacred mountain. There is no way of knowing what will happen to him. The important thing is only to be there, waiting. Maybe he would be scooped up, find peace and quiet in the arms of the god. So many pilgrims died, going round the mountain, or drowned in the rivulets which skirted the lake. This kind of organised tour was different. What were the risks, with Alawat prancing around, and the doctor like a dark hand of protection over their heads at least until Lipu Lekh? After that, the Chinese or the Tibetan guides would take care of them. The travel agency has arranged all that.

His mind keeps going off into arrangements, but these are merely a way of getting there. If he could only concentrate on each moment of being, each moment. If only he could focus on the way, for example, Bhilwara's hand is going out towards the flap of the orange tent, and then his head bending to peep in, or Sharda Behn getting off her horse, with little cries of fear, though details will be a trap, a net to catch him, and destroy the movement of his mind. He does not really know the nature of enlightenment, he searches up and down the cells of air in his blood, following his breath as it moves through his body, controlling its arrival and departure. It is supposed to be a key, but they also say that you can spend many lifetimes, and nothing might happen. Time is a collapsible tent, a life could be as short as the flicker of an eyelash. Or it could go on for ever, as you toiled up the slope to Lipu Lekh Pass.

'Girish, don't go yet, we have to wait for all the pack animals to arrive. They're late, they took a long time loading this morning. But we all have to go over the border together.' Chitra is calling out to him.

The wind has dropped, and a small rain has begun without his noticing; he is already at the edge of the glacier.

All the pilgrims have arrived now, the horses are a sombre knot by themselves, umbrellas are opened, and Chitra retrieves her yellow raincoat from the saddle. Girish Dhume puts on extra layers of clothing, everything he has. It is cold now. Small movements begin up the glacier, a little hazy now with increasing rain. The pack animals are a heavy line bringing up the rear, the contractor's men hover over them, pulling anxiously at their bridles. PK, who is the elder Bhilwara brother, passes Girish Dhume.

'There is a problem with the mules, they are afraid of this ice. I just went back to check if our bags were there, sometimes luggage gets left behind, and then there is no way to catch the contractor, once you're over the border. Imagine, if we are in Tibet without our sleeping-bags, we would die of cold!'

Why have the Bhilwara brothers come on this trip? They have never been on a trek before, and yet they move smoothly like a flowing wave over the mountainside. Maybe one day he will dare to ask them why they have come. It takes a lot of trouble, getting everything together; going to Kailash is not a moment's impulse. What is his reason? He acknowledges it to himself, but would he tell the Bhilwara brothers, if they asked him, 'Oh I'm going to Kailash searching for enlightenment'? Maybe he would. The knowledge must be lying in different places. It's just a question of getting it out in time, when the question is asked. To pull it out together and lay it on a plate, before it becomes untrue.

He has no choice, he must concentrate utterly on the path, or lack of a path, through the ice below his feet, which sink a little with the weight of his body, and then stay, that's when the slip can come. Some rain has got in through the top of his jungle boots, and the green canvas is damp. Slowly, without warning, he had almost not noticed the transition, the rain is becoming snow, soft, white, hazy.

A loud cry comes from some point lower in the glacier. He stops, there is a degree of commotion, then slowly he goes back. One of the mules, heavily laden, has slipped and fallen in the ice. The thongs of the baggage pack have broken and small khaki bundles, standard packing for the pilgrims, are scattered over the snow. Two men bend over the mule, try to lift it. As the body raises slightly, a quick patch of blood, red and silent, spreads on the snow, where the animal's head had lain.

'Its leg has broken.' The doctor is bending over the mule. A white splinter of bone pushes out through the skin at its foreleg. The mule is unconscious. Pain runs through the mule, broken and freezing in the snow. Girish Dhume cannot move. He feels Chitra come up and stand beside him, he cannot turn to her.

'Oh, how dreadful! The poor thing! I can hardly bear to look. Alawat! Where is the commander? Can somebody fetch him? Doctor, you must know where he is.'

But the doctor concentrates on pushing the bone back under the skin. Girish Dhume feels a faintness in his head, and sits down in the snow. The legs of the horsemen rise around him like wands.

'It's no use, there's nothing we can do for it.'

Chitra is turning the slope of the glacier, walking towards them, with Alawat in tow. He is a tall, snowy figure in a long regulation cape, and he has donned enormous snow gloves, sort of spaceship gear, like a moon-traveller. 'Oh God, why can't you be more careful?' The bite of his voice cuts at all the grieving horsemen, they murmur faintly. Then he says, 'You know what I have to do,' and a small involuntary groan comes across the snow.

Girish Dhume clambers up and moves back to join the shifting ring that watches Alawat prepare his gun, he holds it to the mule's head. The shot is a dull, feeble thud. All its power, death and sound muffled by the brain of the collapsed mule.

'It's no use standing around now, we have to move. Pick up the luggage.'

The pilgrims come out, materialising from nowhere, they are rabbits who have been hiding in holes and burrows. The bundles belong to different people. Those who have hired horses give them to the horsemen to carry. But four large, heavy-looking pieces still remain in the snow, a dark cairn, silent testimony to the dead mule.

The Bhilwara brothers come striding across the snow. 'Oh those. They belong to us. How will we get them across?'

'Where's your horseman?'

'He's around. There he is. But he refuses to carry them.'

'Why?'

The Bhilwara brothers shrug helplessly.

'We'll see about it, Nabha Singh!' Alawat calls to a distant knot of people already beginning to scatter over the slope, following the line of pilgrims which has begun the ascent.

A bony man in a tight sweater with a ragged coat thrown over it, his face wrapped in a decrepit scarf, steps away towards them. His arms are wound around his body against the cold. Everyone wants to begin moving, standing still could mean disaster. The feeling pervades all the snowy particles, the grey, veiled sky.

'So, Nabha Singh, why don't you take their luggage?'

'They haven't paid me, and I won't carry this luggage unless I am given Rs 500.'

'The contractor will pay you. He has to make alternative arrangements, and pay for them, since his mule has died.'

'The contractor is a bastard. I know that he will acknowledge nothing, pay for nothing. The bloody man. He is supposed to accompany his mules, in case something goes wrong. Like this.'

The other pack mules are beginning to move. The Bhilwaras' ex-horseman attempts to join the shift. 'Where do you think you're going? Pick up those bundles. And if four is too many, one of the other mule men can carry it.'

The man stands still.

'Don't worry about the contractor. I'll see that he pays you a reasonable amount.'

'No, sir, the contractor is not here. Afterwards, he will not pay me. I have Rs 500 owing to me from the two Sahibs.'

'Stop all this, I have no more time to waste. Pick up those bundles.' Everyone else has left; only Girish Dhume stays back, watching the two men and the pile of luggage. The

Bhilwara brothers stand steadily beside their off-loaded luggage.

'Oh, this man is a terrible rascal. A cheat. We don't owe him any money.' One of them moves threateningly towards the horseman, but he still makes no move to pick up the luggage.

'Show me your permit. Your border permit.' Alawat is decisive.

Nabha Singh searches in the recesses of his ragged clothing, and pulls out a slightly damp, curling piece of paper carefully wrapped in a plastic sheet. He unrolls it for Alawat's inspection.

The camp commander takes it with deliberation, and, without a glance, tears it into four slow pieces. The man cries out. 'Please, Sahib. They will never make another pass. Don't do this. I'll lose my livelihood.'

Alawat lets the snow catch the remnants of the permit, thrown over his shoulder. 'Now pick up the baggage,' he commands.

'Why should I, Sahib? Now I have nothing to lose, you've already torn up my pass. I will have to leave the mountain trails.'

'I said, pick it up, or I'll kill you. How dare you disobey me so close to the border?'

The man is stubborn with despair. He makes no move towards the luggage. Alawat aims his gun. Girish is a few feet away. Everyone freezes into a silent tableau, watching from various points along the glacier. Alawat is possessed by his anger. Girish Dhume hears a dry thud inside his head from a recent killing. He dashes forward and pushes Alawat's arm. The gun goes off harmlessly into the air.

He saved the situation. I don't know what we would have done if Alawat had actually fired that shot into the horseman, especially as I am group leader. But nobody thought beyond that frozen moment. Otherwise we're plotting and planning, but when it comes to the important moments, we're end-stopped, we can't emerge. Something rattled Girish Dhume, got him moving, and there he was, deflecting Alawat's arm, stopping the madness. Maybe the weather had something to do with it. We were in the middle of a storm, the rain had changed to snow almost without our knowing, and, climbing the slope, we were pushing against a virtual blizzard. I wondered how the older women would manage to reach the top, Lipu Lekh Pass seemed miles away. The terrible release after Alawat put his gun down seemed to give the party great energy. They bounded up the slope: the Bhilwara brothers were already at the top of the rise, and Alok Sen was helping Sharda Behn, who was crying loudly that this was the end, she would never survive the storm, and heaping heaven's choicest blessings on the kind young man helping a poor widow. When she reached the huddle we formed at the turn of the mountain, she forgot about her saviour.

Alawat's snow gloves were everywhere, turning on the wireless, helping the horses, pushing the company forward from all directions. He was once more in perfect control of himself but I had seen the snap, the easy and sudden entrance which the mountain could make into his mind, and I should be frightened of such possibilities. Girish Dhume retreated once more into his substratum; searching existence. There is something in his eyes which are very bright and curious, as if they darted into empty corners, picking up their space. I felt a small companionship with him right from the beginning. He had latched on to me, I felt.

Alawat's men shepherded us into the shelter of overhanging rocks, the last steep stretch up to Lipu Lekh Pass lay above us. We would not begin to climb until we were certain the party from the other side had appeared. I went looking for Alawat. He was huddled over the wireless set, it made futile buzzing sounds. 'It's no use, I can't contact them.'

'I suppose we can't go over the pass ourselves, and find them on the other side?'

'No, it's not allowed. We have to wait for the Chinese.

And the guides. You'll surely get lost in the snow. I can't go across with you.'

'But we will freeze if we stay out here much longer. You know some of the older ones are beginning to look blue and pinched in the face.'

'Then we must do something.' He went out hurriedly to the assembled, dreary pilgrims, his long coat swirling around him. 'Look here, everybody, we must dance.'

They tried not to laugh, the cold stretched their faces and perhaps they remembered the gun pointed at the horseman lower on the slope.

'Dance?' said Alok Sen.

'Dance,' commanded Alawat, 'or you will freeze to death.' And he began a bizarre jig in the middle of the slush and falling snow, twirling slowly from side to side, his enormous coat opening out around him, and his huge boots stamping queer rhythms. There was fear, a dread of death in the steps which followed his, feelings which lay heavily, as if they would never get out of the blizzard.

I knew I should dance too, but I could not. Instead, remembering my sense of duty, I walked up and down the path, as rapidly as the slope and the thin air would permit, spurring the others on, urging Mrs Karnik to join in, giving Girish Dhume a gentle prod. He did not look at me, just stood there with his head down, moving slowly from foot to foot, that was his dance.

The party from across the border arrived soon after. One of Alawat's men signalled their approach from the top of the ridge, and we all caught the sign. Like a wave, it gathered up the pockets of waiting. We began to move up like a steady stream of pack animals driven by a common anxiety, no longer distinguishable by individual characteristics.

This was not yet a walk on pilgrimage, it was just getting to the top of the pass.

'Sorry we kept you waiting.' Chinese accents made the words sound different. The whole air was strange, full of blizzard, a fumbling in the snow. The Tibetan guides in the group didn't say a word.

'What happened?' Alawat said. 'Why were you so late? It was very difficult for us, waiting here in the snow.'

'Oh, problems with the truck, the road, and then you know, bad weather,' the Chinese guide said. Alawat handed over charge of us, and said goodbye. His dramas in the snow were already a distant memory.

Leaving the border behind, going into new country, a step-by-step progression, we proceeded across banks of snow to horses waiting at the road-head. No question of choosing horses here, or any other preferences. Everything was lost in a fog of language and culture. Relentlessly, we trailed one Chinese guide who spoke English.

Taklakot held out its arms to the weary travellers. We settled into soft quilts and poured hot water from enormous thermos flasks. On the one in my room, there was a picture of a black cat with a circlet of red flowers above its head. A cold wind blew at night, rattling the close-shut windows. My body in all its hidden places accepted the impossibility of a bath, and adjusted to slow, secret washes with ice-cold water from glass bottles which had once held beer and were now lined up outside the verandah.

'When you reach the lake,' Girish Dhume said, 'that's the time for a bath. The holy bath. I'm waiting for that.'

'Why?' I said. 'What will it do for you?' I didn't understand these spiritual people, what they were looking for. I went only from detail to detail, and none of it made any sense. He couldn't explain it when I asked, though he did say something. I guess he just wasn't very articulate.

'Experiences,' he said. 'Just an indication that I am on the right path.'

'Why are you going to Kailash?'

'I'm hoping something will happen. All the books talk about it. The air is pure, the earth there is blessed, so many have prayed and meditated there.'

'And then what?' I'm very safe with conversation, with

words, with events once they're finished, and can be looked at, like capsules of time, with a surface and a structure, like the picture of a molecule; protons, neutrons and whatever, neatly laid out. It's the atoms which bother me, empty open spaces which cannot be broken down into component parts, like looking into a person's eyes and then not knowing what to do, getting lost there, held suspended, as if you would be there for ever, endlessly, until something breaks. Maybe that something breaking is called enlightenment. But he couldn't tell me how you first embark upon the silence.

'Well,' he said, 'anything could happen. Holiness is in the air, and mountains rise up on all sides. Kailash is the most special mountain in the world.'

One evening some festivities were organised in town, to celebrate an anniversary of the People's Liberation Army. Tibetan groups had been brought in from various corners of the autonomous province, the announcer at the mike proclaimed the exact source of each group. For political reasons it had to be broadcast that the whole province was celebrating the event. A soldier got drunk and was hustled off in a jeep. Whole sections of audience, Tibetan women in fancy headdresses, men in brown-brimmed felt hats and children turned casually towards the commotion, and then back towards the stage. Gradually, as evening came, the sun, shining vigorously through the thin, high air, became less strong upon our bare heads. Many pilgrims in our group headed for the rest house. 'This music is boring, monotonous; the costumes all look the same, brightly coloured, thin and gauzy, unrealistic. We're leaving. Please stay to celebrate the sequined glory of the Tibetan fairy tale if you want to.'

'Chitra, will you stay?' Girish said. I moved quickly with him into the vacated seats up front. The chairs were filled immediately. I found our Tibetan guide beside me. He spoke some English and more Hindi. 'This is story of a famous king of this area. The great K–.' How could I remember these strange-sounding names? Sometimes I have difficulty in remembering my own. A man in great armour and shining headdress was the centre of attention. There was music, three women in flowing gowns of different colours floated around him, singing their hearts' tales to him. Birds flew in through the windows, string instruments made sounds of pleading nostalgia, and then burst into festivity when ropes of pearls were drawn from magic caskets as gifts to the women.

It was difficult extracting information from the Tibetan beside me, but I depended on his small stock of language. 'When did he reign, your king?'

'Oh, hundreds of years ago. Tibet was very strong then. But you are collecting information, what's the use of that?'

'I just want to know. Where was his palace, where all the wives lived?'

'Up on top of that hill. Then it was destroyed and a very important monastery was constructed there instead. The Simbling Gompa.'

'Can we walk up there and see it? The ruins of its walls are visible from the rest house.'

'But there's nothing to see. Only those ruins. The monastery was burned down a few years ago. Nothing remains except heaps of charred stones. Even the murals of the Buddha on the walls were scratched out. And it is a steep climb, it will take you two hours, in the hot sun.'

'We will go in the afternoon.'

I knew Girish would come, he would go anywhere in search of enlightenment, even to a burnt-out Gompa. Others would be interested too, like Alok Sen or Dr Karnik. I had not counted on the Bhilwara brothers, crashing up through the rocks and rolling layers of sand.

Cholong, the Tibetan interpreter, was already there in the Gompa when we arrived. I was not expecting him. Maybe he had been deputed to watch us, and for us everything in Tibet must occur under his bronze eyes. He was seated facing a pile of rubble which had once been a huge statue of Buddha. We could still see the outline of a statue on the wall behind, etched deep into its blackened surface. We left him there and wandered around.

Dr Karnik said, 'It makes me feel strange, that man sitting there in the ruins, counting out his prayers on the rosary.'

A series of half-burned walls ran up and down the hill-top. The roof had been destroyed, and no statues now remained. Paintings on the walls had been scraped and fired, faint traces of stubborn paint still showed up on the surfaces.

We found two slabs of stone carved with images, so badly blurred we could barely make out the seated, godly figures. The Tibetans, discovering them earlier, had put little marks of red paint, to distinguish them from the others. Prayer lamps had formed dark patches in front of the slabs. Behind the ruins was a huge stone tank where the monks collected rain water. I was clambering at the edges when I saw the caves on the opposite hillside: a series of hollows carved out of solid stone, a warren of dark spaces which touched something unfamiliar in my heart. Maybe I had been a monk in my last life.

'That's where the monks went for their retreats. They disappeared for weeks, or months, to meditate.' Dr Karnik had come up beside me. 'The monks in the monastery fed them, also checked that the chaps were still alive in there. And brought them out, I suppose, if they had passed away in the course of their meditation.'

'Attained samadhi,' Girish Dhume said. 'That's the word.' He was standing on the hillside, staring across at the caves as I was, wondering how it would feel to enter, slowly, into the heart of its darkness. Then he sighed softly.

The Bhilwara brothers had photographed the Gompa and the town of Taklakot laid out below, with the Karnali River winding across its wide basin. Now they set off on their descent, smiling and nodding to us.

'Maybe we will bathe in that river.'

'Shall we go too?' I proposed.

Alok Sen said, 'I think that our virtuous friend Cholong, praying out there, has been put to spy on us.'

'We should expect it, being the only large group of foreigners here.'

Cholong went on ahead to Tarchen, base camp for the Kailash parikrama. As pilgrims, that was the high point – to complete a clockwise circle around the Holy Mountain. Many of the group wanted to do a parikrama of Lake Mansarovar too, especially the Karniks, but the Chinese officials said it was not permitted and we could not argue with them.

'The Kailash parikrama is far more important anyway,' Girish Dhume told the Karniks. 'That's the one all the holy books insist upon. The ground around Lake Mansarovar is referred to as holy, one must meditate there, but a parikrama is not necessary.'

'You know that it is 164 kilometres around the lake?' The Karniks and Girish were very friendly, both being from Maharashtra. They spoke to each other in Marathi, which I didn't understand.

I kept thinking of monks in the caves behind the Simbling Gompa. As the monks returned from meditation in the dark caves, to the Gompa on top of the hill, reports say they moved fast, as if their feet hardly touched the ground, and they did not feel the stones or snow, the hard, jagged edges of the mountainsides. It was the same all over Tibet, men in a trance, floating, as it were, over difficult ground. Would Girish Dhume become like them? One comes close to areas of no words or details, colourless and without shape. If one could be there without fear, a great strength could enter your body and mind, fill them with inspiration, an intense harmony. And would it disappear when one moved out of that holy space?

Cholong said, 'I will go on ahead, and wait for you at Tarchen, to make all the arrangements. How many yaks will you need? But I will not come on the parikrama around the mountain with you.'

'How will I talk to the yak men? They are notorious for going off and leaving foreign pilgrims in the lurch.'

He smiled, his teeth long and yellow in a sun-blackened

mouth. 'No, no, they will not do that. I'll speak to them.' But he was evasive. I must insist with the Chinese officials on some amount of safety; I was leader of this group.

'Something must be done,' I said.

The rest house in Taklakot was built in a rectangle: four blocks bordering a central space, kitchens and dining-rooms, then the administrative offices, and, on two sides, rooms for visitors with common toilets. You shat, layer upon layer, from a concrete platform on to the ground six feet below. It was bad enough to have such primitive facilities, but to do the parikrama without a guide was inconceivable.

I walked across to the offices in the early morning. Maybe the officials would not be awake yet. I found Girish beside me. 'Will you come in with me?' I said, hoping to send him into the bedrooms, to wake up the Chinese interpreters still wrapped in their women's arms.

But one emerged from a small room beside the office, and smiled to see an Indian woman marching towards him at the crack of dawn. He was a tall young man, very thin, who hardly ever combed his hair. 'Sorry, I cannot decide anything, I will tell manager what you say about the guide, to go around Kailash with your group. But it is difficult, there is nobody,' he replied to my demand.

'Send Cholong,' I said.

'He is not keeping so well. He had pneumonia little while ago. If he is exposed to cold again, he will be sick. With all these batches of visitors, we need his services in Tarchen.'

'Someone else then, to show us the way. The yak men are not enough. You talk to your boss, tell him that.'

The sun was rising as we came out. A huge laminated concave disc of white metal shone at one end, propped against some straggly vegetation.

'A solar cooker.'

Somebody had perched a kettle on the metal frame. It was already very hot, the water almost boiling.

Girish went too close to the bright disc. A broad ray reflected straight into his face. He fell to the ground with a small scream. I leaned down to help him, and he held his face lightly against my leg.

The day passed in relaxing and recovering from our hard journey to Taklakot. In the evening we all sat around at a late dinner. The food was Chinese but vegetarian, in response to a special request from the Indians.

It was healthy and good, but already after two days our stomachs were longing for chapatis and dal. 'Why don't you try a new approach to noodles and chopsticks?' I told the complaining Bhilwara brothers.

'Or the soup.'

'Shall we talk about the food we should take with us on the Kailash parikrama? There will be no one to cook for us there, or even to make tea.'

'Up at those heights, they say, one does not even feel like eating.'

'But we must eat. Or we will lose strength.'

'Did you see the guide they're giving us for the Kailash parikrama?'

There was something very feline about him, as if he would creep up the mountains with us instead of walking, and if we lost sight of him, we would find that he had become only a wet patch on the rock. His skin looked as if it were too soft for these sun-baked regions, and hung in gentle folds at the edges of his jaw. He knew nothing but Tibetan, and communicated with us in sign language, gesturing with his turquoise-laden hands. But I was told that the yak men followed him blindly.

'He's called Nawang. He'll be on the bus with us to Tarchen tomorrow.'

Girish launched into an analysis of the qualities and nutrition content of various items of available diet. 'Nuts are very good. And raisins. Cheese, that's easy to eat, gives strength, and no cooking. My nieces and nephews packed all these in small cellophane packets for me. I slip one in my pocket, and I have enough nutrition for a long walk. Also these pre-packed chapatis with ghee, such as the Bhilwara brothers have brought with them from Gujarat.'

'Which they sometimes share with us when they are wildly generous.' I was not sure that Alok meant injury with his quick sarcasm.

'Dear brother, you can have our chapatis whenever you wish.' AK Bhilwara had heard him.

'Oh, I don't want them. You might have noticed, I eat very little. I was just talking.'

Girish went on about the diet, with inveterate zeal.

'I have discussed this whole food question at great length with Dr Karnik. He plans to write a treatise on carrying food on mountain treks in general, but especially on the journey to Kailash.'

The company was drifting off to their rooms. Dr Karnik was leaving too. 'Yes, that's what I will do when I get back. I am making notes on my state of health as I go along. Every day I make careful entries in my diary. Now I must leave, madam. Tomorrow, what time does the bus go?'

Everybody had left except Girish.

'Six o'clock,' I said to Dr Karnik's retreating back. Then the panic began to come on. I had to speak to Girish. 'It's my father. When I left Delhi he was very ill, in great pain.'

'Why did you come, then?'

'I don't know, I never thought of that. I don't know how it will be when I get back, there's still more than ten days left of the journey.'

'My father died last year but everything will be all right for you,' he intoned like a rishi, a sage.

'How do you know? Do you feel my father will not die?' Faint hysteria was rising in my voice. I wanted to believe him, to accept that he had some other, more simple source of knowledge. His voice was soft and calm, caressing me, encouraging my doubtful faith.

'I just feel that everything will be all right on your return.'

'Oh but he was in great pain, I couldn't bear to see it continue. Maybe that's why I came on the pilgrimage, rushed up to join your group. Maybe I was running away from my dying father. Sometimes, in delirium, when his mind was trying to blank out the pain, he thought there was a human creature under his bed torturing him and that the place was a hotel room from his past, some place where he had been alone and struggling with demons.'

Girish avoided the question. His eyes were bright and clear in the half-light from the dining-hall behind us. Girls wearing clean blue aprons and shiny clips in their hair were clearing the tables. They dragged out huge tureens of soup from the corner, lifted away jugs of water. Their clatter came through the netted windows.

'How is Madhu Rani Gupta behaving with you now?' Girish changed the subject.

'Well, I haven't had any trouble with her since that fracas in Navidang, when she was afraid that she would be left behind on medical grounds. I don't know why she thought I was her enemy. To me she is just like any other member of the group.'

'I have this theory about vibrations between people. Sometimes these are good, when spiritual auras meet and harmonise, make connections unknown to the mind. Sometimes the vibrations are bad, for no particular reason.'

'Bad vibrations then. She makes me very uncomfortable. Waves of animosity flow from her. I can't understand it at all. She's always suspicious of my motives.'

'She doesn't hate you. Maybe she finds you are too similar.'

'You think I am like Madhu Rani Gupta?'

'Not exactly. You're not at all unpleasant. But both of you are strong women.'

I don't know what people mean by 'strong women', but I didn't want to ask Girish Dhume. He said, 'She spoke to Mrs Karnik the other night. She said life is very different for single women, especially on trips like this. The men think they can sit close to her, touch her, all that, and she hates it.'

Maybe she sensed we had been talking about her. Sharda Behn and I were sharing a room, Madhu had been given a separate, small room leading off from ours. None of the women, least of all me, wanted to share with her. She called to me as I was changing in candlelight, her voice peculiarly soft.

I didn't want to go in, but, as leader of the group, it was my duty. Maybe one of the men had been bothering her, you could never tell about men's taste or behaviour.

'Miss Sinha,' she began.

'Call me Chitra,' I said, relaxing.

'Today we're friends, but it might not last even until tomorrow.'

'Maybe you could try not to be hostile. It's disturbing, when you're tryng to make arrangements, especially in a foreign country.'

'I love the country very much. I'd do anything to protect the honour of India. You will have no trouble while we are in China. I'll do whatever you say, since you're the official channel of communication.'

'But also, be nicer to the others. Sometimes you sound so vicious and rude. An accidental touch and you scream curses as if they had tried to rape you.'

'That's what they want to do, really, in their hearts. I can see it clearly. You think they like you? They talk about you all the time, behind your back.'

'It does not matter, I have a job to do. What about you? How do you survive these solitary trips, where you hardly talk?'

'Oh, it's OK. In any case, I'm always alone, even with friends. Don't you find that? Women like you, like me, we don't fit in easily.'

'It's difficult, being alone.'

Sharda Behn's shrill voice interrupted from the next room. 'What nonsense is this? You two are talking, talking, when I want to sleep. Have you no thought for a poor old woman who has to walk a long distance tomorrow? Please go to sleep, at once.'

Madhu was furious, yelling right back.

'Do you hear how she talks? Like a crude fishwife in the bazaar! She has no culture, no sense. Says we are talking rubbish. As if she ever talks anything else.'

Sharda Behn mumbled slow, retreating curses.

'Oh you, shut up, you old witch,' Madhu called out.

The following day Sharda Behn spread the word about our late-night conversation, I could see from the curious glances directed towards us. Only to Girish I tried to explain our sudden friendship, and the fact that it would probably not last.

'I suppose these things happen,' he said.

Cholong was waiting for us when we arrived in Tarchen. It was to be base camp for the Kailash parikrama, the circling of the mountain.

'Here is the mountain.' Cholong takes us to an atoll. 'Take your first view.'

'Oh do you see it?' He is breathing deeply behind me. What is the hope in his heart? It is dangerous, Girish Dhume, to be already expecting the mountain to give you everything. Hope can close the doors to free movement and access. Will the mountain enter straight in? It rises in its own perfection, complete and pretending to nothing.

Madhu Rani Gupta hovers near the kitchen, beside a low wall which skirts the narrow barrack-like complex. 'There's another group here,' she says with anger. 'I thought the Chinese had reserved this place for us, that's what your travel agency said and you took money from us according to that.'

'Well, that's what they told us, but I'll find out. Madhu, don't start the squabbling again, please.'

I go in search of Cholong. An old woman dressed in full-length, filthy clothes, her rough hair in thin plaits behind her head, her ears encrusted with dirt and turquoises, waddles around the darkening compound. The large bulk of her body sways from side to side on arthritic feet. With her finger, she stirs water into dry powdery sampa, going round and round inside a small wooden bowl.

'Cholong?' I ask her.

She stops to peer at me through grey strands of hair. 'Cholong?' I repeated myself, the sound of his name swelling between us.

She gestures towards a side room with a gnarled hand. Cholong appears. 'This is my aunt,' he says from the door. 'She takes care of this place. She can help you in the kitchen but you must cook your own food. There is a stove. And kerosene came on the bus with you from Taklakot.'

'We know about the stove. Cholong, are there other people here, besides us, in the rest house?'

'No. Not here. But outside, near the village, some Europeans have set up tents. They won't bother you.'

A beautiful young woman holding the hand of a child who is wearing a dirty dress and woollen leggings, appears behind him. She is European, with enormous dark eyes, long curls tumble to her shoulders, and she wears layers of exotic clothing. 'Oh yes, maybe you mean her. She's with one of the men in the tent. She came to ask for a bed for herself and for the child. I said she should ask you.'

The woman grins and pushes her hair back. Her voice is gently accented. 'I am from Greece, my husband will do the parikrama in a couple of days. May I have one bed?'

'There's only two rooms, and we need all the beds. We are ten people.'

'Please, I'm pregnant, you see.' She pats her stomach, her voice is casual and conversational. She follows me into the women's room.

'One can't tell, under all those layers of clothing.' I don't want to believe her just yet.

But she has already established herself in the smaller room. Madhu Rani Gupta is the only other occupant.

'Where are the other women?' I ask.

Madhu glares at me, and turns away rudely. She is friendly

enough to the Greek woman, but she has decided to quarrel with me. I resolve to ignore her.

'What's your name?'

'Erithea. And this is Susan. She was born in India.'

'What about the second baby?'

'I'll go to Greece, to my mother, this time.'

'Is it safe for you to be here?'

'I'm not doing the parikrama. But safety, well, who can say? I could lose my baby even crossing the road in Delhi.'

I wake much before Madhu Rani Gupta, who likes to sleep until the very last moment. I lie in bed looking through a crack in the door at the semi-darkness outside. We cannot start until there is a little more light, so that we can at least see the ground under our feet. Cholong is not coming with us.

'Nawang is good enough. He has done the parikrama many times. I will be here when you get back.'

'I don't know Nawang. I'm sure he's OK. But you've been in India, we know you.'

'Nawang is part of the new generation of Tibetans, he studied in Chinese schools. I don't even speak Chinese.'

'Where did you learn Hindi?'

'In Benares. I was in India for many years until my old father, who lived in these parts, got blind and broke his leg. I came back to look after him until he died. Then I just stayed on. The Chinese find me useful, on account of the tourists who come here. Last year there was a Japanese professor from Tokyo. He has invited me to his country. I'll show you the book he left behind.'

It is a diary with a small, neat handwriting, dedicating it to his dear friend Cholong who helped him so much in discovering the legends and histories of Tibet.

'Will you go to Japan?'

'Who knows? I go to India every year. To Dharamshala, to see the Dalai Lama. Then he sends me back here to look after his people who still live in Tibet.'

'The Chinese know about your visits to India?' He did not answer.

I can see Cholong's sparse beard and black Tibetan hat at the door now. He brings a wave of cold air through the half-open door.

'The yak men have arrived,' he says. 'There are only four yaks.'

'But we asked for eight!'

'That's all they have.'

'Wake the people in the other room, we must leave soon, I'll manage her. Madhu, please get up.'

She makes no movement. Erithea and the child are asleep on the other bed, wrapped in each other's arms for warmth, their mouths open, breathing softly.

We'll have to leave Madhu to follow later. She is the slowest walker of us all, and today we cannot leave anyone behind altogether. It's very irritating. 'Why should I follow a neat pattern which you see?' she told me once.

They set off in twos and threes. Girish Dhume walked with Dr Karnik and Chitra Sinha. Initially she had great difficulty in getting her limbs to move, to overcome the early morning inertia. Her muscles groaned and protested, but she had to keep up with the others. They arrived at a large cairn of stones but she did not sit down to rest, it was still too early.

'The remains of a monastery,' she said. 'You can still see inscriptions on some of the slabs, bits and pieces of 'Om Mani Padme Hum' in Tibetan.'

'Let me take your photo here,' Girish Dhume said. 'Dr Karnik, you stand with her.'

Some weather-beaten prayer flags, once pink, fluttered behind their heads, suspended from two tall stones. They continued the parikrama between tall walls of rock. The side of the mountain was a sheer rock face, with holes in which birds nested. A high bird call followed them, constantly repeated. Maybe it was many identical birds, taking over one from the other, as if in a single cry.

'Oh, it's not a bird at all, it's that little animal.'

It was like a prairie dog, small ears standing up on its head, watching them from a hole in the ground, standing on its hind legs.

'I'm very tired,' she said, 'and thirsty. Let's rest here for a while.'

A small rain had started up, and they had pulled the hoods of their parkas over their heads. 'It's too hot in this, but it will be cold and wet if I take it off.' She wanted everything to be perfect and correct, and then her limbs were too tired to want anything at all.

'Have some of my nephews' raisins.' Girish Dhume was offering her little cellophane-wrapped packets.

She and Girish Dhume continued to lie there, with the narrow gorge and a thin shelf of air, a presence of the mountain's rock face, pressing comfortingly on them.

'Tomorrow we have to cross Dolma-La,' she said.

'It's very high, 18,900 feet. How will the women do it? They say the yaks can't carry them up there.'

'Let's see,' she said. 'Soon we must stop for the night. The first stop on the parikrama.'

'Did you know that some Tibetans do it in one day, not stopping at all?'

'Oh yes. There's a special name for them. I don't know if they earn special favours for themselves on the enlightenment plane. Are they saved earlier? I'm afraid we will have to take three nights on the way, there's no way we can do it faster. Tomorrow we have to walk more than thirty kilometres.'

'One parikrama, and you expiate the sins of one life.'

'Do you have a lot of sins, Girish?'

He turned over on to his stomach and rested his head on his arms.

'It would be nice to do the parikrama in one day and one night. Did you notice the Tibetans we passed this morning, doing the parikrama in prostrations, dragging themselves along on their stomachs?'

'That takes them more than twenty-five days. I would advise against it.'

Tonight it is to be tents, no rooms. Last year's pilgrims brought back bad reports about the quality of Chinese tents, thin and scaly, letting in the rain. They look flimsy at the corner of the mountain.

The Bhilwara brothers are here already, and Alok Sen, waiting for me to find out about the arrangements here. 'There is smoke from behind the tent under the cave,' I remark.

The locals are inside, huge fellows in greasy robes, clustered around a fire in the middle of the tent. Where is Nawang? They stare at me uncomprehendingly, on the verge of laughter. Surely they are expecting us? Hefty shadows stand motionless against the walls of the tent, no-one moves. I gesture, holding the flap open, so that the pilgrims waiting outside are visible. One of them stirs reluctantly, deposits his bowl of sampa on the ground, licks his fingers, and offers his services. Just then, Nawang enters, light from the fire reflecting from his spectacles.

He indicates that the big man will come out with us. 'We must have a stove, and he must light it for us,' I say firmly.

Nawang smiles reassuringly, and grabs a stove as he goes out. The two tents outside are so thin, you can see the remaining daylight through the canvas. 'I hope it doesn't rain tonight,' Alok Sen says.

Everyone from the pilgrim group except Madhu Rani Gupta has arrived.

Sharda Behn is opening up the food which came in the advance party with the yaks.

'The luggage hasn't arrived yet,' she groans, 'and I've forgotten my slippers.' Her feet have big red blisters. Mrs Karnik gives her a fresh pair of socks.

'It's more than a week since I had a bath,' Alok Sen says.

'You'll have to wait now till the clear, cold waters of Lake Mansarovar.'

'She left last, you know, as usual, about an hour after me,' the yak men said. Now she's waiting for us to cook the food, so that she can come and eat it,' carps Sharda Behn. We all know whom she is talking about. Girish Dhume is laughing.

'I can't cook, my head is splitting with a migraine,' Mrs Karnik mutters.

'Well, your husband is a doctor and he is taking tender care of you on this trip.'

Nawang wants to show me the other tent, with the big bodyguard who is theoretically in charge of the place. This tent is for the women, small and circular, tied at the top where the canvas meets the bamboo poles. That's probably the place where it leaks.

Neither Sharda Behn nor Mrs Karnik want to come here. 'We'll stay here with the others, that's reserved for you and Madhu Rani Gupta,' Sharda Behn says spitefully. I feel excluded, no-one has asked me to share the big tent.

The Tibetans' greatest saint is Milarepa and we are now in sight of his cave. It seems far above my head. I look for steps or a path up. The inhabitants of the service tent have emerged to watch the luggage-packs being unloaded from the yaks, a scene of great merriment and bonhomie. The yak men are swigging brown liquor from a bottle. Much friendliness is necessary before they are ready to offer it to the sampa-eaters who watch them expectantly.

I wish Girish Dhume had come out with me. I grope for the steps behind a projection of black rock. They are just niches cut into the rock, encrusted with rubble and mud. I slip several times. Statues are still visible inside the cave. Light comes in from a hole set to one side of the rock, a natural opening. I still need my torch. Its light is yellow and hard in the cave.

The statues spring towards me, as if Milarepa is moving. His statue is pale green, to fix his identity. Two other figures stand beside the saint, his disciples, who shared the space with Milarepa. Did he indeed reach the top of Kailash, as in the legend?

The cave is dark and close around me, I must leave soon. But first I must ask the saint's blessing. I touch my forehead to the feet of Milarepa. The metal of the statue is cold against my skin.

Reaching the tents, I am greeted with the news that Madhu Rani Gupta has arrived and set up her sleeping-bag in the women's tent. When I enter, she is huddled against the wall.

'We'll have trouble from up there,' I say, pointing to the obvious opening above our heads.

I am alone with Milarepa in my sleeping-bag, with the cold darkness of the cave against my skin. It gets colder and colder and I cover my sleeping-bag with a couple of sweaters.

Girish Dhume's voice is calling me out of the tent. 'But come fully dressed and well covered, it's been snowing.'

'Snowing?'

The ground is covered already in more than one foot of snow but the night is clear and sparkling, with heavy stars like crystals in the sky. He is grinning at me from the circle of his blue parka. 'The other tent's collapsed under the weight of the snow.'

'No-one's hurt?'

'No, but they're frightened. Nawang and the stalwarts from the kitchen are trying to get the poles up again.'

Three yak men stand in a short ring around the tent, watching the efforts of the local denizens, misty grey forms clad in a soft dusting of snow. They delight in the sounds of squealing pilgrims coming from the collapsed canvas and pass their bottle from hand to hand as they watch.

'The snow just slid off the smaller tent, without causing damage. It's your large tent which collected it in pockets. Then it became very heavy, and just collapsed over your heads,' Chitra Sinha said.

She was furious with Nawang as official representative, but there was nothing to do now except get it back up.

'Have you noticed,' Alok Sen said, 'the great madam, Madhu Rani Gupta, has not even emerged from her tent, in all this time? She couldn't be asleep through all this commotion!'

'Maybe she is asleep.' Chitra Sinha did not want needless hostility at this point. As she watched, some birds darted across the snow, their feet leaving three-pointed patterns. The group was looking to her. She who had authority to decide what to do next. The heavy snow changed the whole situation. Today they were to cross the high Dolma Pass, now suddenly clad in a new mantle of danger. Nawang could not communicate with her well, she could feel his frustration in the half-sentences of Tibetan which he muttered urgently at her. Then he pulled out the one yak man who knew a bit of Hindi, and brought him into the discussion. They used a weary, jerking system of translation. The yak man was enjoying his new role, staring unabashedly at Chitra Sinha, making mouths at her through the rough hairs on his lip. The talk worked up to a vague conclusion. It was too dangerous to leave camp until snow in the upper reaches had melted a bit. They they could just afford to take those risks. But what would she do about the two older women in the team? Nawang's warning gesticulations were towards Sharda Behn and Mrs Karnik. They could not mount the yaks, which had to move without riders up the steep, slippery slopes, and how could they walk through the snow? The ground would be slippery and full of potholes. They could sink any time, break a limb. The whole group was focusing on the two men, their question was quite clear. But nobody said anything. If only the two women would volunteer to return to Tarchen. Chitra longed for that.

Madhu Rani Gupta emerged just then. 'Oh the tent is back in place!'

'Of course without any help from you.' Alok Sen's voice was combative. So far since the beginning of the trip, he had ignored her, and he was the one person she had not complained about. She was surprised but remained silent.

'Why should she help? She considers herself special, and superior to us.' N K Bhilwara was definitely rough and purposeful. As if unanimously, without discussion, they had all determined to push their tensions at Madhu Rani, who now made no attempt to hold back.

'What are you talking about, you fat, coarse man? You're only bothered about getting your sleeping-bag in place and food in your stomach, and you oppress the poor. That horse-man on the border at Lipu Lekh almost got shot because of you. And do you think that I don't notice the way you look at me, and find every opportunity to brush up against me? In front of your village wife at home, among your sheep and cattle, you must be acting like a saint. But your hypocrisies don't work with me. Just remember, nobody can defeat me.'

'OK, that's enough, leave all this alone.' Chitra turned to Sharda Behn. 'Will you two ladies come with me into the other tent? I would like to speak to you.' Everyone was tense. Only Madhu Rani Gupta settled herself comfortably, deliberately, against one of the tent-poles, sipped her tea, and glared at the rest of the company through shiny spectacles. A sudden twitter of conversation started up as the three women left the tent. Chitra took them into the small tent, seating them on her sleeping-bag which still lay unrolled and abandoned from the time Girish Dhume had called her, hours ago. 'You know why I want to talk to you?'

Suddenly each of the two women felt alone, inside the close circle of the tent.

'We have a very difficult choice before us this morning. Especially difficult for you. I know you have come a long way to make this Kailash parikrama, and now the weather has become dangerous. We can do one of two things. Either you come with us and we risk your lives and the lives of the rest of the party, or I send you back to Tarchen with one yak and a yak man. You would be there by this evening, going on exactly the route we took yesterday. You would wait for us in Tarchen for one day, until we got back. No parikrama, that's true, but you can see Mount Kailash all the time, from Tarchen. That is important isn't it?'

'The important thing is to make the parikrama, virtue lies

in that. I am an old woman, a widow, I will not come this way again,' Sharda Behn said.

'But you see how it is, don't you? You cannot possibly walk all that way over Dolma-La in the snow without yaks. There are not enough yaks, but even if there were they could not carry you over the pass. The stones move and under the snow you can't even see them.'

They were both silent. Chitra repeated her whole argument, put the alternative once more to them. 'Still you say nothing,' she said finally.

'What can we say? It is up to you.'

The decision was put on her, it was very unfair. 'OK,' she said. 'You go back to Tarchen. You must move at the first opportunity. Separate out your luggage, take some foodstuff and water for the way. The rest of our stocks are in Tarchen. You will have enough.'

Sharda Behn began to cry softly. Chitra felt awkward, but she put her arms around her. 'I'm sorry about this, I would very much have liked you to go with us. It's just bad luck that it snowed so heavily last night. But you will see again the face of the mountain you saw yesterday: the huge, steep, almost perpendicular face, laden with snow and ice. It is shaped exactly like a beautiful Shiva lingam, and then from Tarchen you will see it again if it is a good day tomorrow, while you wait for us. Maybe you should go out to this place which Cholong mentioned to me, about a couple of kilometres out of the camp? Ask him about it, I'm sure he can take you there.'

'When do we move?' Mrs Karnik said. Her face was grey and flat. 'I want to speak to my husband.'

'You can go as soon as your yak is ready. As for us, we will have to wait until reports come in that the way is clearing in the upper reaches.'

Birds were still active in the few remaining stretches of untouched snow, between narrow slushy paths. Emptiness and a sense of waiting were evident in the large tent. Nawang had disappeared into secret confabulations. The two women were seen off with tearful farewells. Much later, activity was noticed near the group of yaks, and the yak men appeared to be making preparations. Nawang hurried over the snow to her, gesturing that the pilgrims must be ready to leave immediately. There was no way to find out what news had been received of the state of the snow further up, or who had brought the news. The sun was a big, hopeful white ball behind the haze in the sky.

The yak men cast lecherous glances at me, as they sit around their bottle, and thermos flasks of gur-gur tea. Still, they keep offering me tea, and I am touched by their generosity. I can feel myself opening to them. The others here look to me only to provide the arrangements and make their decisions. But I can't bear the tea, faintly salted and smelling of yak milk. They are definitely undressing me with their eyes, and they touch me whenever possible, running their hands over my body under the pretext of helping me over the rocks. Am I getting like Madhu Rani Gupta, suspecting everyone of sexual designs? Except that the yak men don't bother to hide their desires. No taboos and social inhibitions apply on the high slopes of the Himalayas.

All the yak men are there on the slope, and Girish Dhume is beside me when the boy falls. Silently, the snow must have muffled his cries, he drops from a projecting rock into the snow below, unreal, like a feather, as if a boneless doll had been flung down. His body lies completely still where it touches down.

Others in his party appear as if from nowhere, black patches moving sombrely over the snow, slowly, as if they already knew he was dead. They bend over him, holding his hands, turning away. The yak men make the same movements of acceptance, and move on. I cannot move. How can they be so casual and quick? This fantastical death in the snow retains me. I cannot just walk off and leave the dead boy. The yak men are waiting at the turn of the path, talking to each other.

'Come on, Chitra, you must go now. Everyone else has gone ahead, Nawang is calling for you.' Girish Dhume is tugging at my arm but something has collapsed in me, I cannot bring myself to move. How did he die, so silently and casually? How can I go without mourning?

'Girish, my father was very sick when I left him for this trip. Maybe he'll be dead when I get back. They have no way of contacting me here.'

'He'll be all right. Don't worry about him. Not here. Now you are on Mount Kailash.'

'So what. Yes, OK, life goes on, there's the rest of the world. It is very beautiful and cold, and there is snow under our feet, everything seems to stand still. But Sharda Behn and Mrs Karnik have gone back, and the boy there lies dead. It's strange, he's just lying there alone.'

'I suppose the rituals here are different, but he's lucky to have died within the shadow of Mount Kailash.'

'Nobody's lucky to have died, anywhere. Death is the worst thing to happen to you.'

'I don't know,' Girish said. 'It depends. Living is quite difficult. On the other hand, dying finishes off all your chances in this life.'

'To attain enlightenment?'

'Yes, what else? That's the most important thing. Until your next birth as a human being you can make no effort.'

He is in such a hurry to get up to Dolma-La, what does he hope to find there? To be transported instantly into another region? It's important to move, Nawang is fierce in his gestures, we were already so late in starting off. And today is the longest distance to cover. I know all that. The details provide a shelter. What would happen if they were suddenly lifted off and I were left to consider the mountain alone?

The climb is punishing. The recent snow has melted, and the rocks are wet and slippery, though drying fast in the hot sunshine.

Everything is settled for the time being, the boy is dead, my clothes are in place, the two women are despatched towards the safety of Tarchen. Nothing to worry about. The mountain may impose its will. Walking is difficult. I am going slower and slower, the climb is difficult and tedious. The sun is high above us and burning through the thin air. Small new rivulets from the melting snow are looking for passages between the stones.

I turn a corner and find Girish looking down an unexpected slope. A group of men and women gathers near a line of stones arranged ceremoniously beside the barely discernible path up the mountain. Tears roll down their faces. The yak men have stopped too, their bodies weary, waiting briefly. They talk in low tones. Nawang goes among the mourners, touching a man here on the shoulder, embracing another, a short, dumpy figure in Chinese-style jacket and blue trousers.

'They're putting up prayer flags, between the cairns of stones. These are small funeral chortens,' Girish says.

Madhu Rani Gupta has caught up now, and goes on, carefully skirting the group. The priests arrive, and a chanting of mantras begins.

'Why don't you tie a prayer flag too?' Girish hands me a rough triangle of green cloth, with faint letters printed in Tibetan on both sides.

I attach it to the nearest cairn, pressing my forehead against the stones. My brain feels near to exploding from the sun.

Meanwhile all the yaks have run off, and the yak men are full of energy, swearing at them in rough gutturals. Smiling broadly, Nawang presents me with sprigs of a tufty plant with tiny mauve flowers and stiff clusters of leaves. I smile back.

'What is the plant?' Dr Karnik is walking very slowly today. He trails along just behind me, the gap between us beginning to widen.

'Kailash incense. If you dry it and throw it on a fire, it gives off a fine perfume. They say it grows only on these high slopes of Kailash, and nowhere else in the world.'

'I'll try and find some.' Girish is walking with me.

'You can take this, I don't need it.'

He is collecting things, maybe this is important. I feel gentle and soft towards him, I want the best for him. He too is walking very slowly, as if his limbs were weighted. I leave him behind.

The Bhilwara brothers are standing at the edge of a drop, looking down at a beautiful patch of water, half-frozen over, which glitters at the bottom. Then they begin taking photos. This is probably the famous lake of Gourikund. The climb to Dolma-La must be close now.

I stop at the base. Clouds and mist have parted. For a short while the mountain top is visible, perfectly symmetrical, riven with patches of glaciers, heavy with snow. Alok Sen is gesturing to the others. 'Come and see the mountain. It's very clear now. We haven't had such a good view before.'

'Like a benediction.' Dr Karnik stands with his eyes closed and his hands joined in prayer. I look towards Girish Dhume. His face looks yearningly towards the mountain, and he wraps himself in silence.

For a while, the yak men provide jovial company on the way up, but even they have stopped joking and laughing amongst themselves, and, as they heave their lumpy bodies, they are panting from the climb. One of them hangs around very close to me, rushing to touch me and to rub against me each time the slope offers opportunity.

Then he passes a hand over my bottom. This is too obvious to ignore, it's going too far and I shout at him. After that, the others scatter too, and I am alone. I cannot see the top of Mount Kailash any more, there is nothing here to hold me, just one foot going before the other. Somehow I must do that, or I will never reach the top. Each time, the slope plays a trick. I fix on a height, that's the top, Dolma-La, surely. When I arrive there is another slope, and I must go up further. More rocks appear, as if from nowhere, whenever I look up from the ground. Not a chance of sitting to rest by the wayside. I would never rise or move again. But the mountainside is cruel, with its sudden steps and heights; my boots weigh a great deal, my breath comes shorter and shorter. Were my head to get any lighter, I should not be able to give direction to my moving feet. Already there's a blue haze before my eyes, I look through it to the mountain. An idea comes over me that perhaps I will never reach the top, never arrive at that point of absolute perfection. What matters is not the achievement itself, just the getting there. The sun is clawing at me, I do not care now that the yak man touched me. Nothing matters now, supposing I were held and carried up, at least I would reach the top. I have forgotten all their names, those people who are with me, now there is no-one. Maybe this is the way to be alone with Mount Kailash.

I collapse when I get to the top. The blue haze is much stronger now, I sink into it, I never want to look beyond it, never wish to open my eyes again.

The face of Alok Sen emerges through the haze, slowly coming together into a fragrant picture. He is holding me, putting a sweet drink to my mouth.

The the voice of Girish Dhume wafts towards me. 'We are waiting for you beside the rock, the puja, the prayer, has been delayed until you join us.'

'I don't want to pray. Just leave me here. Girish, I thought I would never arrive.'

'You will be all right in a short while.' This is the voice of Madhu Rani Gupta, I have never heard it used with such gentleness before.

'Don't move for a while,' she says. 'All that puja and so on, you can do it later, if you want to.'

She holds my head cushioned in her lap. I go back into the haze. Slowly it fades, and I become a sane person again. Madhu's lap is no longer under my head, a rucksack holds it off the ground. I watch the pilgrims standing before the huge rock which marks Dolma-La. They are in a line, waiting their turn to approach, smear it with red paste, offer incense and a coconut. Coconut. I scrabble in my rucksack.

'Take these two also,' I call out, 'they are for Sharda Behn and Mrs Karnik. I promised them. I have to carry them back, blessed by the presence here.'

It turns out that one of the pilgrims is a qualified pandit, a priest. He is squatting near the rock lighting a tiny fire, chanting all the sacred mantras. I know they are expecting me to join them, but I cannot bring myself to move, a blissful emptiness is in my head which I cannot dislodge.

Nawang is making vigorous signs which indicate that we must move on. He points in agitation to the sky, and it doesn't bother me that I do not understand completely. Is he signifying the passage of time? Finally, the company is parted from the sacred rock. Small piles of remembrance stones surround it, stuck with bits of hair and teeth left by pilgrims who have gone over the pass. To what have these offerings been made? Who has accepted the coconuts of the two women waiting for us in Tarchen? Patches of fresh red paste stare at me from the sacred rock.

'Are you OK now?'

I nod. I am ready to move down the mountain towards the next camp.

I haven't told anyone else, but I want to tell you. I don't know why but I think it is important to tell you. As if, walking up the mountain to Dolma-La, I held you like a stone in my hand, pressing against my palm. I didn't know whether you had gone on ahead, or were coming behind me; I was alone. I didn't see anyone else, though from time to time I could hear the shouts of the yak men as they came around the mountain, spreading over it with flat noise. And then there was only silence, and then nothing; I was nothing, walking up slowly with my lungs bursting, and with you pressed into the palm of my hand.

There is no particular moment that it happened. It does not come after 'then' and there is no 'after'. Just a sudden flame which wrapped around me, and I was in the centre of it, blissful, ecstatic. I have never been happy like that, I was almost floating. I saw nothing except the faint redness, the glow, which surrounded me, as if I were walking in my happiness. And then it was gone. I know the loss. I felt presence, and then absence. This was the first sign.

There were other signs, three in all. The second was a whole picture. I don't know where I saw it, whether my eyes were open or closed, how it appeared. But I saw Shiva and Parvati sitting together just as in the holy pictures. Then they moved closer and closer to me, until finally I saw only the forehead of Shiva, faintly blue, resplendent with the original signs of the faith, the caste marks painted in ash upon his skin.

The third was also a Shiva sign, quite simple, the lingam, but white, as if made of snow, melting rapidly in mountain sunshine. And then it was gone. I never thought I would reach the top of the pass so easily. I saw you there, sprawled out exhausted on the ground. You had always been stronger than I am, I wondered that you were so worn out, and I felt nothing, no fatigue, no exhaustion, just a slow ache all over my body, just this beautiful, floating sensation, as if I had been freshly born, and was looking at things with new eyes. I did not want to touch you or to help you. I was very glad to see Madhu Rani Gupta take you in her lap, that freed me to watch you from a distance, you were alone in your exhaustion, and yet not separate from me. In fact, funny thing, nothing felt separate from me, not even the line of pilgrims making their offerings at the big rock, and you remember how much they had been irritating me, with their jealousies and meannesses?

But Chitra, I don't know, is this enlightenment? I want it so much.

How do I know? Maybe it's the first step, these visions you saw on Mount Kailash, this is the way it goes. Perhaps. Why don't you wait? But listen, thank you for telling me, I understand and believe that you have not told the others about it, and that this is the most precious thing in your life.

I was really exhausted, up there. I thought I would not be able to move one inch ever again in my life, my limbs were heavy. Then I slept, with Madhu Rani Gupta's lap under my head. What made her suddenly so kind to me? When I awoke, I wanted to move down the slope; in fact I was the first to begin moving, the others were still praying and collecting their coconuts from the big rock. Going downhill was so easy, I leaped from rock to rock, like a goat gambolling through familiar territory.